RAG MEN

ROCKY ALEXANDER

For Jerry and Idgie

"The world dies over and over again, but the skeleton always gets up and walks." -Henry Miller

1.

Colin Ross sat on the edge of his bed and withdrew the revolver from the black leather holster on the nightstand. He snapped open the cylinder and from the rectangular box beside the holster, he removed five rounds of high pressure .38 Special ammo and loaded them into the chambers. For the next minute, he only stared at the stainless steel frame of the weapon and felt the weight of it in his hand. He wondered if it was going to hurt when he did it and for how long. He imagined it would be quick; most likely he would be dead before he heard the shot.

He lifted the gun and placed the two-inch barrel into his mouth, wincing at the coldness on his lips. Perhaps this wasn't the best way. He recalled a time when he was a teenager, taking potshots at an old, rusted body of a Mercury Cougar that rested on concrete blocks in the weeds behind a hay barn on his grandfather's farm. The gun he had fired had been a .38 revolver similar to the one he held now. He remembered the first shot ricocheting off the front windshield without leaving more than a chip in the glass. It didn't seem like the most reliable caliber of bullet to completely trust with the task of killing himself. The possibility existed that he could shoot himself through the mouth and the bullet could fail to hit anything crucial to life, while still causing an unforeseeable amount of brain damage, and the muzzle blast between his jaws would probably leave his face horribly disfigured. The last thing he wanted to do was spend the rest of his life ugly and stupid and being spoon-fed oatmeal and mashed vegetables by some fat, hairy guy in a nursing home.

He took the barrel from his mouth and placed it behind his right ear. His hand began to tremble as he cocked the hammer back. *Do it, you fucking coward. Just do it.* He closed his eyes and took a deep breath and tightened his finger on the trigger. He saw her face in his mind. He saw her smile and heard her laughter and wanted to hold her more than he had ever wanted anything throughout his entire existence. He didn't believe in God, or Heaven, or an afterlife. He held no illusion that he would be reunited with her in death. What he did believe was that he couldn't live without her. He didn't want to even if he could. *There's nothing left for you here. End it. End the pain. It can all disappear in the blink of an eye. It can be just like before it ever was.*

The hand in which he held the revolver became even more unsteady and he clutched it against his chest and tried to control the shakiness. Deep within his consciousness she whispered, *I love you, Colin*, and he felt her there. Inside. The thought struck him that if he should remain alive, then she might continue to exist as well...as a part of him. *Except it isn't her, but only your memories of her.*

Well, maybe that was better than nothing.

Fucking excuses.

He screamed into the dark, empty room, drew the gun back to throw it, then reconsidered and uncocked it and stuffed it back into its holster. He sat there silently for a long time with his hands on his forehead, then got up and grabbed his cell phone and car keys off the dresser and went outside to his cargo van that was parked in the driveway.

Five minutes later, he pulled up in front of the brick building with ROSS BOXING CLUB stenciled across the streetside wall in huge, white letters. He unlocked the door and went inside, crossed the lobby in the darkness and flicked on the overhead fluorescents in the area behind the counter, then ascended the stairs to his office. Each step sent sharp slivers of pain through his knees. He was in great shape for forty, but years of intense athletic training and competition were slowly catching up with him. Every trip up the staircase, and there had been hundreds, if not thousands since he had opened the gym six years ago, was a reminder that he wasn't immune to getting old, no matter how much he resisted.

He snapped the office light switch and stood in the doorway for a moment looking the place over. Empty cardboard boxes and plastic wrappers were scattered randomly over the wood floor. On various surfaces sat unfinished drink containers, and the two garbage cans were overflowing. He kicked a couple of boxes out of his way, took a bottle of water from the refrigerator, and studied it briefly. It was partially frozen. It was 12:01 a.m. on the fourth of February and cold enough in the office that Ross could see the misty plume of his breath in the air. He cranked up the thermostat, pulled an electric space heater close to his desk, then sat and ate tuna fish out of a can with a plastic fork and sipped the water and browsed internet news articles on his computer display monitor. The current updates made him wish he had gone ahead and pulled the trigger of his handgun when he had the chance.

The riots had gotten worse. News sites were flooded with images and video footage depicting police and National Guard troops clad head to toe in protective biological suits, their faces covered by polycarbonate visors or gas masks, striking civilians with batons and rifle butts. Exchanges of tear gas and Molotov cocktails. People bleeding in the street or being carted off like cattle aboard military trucks and paddy wagons. Mouths open, screaming. Machine guns mounted atop Humvees. Entire city blocks cordoned off with eight-foot chain link fencing crowned with razor wire. Smoke and fire and violence and chaos of the sort felicitous to the biblical Book of Revelation.

Ross pulled up a website which featured a zoomable map of the United States peppered with tiny, red dots. Above the map was written: QILU VIRUS PANDEMIC. Each red dot represented a laboratory confirmed infection. On January 14, there had been thirteen dots on the map: seven in Los Angeles, one in San Diego, two in San Francisco, with one over each of the cities of Seattle, Las Vegas, and Chicago. Now, only three weeks later, there were too many dots to count. Red clusters all across the map, in nearly every state, with the heaviest concentrations on the west coast. The Dakotas had so far been spared, as well as a few of the smaller New England states, but Ross didn't think that would last much longer. The virus was spreading like a wildfire in a hot summer wind, and there didn't seem to be a damned thing anyone could do to stop it.

He moused over the map and zoomed in on the central region of Washington State, and was relieved to find that the city of Wenatchee and the surrounding vicinity were clean, at least for the time being; the situation was subject to change at any time. He considered loading up his van with supplies and leaving town, going somewhere secluded to wait things out, but he wasn't sure where that might be. Where do you go when the whole world is dying? His uncle, Charlie, owned a summer cabin on a small fishing lake near Eatonville, two hundred miles to the west, but getting there could prove to be a challenge. The route would take him across the Cascade Mountains and through the outskirts of Seattle, a city currently synonymous with Hell. Even if he should decide to brave it, the roads leading in and out of the area were closed to all but essential traffic.

It was probably best to stay put. The gym storeroom was stocked with cases of water and energy drinks, protein shakes and power bars. A full drink cooler downstairs and an office refrigerator packed with frozen lunchmeats and cartons of soymilk. A case of tuna fish atop the refrigerator. He had some provisions at home as well, but he held no intention of staying there; it reminded him of *her*. He planned to go back for his gun and whatever else he might need, and return to the gym and see how things played out. The worst that could happen was that he could die, which was not a problem at all. With some luck, he wouldn't even have to do it himself.

He stretched out on the sofa at the back of the office, pulled a thick blanket up to his chin, and closed his eyes and drifted off into deep, merciful sleep. He dreamed of her, and in his slumber, he wept.

2.

Rooster stood on the front porch of the one-story Craftsman bungalow on 57th Avenue in the Rainier Beach neighborhood of Seattle. The place hadn't changed at all in the months since he had last been here: same growing heap of cigarette butts on the ground by the porch steps; same faded and peeling paint on the siding, exposing the aging gray wood beneath; same damned garbage in the front yard. He flicked his burning Marlboro onto the butt pile and knocked on the door.

A black man approximately the size of King Kong answered. "Yeah, what you want?"

"I'm here to see Timbo."

"Who the fuck are you?"

"I'm Rooster."

"Rooster? What the hell kinda name is Rooster?"

"Just tell him."

Kong looked him up and down suspiciously, and then closed the door. A few seconds later, he opened it and motioned Rooster inside.

The interior of the house smelled like marijuana and methamphetamine and Fritos and assholes. The windows in the living room had blankets crookedly tacked over them. In the walls were several fist-sized holes and do-it-yourself patch jobs covered with paint that didn't match the original wall color. A fish aquarium in a corner with water so filthy that Rooster didn't imagine there was anything alive in there. On a stand in front of a non-functional fireplace was a forty-two-inch LCD TV that displayed nothing but a blue screen. The stained carpet floor was littered with food trash and beer cans and God only knew what else.

Timbo sat in an orange recliner opposite a sectional sofa that was arranged around a large coffee table in the center of the living room. He wore a red and white flannel bathrobe open over a dirty white t-shirt and black shorts. Three skinny, tattooed women were on the sofa. Rooster knew Christie and Timbo's wife, Susan, but he didn't recognize the black woman with the dyed blonde dreadlocks. He figured she must be with King Kong. Sitting between her and Christie was a guy with long hair and ridiculous sideburns. Rooster knew him too; he was Mark Rogers, one of the most intelligent people Rooster had ever met, and also a loony, self-loathing, junky hermit. Rooster couldn't stand him.

"Hey, Rooster!" Timbo said without getting up from his seat. "I didn't expect to see you 'till around summertime, if ever again."

"They let some of us short-timers out early. They gotta make room for the rioters."

"Well, lucky you! I guess every cloud has a silver lining. It's good to see you." To King Kong, Timbo said, "Hey, Jamel, why don't you grab a chair out of the kitchen so the Rooster can sit down."

Kong grunted and lumbered into the kitchen and returned with a chair upholstered in cracked, red vinyl, then sat on the sofa next to the woman with the dreadlocks. Rooster exchanged greetings with everyone, and then Timbo lifted an open magazine from the coffee table, revealing a glass pipe and a baggie of tiny meth rocks. He passed the pipe and a cigarette lighter to Rooster. "Have a hit of this."

Rooster took the pipe and drew from it, savoring the rush of warmth that instantly engulfed his neck and shoulders and set his scalp atingle. *Oh Damn, that's good.* The intensity of the euphoria that flooded his mind was such that, when he closed his eyes, he felt as if the slightest breeze could have liberated his consciousness from his worn body and carried it away to some far away, blissful Arcadia. He doubted there was a better sensation to ever be had. Timbo told him to have another hit, and so he did.

"When did you get out, Rooster?" Susan asked.

"Ten o'clock yesterday mornin'," he said in an exhalation of foul-smelling chemical smoke. "They didn't even give me a heads up that they were turning me loose. They just came to the door and told me to roll up my mattress and stuff. An hour or so later, I was walkin' down the street."

"Jesus man," Mark said. "They just sent you walking in the middle of all that anarchy? The least they could have done was spring for a cab."

Rooster took a pack of cigarettes from his coat pocket and tapped it against his palm. "There ain't no cabs runnin' right now. In fact, there ain't much at all runnin' west of I-5, not that I seen anyway. A lot of streets are blocked off by cops and soldiers, and those that ain't are cluttered with wreckage and debris and crowds of pissed off people that look like they'd kill you just to see what color your blood is." He lit a Marlboro and leaned back in the chair. "You been hidin' under a rock or something?"

"We don't go out much," Timbo broke in. "All we really need is dope and cigarettes and a little bit of food. We have enough to last us a while if we go easy on it. When we run out, well, then I guess we'll just have to make do. That's the world we're living in right now, Rooster. You have to make do with what you got. To go gallivanting around out there is to risk getting sick, and I've seen the pictures, man, I've seen the videos. No way do I want to end up like that. They say it's like rabies. It'll make you foam at the mouth and chew your own damn hands off, make you batshit crazy. Just the other day there was that guy in Spokane. Walked into a bus station–naked as a damn jaybird mind you–and attacked four people, biting them in the faces and throats. He *killed* two of them. Chewed them up like a rabid dog. Don't know what became of the other two. He might have killed even more if the cops hadn't shot him dead right there in the bus station. I hear it took ten shots to kill the bastard. I don't want to end up like that. No sir. Hell, if you had been anyone else, I wouldn't have ever even opened the door for you. You can't be too careful. What are you doing running around in the middle of the night in the first place?"

"It's easier to get around in the dark," Rooster said. "You can stay in the shadows and not draw any attention to yourself."

Timbo took a hit from the pipe and passed it to Susan. "Where did you walk here from?"

"I'm staying with a friend up on Beacon Hill. I just wanted to come by and see how you all was doing."

"Beacon Hill. That's gotta be five miles from here. Are you fucking nuts?"

"To tell you the truth, I borrowed my buddy's car but I left it parked up north of Cloverdale. There's a big military camp up by there–helicopters and everything. I didn't want to get pulled over; they got that curfew going on. I just pulled the car up next to a curb and left it sit. I didn't have to walk very far from there."

Timbo nodded. "They're using the school up there as some kind of hospital or something. They got all them soldiers guarding it, at least that's what I heard. Who knows what's really going on? I hear they got a bunch of soldiers guarding the jail too. Is that true?"

"Yeah, the whole area of Pioneer Square is swarming with military, protecting the jail, the courthouse, Public Health, all those buildings around there. Harborview Hospital is there too, right across I-5. I'll bet it's jammed full of people who are infected with that Qilu Virus."

"*Chee*-lew," Mark said. "You're pronouncing it kee-lew but the proper pronunciation is *chee*. It's Chinese. They say the virus originated somewhere along the Yellow River in the Shandong Province of China, that's why you hear some people call it the Yellow River Virus. 'Qilu' is a nickname for Shandong though; that's how it got its name."

Well thank you very much, Mr. Know-it-all, Rooster thought contemptuously. "I know where the virus came from, I read the damned news. Chee-lew, kee-lew, Quaalude, tequila, it don't matter how you say it; there's a whole lot of people sick from it. I highly doubt they're laying around on their death beds pondering the correct pronunciation."

"I was just sayin', man," Mark said.

"*All* the hospitals are full up," said Christie. "They're using the schools to handle the overflow. I heard it on the radio."

"The world is truly going to Hell in a hand basket," Timbo said. "I guess all we can do is ride it out." He carefully rolled up the bag of meth and placed it in the pocket of his shorts. "I'd give you another hit of this crank, Rooster, but like I told you, we have to make it last."

"It's all good," Rooster said. "I'm pretty high. I feel like a bit of a lightweight after spending some time in lockup."

"Yeah, I suppose it has been a while since you've had any kind of fun." Timbo glanced at Rooster, then Christie, then back at Rooster. "Hell, man, why don't you go ahead and take Christie in the back bedroom and let her show you some lovin'?"

Rooster glanced at Christie, then back at Timbo and chuckled. "You serious?"

"As a heart attack. How long were you locked up? Six months?"

"Seven."

"Well, that's a long time to be without a woman. Go ahead. Just don't make a mess."

Rooster raked his eyes over Christie's pale skin and bony physique, the spattering of meth sores on her face and forearms. She smiled, exposing a mouthful of rotting teeth. He considered the offer for a few seconds, then shrugged and said, "Might as well." Timbo was right: Seven months was too long. "Put on some music though, so I know you all ain't out here listenin' to us moan and holler."

He led the girl into the familiar bedroom and did her from behind as Pink Floyd played from a stereo in the living room. A couple of minutes into it, he reached over and lifted a ceramic lamp from a dresser close to the bed, yanked the electrical cord from the wall socket, smashed Christie in the back of her head as hard as he could with the lamp, then strangled her with the cord. He continued to have sex with her after she was dead, and when he finished he stood over her body and stared at the butterfly tattoo on her lower back–her "tramp stamp." *Fly away, little butterfly*, he thought. *Fly away.*

He pulled up his pants, picked his coat off the floor and removed the SIG Sauer .380 semi-auto pistol from a zippered inside pocket. He produced a four-inch sound suppressor from another pocket and carefully screwed it onto the barrel of the SIG. He checked the seven-round magazine, took a second magazine from his coat, removed one round from it and chambered the round in the gun. He held his coat over the pistol and calmly opened the bedroom door and crossed the narrow hallway into the living room.

The six of them looked up at him through meandering tendrils of cigarette smoke with mischievous smiles and wide, glassy eyes. "How did that feel after seven months?" Timbo asked playfully.

"Felt good," Rooster answered. He moved toward the stereo system on a shelf beneath the flat screen TV. An ancient Led Zeppelin song that Rooster didn't recognize was emanating from the speakers; he gyrated his hips to the rhythm of it. "I love this song," he lied. "Mind if I turn it up?" He didn't wait for a response. He cranked the volume knob a few notches, then turned toward the sofa, his body swaying comically to the music.

They chortled and cheered as he danced closer to the sofa, and Timbo said, "What's Christie doing in there? Recovering? I hope you weren't too much for her. I was just telling Jamel and Candace here why they call you Rooster."

Rooster let his coat fall to the floor. The laughter faded, and Rooster saw awareness in their glossy eyes; they knew what was coming. He was closest to Susan and Mark, so he shot them first. One round in each of their heads. *Pop! Pop!* The shots were loud despite the suppressor, the sound like a sledgehammer striking concrete. King Kong was on his feet instantly, and Rooster pumped two bullets into him. The big man bolted for the front door without even flinching, but Rooster shot him twice more in the back, and he collapsed before he made it. The woman with the blonde dreadlocks was next. *What did Timbo say her name was? Oh that's right: Candace.* "So long, Candace." She screamed and held her hands out in front of her, and Rooster shot her between the eyes. He then turned his attention to Timbo, who had dove from his chair and was on his hands and knees, crawling toward the hallway from where Rooster had just come. Rooster walked over to him and pointed the gun at the back of his head. "Where do you think you're going, asshole?"

Timbo froze in place and began to whimper. "Rooster, p-p-please...please don't kill me, man. I'm your friend."

"No, you're wrong about that, Timbo. You ain't my fuckin' friend. Now I want you to crawl on over to that stereo and turn the music off, so I don't have to shout."

"Okay, okay...anything you want, Rooster. Anything. Just please don't shoot me, man."

Timbo crab-walked across the dirty living room floor as Rooster followed closely and removed the empty magazine from the SIG and replaced it with the fresh one from his back pocket. Once the music was off, Rooster heard moaning from across the room near the front door. "Well, I'll be damned," he said with amusement. "Looks like your boy Jamel is still alive. How 'bout you slither over there with me, Timbo, and let's have a look." Timbo did as he was told.

Jamel lay on his left side on the tiled floor of the entryway. Blood streamed from holes in his back, neck, and right shoulder into a widening pool beneath him. His eyes were half-open, and a soft gurgling sound accompanied his breathing. "Help me," he pleaded weakly, his voice barely more than a whisper. "Oh God *help me*. I need a ambulance."

Rooster scanned the room for something he might use to crush Jamel's skull, and when he saw nothing he thought would be substantial enough, he raised his right foot and brought his boot heel down on the man's neck. Again and again, he stomped savagely until he was out of breath, and then, for good measure, he leaped into the air and landed with both feet on Jamel's head. He slipped and fell against the wall but quickly righted himself and trained his gun on Timbo, who was sobbing on his knees a few feet away. He looked down at Jamel and was astonished to see that his massive chest was still heaving up and down even as he twitched and shuddered in the now rapidly spreading blood pool. *Un-fucking-believable, this guy.* Rooster watched, fascinated, until Kong finally let out his last bubbling breath and his legs stopped twitching. He then turned to Timbo and, with a maniacal nonchalance, said, "Whatcha got to eat around here?"

3.

He relaxed at the flimsy kitchen table and ate ramen noodles and stale cheese puffs while Timbo sat cross-legged close by on the floor, his hands duct taped behind his back. The sweet-sour smell of blood coalesced with the other rank odors in the house, fouling the air like road kill under a summer sun, but it didn't affect Rooster's appetite in the least.

"Why didn't you just shoot him?" Timbo asked, timidly.

Rooster continued to chew his food without responding. He had confiscated Timbo's bag of meth after he had bound the man's wrists, and he now held it up across the kitchen light and examined the contents. The dirty-looking, yellow pebbles reminded Rooster of extricated gallstones.

"Seriously, man, why did you have to stomp his head in like you did? Jamel was a pretty cool dude. He didn't deserve to go out like that."

Rooster placed the baggie in his pocket and emitted a frustrated sigh. "For one, the fucker wasn't worth another bullet; I'd already put four in his fat ass. Bullets are hard to come by at this current point in time. And two, you have neighbors twenty feet on both sides of you. They likely didn't make out the gunshots with the stereo blaring and all, but without the music playing, a gunshot might sound too much like a gunshot, even with the silencer, which don't really silence nothin'."

Timbo was quiet for a minute, and then he lowered his head and began to cry. "What are you gonna do to me, man? I can help you, you know? Whatever it is you want, I can help you. I'm scared, man. You're really scaring me. What can I do? Just tell me, Rooster. I'll do anything. I'm just...so...scared right now." He was blubbering like a frightened child. A strand of mucus swung from his nose, and rivulets of saliva dribbled down his chin before dropping onto his lap.

Rooster couldn't help chuckling. "Stop crying, you damned pussy. Have a little fuckin' dignity." He pushed his chair away from the table, stood and bent over, pressing his face only a few inches from Timbo's. "Listen up," he said softly. "There's something you don't know about me. Do you think you can handle it if I tell you?"

Timbo nodded vigorously, his lip quivering. "Y-y-yeah, man. I can handle it. Whatever it is, it's cool with me."

"Good." Rooster looked Timbo dead in the eyes and leaned in closer. "I'm a vampire. The only thing I want from you is your blood."

Timbo's face went pale. He opened his mouth as if to say something, but the only sound that came out was a frail squeak. Rooster took a few seconds to revel in the man's terror and bewilderment, then bared his teeth and chomped at Timbo's neck, releasing a vicious growl as he did. Timbo shrieked wildly and fell backward, as Rooster howled in laughter.

"I'm just messing with you, you fuckin' idiot," Rooster roared. "Even if I *was* a vampire, the last thing on Earth I would want is your nasty-assed blood. I *will* take your dope stash though, along with your money, whatever guns you have in the house, and the keys to the vehicles parked outside."

"S-sure, sure, Rooster," Timbo whined. "You can have anything you want. I only want to be helpful to you, man. You're like a brother to me."

"Then get your sorry ass up and show me where you hide your *shit*."

Timbo struggled to his feet and led Rooster into his bedroom. "There's a lock box on the floor in the closet," he said, "underneath some folded blankets. The keys to my Jeep are on the dresser. I don't know about the keys to Jamel's Impala; they're probably in his pocket."

Rooster pushed him onto the bed and told him to roll over and stay on his belly. Timbo did so without hesitation as Rooster snatched the car keys off the dresser and ransacked the closet.

"What's the combination to the lock?" Rooster demanded after he found the metal box. Timbo told him, and he opened the lid to reveal a loaded Smith & Wesson short-barreled .357 Magnum revolver with a nickel finish, a fifty-round box of hollow-point bullets, three rolled bags of marijuana, one rolled bag of crystal meth, and a hundred twenty-seven dollars in cash. There were also three capped vials of pills, some empty syringes, and some loose change. "What are these pills in here?" he asked.

"Uh, some OxyContin, some Vicodin, and uh...some Rohypnol."

"What the fuck is Rohypnol?"

"It's uh, it's a tranquilizer. Sorta like Valium."

"Which ones are the Rohypnol? These containers aren't labeled."

"The Rohypnol are the ones that say 'ROCHE' on the back of them. The yellow ones are the Oxy, and the long ones are the Vicodin."

Rooster stuffed the Magnum into his waistband and emptied the remaining contents of the box into a stained pillowcase. He also took from the closet a 12-gauge pump shotgun and a long-handled metal flashlight. He eased the slide of the shotgun back partway to check if the weapon was loaded. It was. "Where are the extra shells for the shotgun?"

"Top shelf. Right corner."

He tossed the box of shells into the pillowcase and demanded the rest of Timbo's money.

"That's all I have, Rooster. I swear."

"If I have to ask you again, I'm gonna start cutting your fingers off."

When Timbo didn't respond, Rooster leaned over the bed and grasped his thumb and wrenched it until it broke with an audible *snap!*

Timbo squealed in pain. "Okay! Okay! My wallet is in the top dresser drawer. There's about a hundred bucks in it. I just forgot about it, is all. I just *forgot.* Please don't hurt me anymore."

Rooster found the wallet and removed the money. He rifled through the other dresser drawers, peered under the bed, and rummaged through a purse that hung from a hook on the bedroom door. After finding nothing of interest, he told Timbo to get off the bed and go into the kitchen. Once there, he ordered Timbo to get on his knees, and then pulled a butcher knife from a wooden rack on the counter. "Well, looks like this is the end of the line," he said coldly. "Any last words?"

Timbo looked up at Rooster, his teary eyes pleading. "Wha—"

Rooster swept the knife blade across Timbo's throat before he could say anything else. He left the man writhing and kicking on the floor while he filled a large garbage bag with food from the kitchen cabinets and a couple of twenty-ounce bottles of Pepsi from the refrigerator. After he had collected all that would fit inside the bag, he put on his coat and placed a few additional food items into his pockets, then went into the living room to search the bodies in there. He spent a couple of minutes pillaging the corpses, his effort rewarding him with another seventy-eight dollars in cash and Jamel's car keys. A red-dyed rabbit's foot dangled from the key ring. *So much for luck*, Rooster thought.

He placed the garbage bag, pillowcase, and the shotgun near the front door, and headed outside to check the fuel levels in the vehicles. The door thumped against Jamel's swollen, bloody head when he opened it, but Rooster was able to force a wide enough gap to squeeze his lanky frame through without too much trouble. The gas gauge in Timbo's Jeep Cherokee registered just under a quarter of a tank. It was likely enough to get him to where he needed to drive, but fuel was rapidly becoming a rare and valuable commodity these days; he would hate to leave Jamel's Impala sitting there if it happened to have a full tank. He was, however, only mildly disappointed when he discovered that it contained only a quarter tank as well. He decided that when it came time to leave, he would take the Jeep. He didn't know what or whom he might have to drive over on the way to his destination, but in any case, the Jeep was more suited for the job.

He glanced at his watch. 1:51 am. The area-wide curfew was in effect from dusk to dawn. Anyone caught out on the streets at night would be arrested. Or worse; he had heard rumors of soldiers and police officers shooting people. He didn't know if there was any truth to it, but he'd already risked it once this night. He wasn't willing to gamble further just yet. He figured that sunrise would be around 7:30, over five and a half hours away. *Might as well make myself comfortable*, he thought. He went back inside the house and locked the front door and waited for the sun to come up.

4.

The little boy stands in line with his stepfather. He is eight years old and excited to be signing up for his second season of Little League Baseball. He has worked hard to improve his skills since last year and cannot wait to show everyone how much better he has become. His mom keeps telling him that if he keeps practicing, he might even be good enough to play with the pros someday. He believes her because he knows she loves him and she would never lie to him. Yes, Mom, I really can be a pro someday, he tells her. I know I can be anything I want if I get good grades and work hard, right? That's right, son. That's exactly right.

The line is moving slowly and Lyle, his stepfather, is growing impatient. He is beginning to curse under his breath. The little boy prays to God to make the line move faster, before Lyle starts to get mad, but several minutes pass and the registration table still looks so far away. Some of the other parents are talking and laughing with each other, but Lyle is shifting back and forth on his feet and rubbing his forehead and whispering things to himself that the boy can't hear well enough to understand. Finally, the man grabs the boy by the arm and tells him they are leaving. The boy doesn't want to go. If they leave without signing the papers, he won't get to play in Little League, but Lyle doesn't care. You can play next year, he says.

The boy is crying as his stepfather drags him outside into the parking lot. There are people standing all around and he notices some of his classmates playing catch on the sidewalk. One of them asks him if he got signed up for Little League, and he answers no and turns his head to hide his tears. He begs Lyle to stay just a little while longer. The man isn't listening. The boy knows that if his mom were here she would wait as long as it took, but she isn't here, and the boy longs for the time before his stepfather came along, when things were better.

I hate you, the boy says. In front of everyone, Lyle punches him hard on the cheek with his fist. The boy feels dizzy and the only thing that keeps him from falling is Lyle's painful grip on his arm. He looks around at all the watching faces and wonders why none of the adults try to help him. Some of them pretend not to notice, but the boy can see the uncomfortable expressions on their faces. He hangs his head in embarrassment as Lyle drags him to the car. Don't you ever tell me you hate me, the man says through gritted teeth.

Not a word is spoken during the ride home. He runs into the house and his mom asks why he is crying. He describes to her what happened and sees her face grow red with anger. Don't worry, son, I'll take you back and get you signed up for Little League. She does, and the boy is thrilled, but when they return home, Lyle meets them at the front door and punches the boy's mom in the mouth. She falls and he kicks her over and over as she screams, then he yanks her up off the floor and punches her again in the face. Blood is streaming down her chin and Lyle curses her for making him do this to her. The boy watches from across the room and wishes he could help his mom, but he knows that if he tries to interfere, he will be beaten as well. So he closes his eyes and covers his ears and dreams about Little League Baseball.

*** *

Ross awoke from a nightmare in which he had been walking down the cracked pavement of a street in a long-abandoned town at the foot of a mountain range as dozens of ghostly arms reached for him through the windows of the dilapidated buildings that lined the street on both sides.

Thunk! The sound came from the large fixed window in the wall that ran perpendicular to the sofa on which he lay sweating despite the cold. He heard it twice more before he forced himself to sit up and take a look. He thought it might be someone tossing an object up against the two-story window in order to get his attention, but then he saw the bird—a little brown sparrow—fly head-first into one of the glass panels.

Thunk!

"Go *away*," Ross shouted hoarsely. "It's too early for this shit."

Thunk! Again, the sparrow ricocheted off the window, leaving behind a smudge of blood. Ross watched in bewilderment as the bird continued to bounce off the same spot on the glass every few seconds, each time leaving behind a further remnant of blood and goo, until finally, the little creature dropped out of sight and did not return. For a moment, Ross wondered what was out there that so fervently compelled the bird to want to come inside, but he thought he might know the answer:

It's the fucking end of the world.

He gnawed on a chocolate protein bar, which had the approximate consistency of a brick, as he made his way downstairs to the training area. Out of habit, he grabbed a push broom from the maintenance closet and started sweeping the six thousand square-foot concrete floor, but reconsidered. The gym had been closed for a week, and there was no telling how long it would be before Ross could reopen it, if he could *ever* reopen it. Nobody other than Ross himself was going to be using the facility, and he didn't give much of a damn about a dusty floor.

He set the broom aside and took a pair of black hand wraps, a jump rope, and a pair of black and white Grant boxing gloves from his locker in the shower room. He laid the gloves and jump rope on a weight bench while he wrapped his hands, then clicked on a 3-minute round timer and began his daily training ritual. Even though he had not boxed professionally in over six years, his workouts had been a constant in his life since he was a teenager. In fact, it had been the only constant in his life, at least until he had met Monica.

He remembered the first time he had laid eyes on her eight years ago, back when he had trained regularly at Cam's Boxing Club in Seattle, putting in three or four hours a day, six days a week in preparation for his fights. One evening she had come in looking to purchase some boxing lessons. Cam had given her an unbeatable rate. He was always bitching about never having enough females in the club, and Monica was the most beautiful thing to have ever walked through the door. Her looks were certain to draw an increase in male memberships, and she promised to tell her girlfriends to give it a try as well. Ross didn't think she ever brought in any more women, but after a few days he could always tell when she was in the gym because almost every guy present would be huddled around her like bees on a honeycomb. Ross himself, normally very focused and disciplined, had once let his attention drift toward her while he was sparring a heavy-handed pro boxer from another club. He had, in an instant, been mesmerized by the sight of her striking a punching bag about ten feet from the ring; her silky blonde hair pulled back into a ponytail, revealing the sexy line of her neck; her sapphire eyes sparkling with determination; her milky skin glistening with perspiration—

Then everything had gone black.

Ross had not felt the left hook that rocked his chin, nor had he felt the impact of his head striking the canvas. He had only heard the voice of Big Al, his coach, screaming, "—the hell are you *doing*, ya damn palooka? Get your sorry ass up off the mat and keep your eyes on the *prize*." It had been one of Big Al's favorite expressions. Keep your eyes on the prize. But Monica *was* the prize, and Ross had found it increasingly difficult to keep his eyes *off* her. As time went on, he had been delighted to frequently catch her eyeing *him*.

At some point, he had begun giving her boxing lessons, creating the opportunity for the two of them to get to know each other. It turned out that she was as brainy as she was beautiful, holding a master's degree in psychology, and at the time, working toward a doctorate through the University of Washington. Before long, they had started dating. Twenty months later, after Monica finished her program at the university, they married. At the same time, Ross, then thirty-five years old, retired from his career as a professional boxer due to his ailing knees. They moved away from the hustle and bustle of Seattle to settle down in Wenatchee, where Ross opened the gym, and Monica began work at the Valley Hospital's Rehabilitation Center. The next six years had been glorious beyond anything Ross could have imagined, but it had all changed in the space of a single moment, when he had received the phone call seven days ago.

Now he stood on the cold concrete floor and tried not to drown in his grief. He was no stranger to suffering, but the loss of Monica was beyond what his strength could bear. When she died, his dreams and vision of the future had died with her. Now he was alone in a whirlwind of chaos and uncertainty, writhing in the torment of his very existence. *What* are *you?* asked a voice deep in his mind. It was a question he frequently asked the fighters he trained when the fire in their eyes began to dim. "I'm a fucking warrior," he answered aloud. But he didn't feel like a warrior; he felt more like the guy who gets carried out of the ring on a stretcher.

His mind shifted to the pandemic that was currently engulfing humanity like the darkness of night. He wondered what it would feel like to be infected. The talking heads on the news channels had described the first symptoms as closely resembling those of influenza, but within three or four days a victim will, in all likelihood, go violently insane and die. He thought of the sparrow at the window. Were birds carriers of the virus? Perhaps it had originated with them–some sort of avian flu that had mutated into an unstoppable super bug that would continue to decimate mankind until there was no one left to infect and kill. Scientists didn't seem to think so, but Ross wasn't convinced that anyone knew for sure.

He switched on the radio situated on a shelf near the entrance to the front service counter area. The faceless voice of the on-air announcer erupted from the network of speakers that hung on the walls throughout the building. "—Department of Homeland Security denies that the mandatory shutdown of video-hosting, peer-to-peer, and social networking websites is an effort to censor information or free speech, saying that the measure is, in fact, being implemented in order to free up bandwidth crucial to the continuity of essential services. The President is expected to speak on the issue at a press conference sometime this afternoon.

"In local news today, a Wenatchee police officer shot and killed a man who allegedly attacked him at a trailer park on

Crawford Avenue. Police spokesperson, Cheryl Rodriguez, says the officer, whose name has not yet been disclosed, was responding to a suspicious person call at Shady Groves Trailer Park early this morning, when an unidentified man attacked the officer and wrestled him to the ground. During the struggle, the officer pulled his gun and shot the suspect several times. The suspect died at the scene, and the officer was taken to Valley Hospital with undisclosed injuries. Rodriguez says the incident is being investigated, but so far, there is no evidence of wrongdoing on the officer's part."

The radio announcer's voice could not have been more devoid of emotion if he had been reading a fast food menu as his report went on to address food and gas shortages, increased crime and civil unrest, and a plea from the mayor for local residents to "pull together and help one another through this unprecedented but temporary crisis."

Ross listened until he could take it no longer, then inserted a disc into the CD player and submerged his misery in the driving, industrial rhythm of Caustic's "White Knuckle Head Fuck." Even with the music blasting from the wall speakers, the gym felt eerily quiet. He missed the cacophony of a packed house; twenty or thirty pairs of boxing gloves smacking against the swaying leather bags that hung from steel support beams sixteen feet overhead. The clattering of wood floorboards as fighters slipped and shuffled within the ropes of the two twenty-foot rings that graced the center of the wide floor. The staccato cadence of speed bags rebounding against their Formica-coated platforms; the clanging of iron weights and chrome barbells; the grunts and groans and gasps of men, women, and children from various walks of life, with unique, individual motivations that commingled into a collective symphony of dreams. On those days, the music, no matter how loud, was only background noise.

A half-hour into his workout, Ross heard someone pounding on the front door. He removed his boxing gloves, turned down the music, and made his way to the front of the building. Through the plate glass window in the lobby, he saw a dark blue police cruiser parked next to his van. The officer at the door wore a white particle mask over his face. He waved when he saw Ross through the window.

"Good morning, Coach," the cop said, after Ross opened the door.

Even through the facemask, Ross recognized the voice of Mickey Rivera, an amateur boxer who had been a regular at the gym for nearly two years, and had worked security at a few of the fights Ross had promoted. Mickey was a five-year veteran of the Wenatchee Police Department, and had recently become a member of the county SWAT Team.

"What the hell are you doing with that bra cup on your face?" Ross asked. "Don't you know the virus can get in through your eyes?"

Mickey chuckled. "I'm not sure anyone knows that for a fact, but in any case, the mask is more for *your* protection than mine."

Ross considered that for a few seconds, and then asked, "Are you sick?"

"Not at all. I'm as healthy as a horse."

"Then take that goofy thing off."

Mickey pulled the mask down beneath his chin, exposing a broad smile. "I haven't seen you in a while, Coach. I noticed your van out front and thought I'd drop in for a quick visit. How are you doing?"

"I've definitely been better," Ross said. He motioned Mickey inside and pulled the metal door closed behind him.

"I can't stay very long," Mickey said. "I just wanted to see how you're holding up."

"Like I said, I've been better."

Mickey shifted nervously on his feet and lowered his eyes. "I heard about Monica. I'm really sorry, man."

Ross nodded solemnly and scratched the stubble on his chin. "I appreciate you paying your respects. Right now, I'm just trying to work things out in my head, you know? This...everything...it's a lot to deal with."

"I understand, Coach. It *is* a lot to deal with. I can't even imagine what you must be feeling. But if there's anything I can do, please don't hesitate to let me know."

"Thanks, Mickey. You don't need to be worrying about me though. I'll manage. I always have. How about you? This whole pandemic thing must be taking its toll on you and your family."

"We're doing okay. My son is enjoying the time off from school. Things haven't been too bad as far as police work goes–not too many people out running around. There was a shooting this morning though. Some guy jumped on an officer and ended up getting himself killed."

"I heard about that on the radio. What happened?"

"Well, about three o'clock this morning, Officer Morris, a friend of mine, got called to check out a suspicious person report at that trailer court over by Lincoln Park, and when he got there, some guy in his underwear jumped on him...tried to take his gun away. They were grappling on the ground, and Morris was getting beat up pretty bad, and finally he got into position to fire and shot the guy four or five times. Witnesses said the guy looked like he was jacked up on meth or something. They said he kept on fighting even after Morris started shooting."

"That's pretty crazy," Ross said. "You don't think the guy was infected with the virus, do you?"

"God, I hope not. We'll know pretty soon if he was."

"How soon?"

"I don't know how the testing procedure works. I'm a cop, not a doctor. I'm confident the medical examiner is prioritizing it though."

"So what happens if it turns out he *was* infected?" Ross felt a knot forming in his stomach. "What does that mean for Wenatchee?"

"If that ends up being the case, Wenatchee is prepared for it." In his mind, Ross saw images of the chaos in Seattle, Los Angeles, Chicago, and the countless other cities around the nation and the world. "I hope you're right, Mickey. I hope you're right."

5.

Rooster had driven less than half a mile before he found himself bogged down in traffic that was all but stationary. Several car lengths ahead on the right of the street was a large, flashing sign which read: "ROAD CLOSED" and "DETOUR AHEAD" in an alternating sequence. Both the southbound and northbound lanes were clogged with southbound traffic—everybody wanted out of the city; nobody wanted in—and with no room to turn around, Rooster had no choice but to follow the creeping flow of the vehicles in front of him. He shut the Jeep's engine off as much as possible to save gas, but his frustration brewed as the needle of the fuel gauge dropped steadily closer to the red "Empty" mark.

He had slept very little since his release from the county jail, but thanks to periodic tokes on the meth pipe, he felt fully awake. Still, he knew better than to allow his false sense of alertness to fool him. He understood that his mental clarity was dulled significantly by his intoxication and lack of sleep. Occasionally, he would catch himself dreaming, even though his eyes were wide open. When he noticed the red and blue police strobes about a hundred yards beyond the detour sign, he could feel the familiar prickle of paranoia beginning to pervade his mind, and he had to struggle to keep it in check. *Everything's cool. Traffic cops enforcing the detour, is all. Don't sweat it.* Nonetheless, he took the .357 Magnum from below his seat and placed it beneath his right leg. Just in case.

As he drew closer to the roadblock, he could see four police officers directing traffic. All were dressed in black riot gear with gas masks and helmets with raised face shields. Two of the officers each held a shotgun pointed at the ground. Behind the orange traffic cones and flimsy road barriers two patrol cars and two motorcycles were parked. Rooster briefly entertained the idea of shooting it out with the cops and stealing one of the motorcycles, but he didn't think he stood much of a chance in that scenario. This was not like the movies where Hollywood tough guys single-handedly dispatched hordes of armed enemies; this was reality, where you were likely to be shot to pieces in seconds for trying something so foolish.

Stay cool, Rooster. Stay fucking cool.

When he finally reached the roadblock, an officer extended his arm and pointed for Rooster to follow the traffic right, onto 132nd Street. Rooster did, and that was that. Simple. Easy. No exchange of gunfire necessary. He did, however, still need to get to where he needed to go. He would have to find another way.

He drove on 132nd until he came to Black River High School on the north side of the street. He pulled into the entranceway, parked, and looked over a map while he sucked on the meth pipe. Across the road was a densely wooded area which separated him from 134th Street, three hundred yards to the south. If he cut through the woods on foot, he would come out south of the roadblocks and about a mile west of Downtown Renton, an area through which he needed to travel to reach his destination. He didn't at all like the idea of abandoning the Jeep, but he thought it would be easy enough to steal another car later on, and it was nearly out of gas anyway. He would be forced to leave the shotgun behind as well; there was no way he would be able to carry it without drawing unwanted attention.

He opened the back door of the Jeep and pulled out the garbage bag full of goods he had taken from Timbo's residence. He removed some of the heavier food containers to lessen the chance of the bag breaking during his walk, and emptied their contents onto the asphalt. He didn't see any reason to leave it for the benefit of someone else. He also emptied the shells from the shotgun and dropped them into the pillowcase with the others. He had the idea that, as time went on, it might be easier to find another shotgun than it would be to find shells for it. He raised the gun over his head and smashed its birch stock against the ground, then tossed it back onto the Jeep floorboard. He took the Magnum from the front seat and stuck it in his waistband. When he was certain he had everything he needed, he locked the doors from the outside, flung the keys into the woods, and punctured all four tires with a flathead screwdriver. He then hoisted the pillowcase and garbage bag over his shoulder and headed into the trees. Once on 134th, he walked east on the narrow street past large, multi-floored homes with yards lined with meticulously manicured shrubbery and American flags fluttering at the tops of tall poles. At one home, a man who looked to be in his fifties stood by a black pickup truck and watched Rooster with apprehension. Rooster felt an urge to shoot the man in the face with the .357 and take his truck, but instead, he kept walking. He turned right on Langston Road, which would lead him downhill through a residential area and into Downtown Renton.

At the bottom of the hill was what would normally be the busy intersection of Sunset and Hardie, eerily void of traffic despite morning rush hour. A convenience store was on the right, closed, its windows boarded up. A used car dealership on the right, its windows boarded as well. Many of the little Japanese cars on the lot exhibited ugly dents, and glass from the shattered light covers and windshields littered the pavement like crushed ice. Across the intersection was a huge Fred Meyer store, a bank, a strip mall, a massive parking expanse, empty. There were fires burning in the distance, and Rooster watched the smoke drift up to imbue itself into the low blanket of dark winter clouds.

He continued east along the sidewalk, marveling at the vacant grocery stores, fast food restaurants, and various shops and offices that bordered the one-way street. There was broken glass here and there, and graffiti was painted across the walls of a number of buildings—phrases such as TRUST JESUS and JUDGMENT DAY IS UPON US, along with assorted gang symbols. There were vehicles that passed occasionally. After a while, he stuck out his thumb in the hope that someone would be stupid enough to give him a ride, but when he spotted a police car at an intersection, he decided that hitchhiking was probably not conducive to avoiding the attention of law enforcement, and cursed himself for not considering that to begin with. Fortunately, the cop paid him no notice.

Every so often, he would come across a pedestrian or two. Some wore surgical masks, and most went out of their way to maintain a safe distance from him. Sitting against the wall of one coffee shop was an old Native American man with long gray hair, dressed in an army jacket and blue jeans. Against his chest, he held a cardboard sign which read: GOD WON'T SAVE YOU in bold, black letters. Rooster laughed and drew a wad of cash from his pants pocket and tossed the man a crumpled five-dollar bill. "Here you go, old man. You're probably the most truthful sumbitch I've come across in a long time."

Farther down the street, he encountered three black men in baggy pants and bulky, black coats. One of them held a large, blue-gray pit bull at the end of a leash. The men straightened and puffed out their chests as Rooster drew near. "Yo, man, what you got in the bags?" The guy with the dog said.

"Nothing you need to concern yourself with," Rooster replied.

The three of them spread out, blocking Rooster's path.

"I asked you a question, fool. What the fuck is in them bags?"

"I answered your question...fool. Maybe you should dig the shit out of your ears so you can hear better."

At that, their eyes grew so big they looked like they might pop out of their skulls. The dog handler's mouth dropped open, and he began bouncing around and flinging his arms in a showy display of anger. "*Motherfucker!* Bitch, I'm gonna count to three—nah, fuck that. I'm gonna count to *two*, and then you're gonna give me them bags or else I'm gonna set my dog on your punk ass." He slapped the dog on the back and yelled, "Watch him, Lotto!"

Lotto lunged forward on the leash and bared his teeth and barked viciously.

"*One*, motherfucker," the man said.

Rooster remained calm. "If you turn that dog loose, I'm gonna take out my gun and shoot all three of you before he has a chance to bite me."

"Bullshit, Reggie," one of the other guys said, throwing his arms into the air. "If this fool had a gun, he would have already had it out."

Rooster locked eyes with Reggie. "I know what you're thinkin', dude. You're thinkin' that this scruffy white boy is bluffin'. But think about this: if I'm *not* bluffin', then you get to die a slow, agonizin' death right here on the sidewalk in this godforsaken ghost town, because I'm gonna shoot you directly in the nuts. Is it really worth taking that risk just to see what's in these bags? They could be full of dirty underwear, for all you know."

"This motherfucker all thinking he's Clint Eastwood," jeered the loudmouth on Reggie's right. "Motherfuckin' Dirty Harry. Bitch, you ain't no Clint Eastwood, you just a skinny-ass punk. If they was underwear in them bags, you wouldn't be trying so hard to protect it."

"Well, Einstein," Rooster said, "I ain't made the slightest effort to protect *anything* yet, but if y'all don't take your dog and back the fuck up on outta here, then you're gonna find out just how far I'm willing to go."

Reggie stood still and silent, his right hand tightly gripping the leash. Rooster knew there was a battle raging in the man's mind: pride versus survival. The dog continued to lunge and snarl. The guy on Reggie's left was nervously switching his attention back and forth between Rooster and Reggie. Then Reggie lifted his chin defiantly, a crooked smile forming on his lips. "*Two,* motherfucker."

He let go of the leash.

The big dog launched like a racehorse fresh out of the gate. Rooster dropped his bags, spread his feet to balance himself, and thrust his left arm out in front of his body. Lotto hesitated briefly, then attacked Rooster's arm at the urging of his owner. Rooster winced as the dog's teeth clamped down just above his wrist. With his right hand, he reached beneath his coat and brushed his fingertips across the butt of the Magnum, but before he could get a grip on it Lotto jerked him off balance, and he was forced to grasp his left hand to counter the violent tugging on his arm.

"That's right! Get him, Lotto!" Reggie screamed.

A red Honda Civic approached, slowed to a crawl, and then sped away. "Oh shit, Reggie," one of the thugs said, "we gotta go. Those fools are gonna call the cops."

Rooster heard ripping sounds and hoped it wasn't his skin. A section of thick fabric tore away from his coat sleeve, and he staggered sideways as Lotto lost his grip, but the dog lunged again and found another hold higher up on Rooster's forearm before Rooster realized he was free. Lotto flung his head from side to side as if he was shaking a dead rabbit, and then yanked backward, working his neck like a spring-loaded piston. With every ounce of his strength, Rooster straightened his back and lifted the dog high enough that his front legs were off the ground. Then he quickly reached beneath his coat and this time, grasped the handle of the Magnum.

In the next instant, Reggie was there, trying to pry Lotto's jaws open with his hands while Einstein pulled the dog by his hind legs. From the corner of his eye, Rooster saw the third guy snatch up the bags that the three bastards were obviously willing to die for. The roar of a large engine. The whoosh-whine of air brakes. A yellow utility truck with a folding boom on top pulled up alongside the curb. Two men wearing white surgical masks jumped out and asked if they could help, just as Rooster thrust the barrel of the .357 into Reggie's crotch and pulled the trigger.

6.

Ross didn't finish his workout after Mickey left. Instead, he took two large duffel bags from a storage closet and tossed them into his van, locked the front door of the gym, then climbed into the van and was backing out of the parking space when he saw Andre Wallace roll up on a bicycle.

"Hey, man," Andre said, cheerfully, "what's goin' on?"

"I'm sorta busy right now, Dre."

"Oh come on, man. I gotta talk to you."

Ross sighed. "You sick at all? Even a little bit?"

"Nah, I ain't sick. I feel good."

"Alright, throw your bike in the back and hop in."

Andre wrestled his bicycle into the back of the van, then climbed in and shut the doors behind him. Ross waited for him to make his way forward to the passenger's seat, but after several seconds, Ross looked over his shoulder and saw the youngster sitting on the floor.

"Dre, come on up front. You don't have to sit back there."

Andre came up and buckled himself in as Ross reversed the van into the street. "Yo, where you goin', man?"

"I have to run home for a few minutes," Ross said. "I need to pick up a few things."

"You gonna open the gym back up?"

"No. Not anytime soon."

"Are you *ever* gonna open it back up?"

"Why? Are you in a hurry to go back to washing the windows and scrubbing the toilets?"

"They ain't been cleaned in a week, have they? They prolly need cleanin'," Andre said, matter-of-factly.

Ross couldn't help but to smile. He liked Andre. He had liked him since the first day he had come into the gym over four years ago. The kid had been sixteen then, still in high school. He never had any money to pay for gym membership, but he had shown such an eagerness toward boxing that Ross let him assume some of the custodial chores in exchange for lessons. His physical awkwardness and mental disability prevented him from being proficient at either boxing or custodial chores, but Ross appreciated his determination and enjoyed having him around, even if he had a tendency to get on Ross's nerves occasionally.

"So what did you need to talk to me about?" Ross asked.

"I was just gonna ask you for a favor."

"You're always asking me for favors."

"I know, but you ain't ever turned me down."

"What is it, Dre?"

"I was just gonna ask if I could maybe stay with you for a little while."

"I don't know if that's a good idea, I'm dealing with some major personal issues right now."

"Man, we *all* dealing with personal issues. They's people starvin' in my hood. People can't even feed they own babies. Ain't no gas for people's cars, can't get no medicine, all the jobs are shut down, and the little bit that people *do* got, other people are tryin' to take away. A friend of mine got jacked just the other day."

"The fact that everybody has their own problems doesn't make mine any easier to deal with, Dre. I doubt there are many people who would trade places with me. If you need money or food or anything like that, I can help you out some, but—"

"*Look*, man, you don't understand. My momma done locked me out the house. I been stayin' over with my ex-girlfriend and *her* momma, but they wantin' me to go too. I got nowhere else, and it's cold outside. You like a father to me. That's why I'm asking you."

"Why would your momma lock you out of the house in the middle of winter? That makes no sense to me at all. It has to be some kind of misunderstanding. I know you take things the wrong way sometimes."

"They ain't no misunderstanding. She sent me to the store to get some groceries a few days ago. The store was closed, so I went back home. When I got there, they was a bag of my clothes on the front porch. I tried to get back in the house, but my momma came to the window and said I couldn't come back in. Told me I had to find someplace else to stay."

"She didn't tell you why?"

"No, she didn't say why."

Ross pulled the van into the driveway of his two-bedroom house and shut off the engine.

"Have you tried going back since then?"

"I went back yesterday, but she wouldn't even come to the door."

"Well, let me gather up a few things inside, and when I'm finished, I'll drive us over to your momma's house and see if I can get her to let you come home."

Andre seemed satisfied with that. Ross grabbed the duffel bags from between the seats and got out of the van. "You coming in, Dre, or do you want to wait for me?"

"Nah, man, I'll come with you. I can say hi to your wife. Or is she still over there in England?"

Ross felt his throat tighten. "France. She went to France, Dre, and...essentially, yes, she's still over there."

"Oh. When is she gonna be back?"

Ross bit his lip and took a deep breath and fought the compulsion to collapse in the driveway and cry like a baby. *What are you?*

I'm a warrior.

"You coming in or what?" he asked.

Inside the house, he handed one of the duffel bags to Andre and instructed him to stuff it with non-perishable food products from the kitchen while Ross went into the master bedroom to gather some clothes, his handgun, and two boxes of .38 cartridges.

"Yo, you takin' a trip somewheres?" Andre asked.

"No. I'm going to be staying at the gym for a little while."

"You get evicted from your house or somethin'?"

"No, Dre, nothing like that. That's just where I want to be right now."

"Why can't I stay here then, if nobody gonna be living here?"

"Because you need to look after your momma."

"But my momma locked me out the house."

"I'll explain things to you later. Right now, I'd like to pack up some things and get out of here."

Ross filled his bag and grabbed an armload of tee shirts off a rack in the closet and took it all out to the van. Then he returned and collected towels and blankets, some fishing and camping gear, batteries, a video game console, video games, CDs, DVDs, a gallon of bleach, soap, toothpaste, and other basic necessities, loaded everything onto the van, then went into the kitchen and prepared two frozen dinners in the microwave while Andre continued to bag non-perishables at a snail's pace.

"Dang, man, you look like you takin' everything but the kitchen sink," Andre said.

"I don't know how things are going to play out. I don't know if I'm going to be holed up in the gym for six months or a year, or if I might have to go camp in the mountains. I don't know how death is going to end up taking me, Andre, but I can tell you that it's not going to be by way of thirst or starvation or some fucked up virus that was probably created in a lab somewhere. It's only a matter of time before sick people start turning up here in Wenatchee, and when they do, things are going to get a lot worse than they are now." Ross shoved a tray of spaghetti and meatballs on the counter in front of Andre, passed him a fork. "Here, man, eat with me."

They ate on their feet, and when they finished, Ross took a bed sheet from a linen closet and spread it over the dining room table. What food remained in the cabinets, he placed on top of the sheet and tied the four corners together. Then he transferred the contents of the kitchen freezer into two plastic grocery bags. "This is going to be a peace offering for your momma," he told Andre. "Whatever you did to piss her off, she'll forget about when we show up with all this food."

"Thank you, sir. I figured you would know how to handle the situation."

"Don't thank me yet; she still might not let you back in the house. And don't call me 'sir,' it makes me feel old."

"Okay, sir."

Before they left the house, Ross took a framed photograph off a shelf in the living room. It was a picture of him and Monica on their wedding day, the two of them holding hands in front of a thirty-foot waterfall in the Cascade Mountains, Ross in an ivory tuxedo, a Calla lily boutonniere on his lapel, Monica in a sleeveless, white chiffon gown and a smile that could warm the coldest of hearts. His eyes lingered on that smile until his sorrow was nearly too much to overcome, then he tucked the photo under his arm and walked out the door.

He drove on the back streets, avoiding higher-traffic routes out of habit—not because there was substantial traffic to be avoided. Andre's mother lived in a small house in the low-income neighborhood of Appleyard, just south of Wenatchee city limits. The drive took less than ten minutes. Ross pulled into the graveled parking space in front of the run-down detached garage and helped Andre carry the foodstuff to the front door. He knocked a few times but no one answered. "Miss Wallace?" he called. "Miss Wallace, it's Coach Ross. I have Andre with me. We've brought you some groceries."

No answer.

"Come on, Momma," Andre shouted impatiently, "open the door."

Ross leaned over to his right and peeked through the living room window. The interior was dark, and he had to press his face close to the glass to see past his own reflection. "I don't think she's home, Dre."

He pulled away from the window, and an instant later, heard a rapid pounding from inside the house, heavy footfalls thundering across the floor like those of a stampeding bull. The window panes vibrated, and then Ross jumped in astonishment as Miss Wallace threw herself against the glass and began clawing at it with mangled fingertips, painting the inside of the window with streaks of red.

Her lips were caked with a white, powdery substance and what appeared to be blood, and embedded in them were small shards of wood. Some of her front teeth were missing from her black gums, and those that remained were broken and jagged. Her dark skin was colored even darker around her eyes—eyes that bulged from their sockets and stared at Ross with an intensity that made the cold winter air feel even colder. The woman snapped her jaws at the glass a few times and then unleashed an animalistic scream that increased in pitch and volume until Ross thought his sanity might shatter like fine crystal.

Ross was dimly aware of Andre yanking frantically on the knob of the front door—apparently oblivious to the fact that the door opened inward—and yelling things that to Ross, in his bafflement, might as well have been in another language. Miss Wallace's ungodly scream abruptly terminated in a series of chokes and sputters, and a surge of blood erupted from the woman's mouth. The scene widened in Ross's vision, and he realized he was backpedaling into the yard. He called to Andre, who was now kicking at the door, to "Stop! Wait!" but his words held no authority. *She's got it. Oh fuck oh fuck oh fuck, she has the virus.*

The window glass shattered and Miss Wallace thrust her arms through, reaching toward Ross like a drowning victim pleading for rescue, her hands grasping at the air. She let out another blood-curdling screech, and then Ross saw Andre step toward the window and extend a hand to his mother. The woman's eyes shifted to her son, and her thrashing ceased. For a moment, there was an eerie calmness that Ross imagined might be comparable to being inside the eye of a hurricane. But when Andre placed his tender hand on his mother's forearm, a deep, guttural groan issued from her throat, followed by a recurrence of the abhorrent screaming. Miss Wallace seized her son by his wrist and pulled furiously. At the same time, she smashed her head through the thin, wood muntin bars and bit at Andre with her jagged teeth.

Ross leaped forward and grasped Andre in a bear hug and jerked him free from his mother's grip. Andre struggled, but Ross was a strong two hundred-thirty pounds and outweighed him by seventy-five. Ross hurled him onto the lawn and told him to stay there. "Your mom is sick. I'm calling an ambulance." He frantically searched his coat pockets for his cell phone, and realized he had left it in the van. "Don't fucking move. Dre. I'm just going to get my phone. We'll get some help out here." Andre got back on his feet, but showed no intention of moving from where he stood.

Ross grabbed his cell phone from the van console and explained the situation to a 9-1-1 operator as he rummaged through the rear cargo section for a first-aid kit. He found a six-pack of pump bottles of hand sanitizer lotion, tore one of the bottles from the plastic wrapping, and rushed it, along with a bath towel, back to Andre. On return, he saw that Miss Wallace had disappeared from the window. He could hear her beating and scratching at the inside of the front door as he tossed the towel and sanitizer to Andre and told him to clean himself. From the distance came the howling of police sirens. The emergency dispatch operator instructed him to stay on the line until the officers arrived.

He stood on the grass and spoke with the dispatch operator and listened to the soul-shriveling screams emanating from inside the house, and then there were more thundering footfalls just before Miss Wallace's entire body came crashing through the window. She toppled onto the ground in a shower of glass and wood, and lay there for a few moments, her head and limbs jerking convulsively as if she were caught in the throes of death. Then she raised her head and slowly scanned her surroundings with a look of maniacal wonder, like a woman being born into another world, pressed her bloody palms onto the glass-strewn walkway, and pushed herself up onto her feet. Ross stared in awe as the old woman took a couple of wobbly steps in his direction. With her next step, she broke into a run.

7.

The boy stands spread-legged behind the imaginary line between second and third base and studies the prints of his cleats in the soft, powdery dirt. The lights glaring from high up on the poles that surround the field are so bright that if he stares directly at them it will cause him to see white spots that take a long time to fade away. Still, he can't help but to glance up at them from time to time; he's not sure why. The stands are packed tonight—the whole town must be here watching this game. Lyle is here too, up in one of the middle rows behind home plate, where the tall fences come together. The boy doesn't like Lyle, but he still wants Lyle to be proud of him. Maybe if Lyle were proud of him he wouldn't be so goshdang mean all the time. Maybe. He wishes his mom were here instead of having to work at the steel factory. He always wanted to play shortstop and tonight he gets to and it's just too flippin' bad that his mom doesn't get to be here to see it. It's okay though; he'll tell her all about it when she gets home. Suddenly, there is the exciting crack of the bat hitting the baseball, and the fans go crazy. It's a line drive. Coming straight at him. Fast. He lifts his glove to catch it but it's hard to see the ball because of the white spots in front of his eyes. It hits him on the right cheekbone and it feels like he is dying. He drops to his knees and holds his face and tries hard not to cry but the tears come anyway. People are yelling at him to get the ball, but he can't. He just can't. It hurts too bad. Finally, the crowd noise dies down, and then his coach is there, asking him if he is okay. I think my whole face is broken, he tells the coach. Then Lyle comes walking out onto the field. The boy doesn't think parents are allowed on the field, but

Lyle keeps on coming, and nobody tries to stop him. Probably, they are scared of him. The boy can understand why, even though Lyle is smaller than a lot of guys. He heard someone say once that Lyle is as mean as a snake. The boy couldn't recall ever meeting a snake that was as mean as Lyle. Are you alright, Lyle asks him. I'm busted up pretty bad. I think I might need a ambulance. Lyle looks at his face. You don't need no ambulance. You just got a little shiner is all. Get up and shake it off. The coach asks the boy if he can keep playing, and the boy says no, so Lyle tells him to get his stuff and go to the car. On the way home, the boy asks Lyle what a shiner is. Lyle doesn't answer.

The next day, when the boy is getting ready for school, Lyle comes into the bedroom and hands him a raggedy old dress that looks like it was made out of a man's shirt, and tells him to put it on. What? You heard me. Put this on and don't make me tell you again. If you're gonna act like a sissy, then you're gonna dress like one too. The boy says he doesn't want to put it on, and Lyle slaps him in the mouth. Through tears, the boy says, I want my mom. Lyle slaps him again. Harder. Your mom is sleeping. If you wake her up, you'll be sorry you were ever born. The boy does as he is told while Lyle watches to be sure. After he has changed into the dress, Lyle walks him to the end of the driveway and waits with him for the school bus to arrive. Please don't make me go, the boy cries. Lyle tells him to shut his goddamn mouth, and when the school bus comes, all the kids laugh and laugh.

***

The gun bucked in Rooster's hand, and Reggie instantly dropped to his knees and fell over onto the sidewalk. The loudmouth who had been pulling on the dog's hind legs let go, backed up a couple of steps, and froze in place. Rooster immediately turned his gun on the third guy, intending to shoot him before he could escape with Rooster's supplies, but the bastard had already dropped the bags and was sprinting down the street like a track star. Surprisingly, Lotto lost interest in Rooster's arm and took off after the runner.

The passenger of the utility truck ducked behind the far side of the vehicle. The driver leaped onto the truck's running board and began to open the door, but stopped when Rooster pointed the gun barrel his way. Rooster applied pressure to the trigger but decided against killing the man. He remembered an old movie quote by a character played by actor James Caan, "One's backfire, three is gunplay," referring to firing a gun where people might hear. The shot that had put Reggie into the final few minutes of his life had certainly caught the attention of anyone within earshot, but likely, most would question whether it was gunfire or something else, such as a common engine backfire. Additional shots were sure to diminish any doubt. Rooster still had the SIG, but he had removed the sound suppressor in order to make the weapon easier to conceal. *I guess it's your lucky day, fucker.* He ordered the man to get into his truck and go, then turned to the thug who stood, trembling, on the edge of the sidewalk, and told him to go too. The guy didn't hesitate.

As the utility truck pulled away from the curb, Rooster promptly moved to regain possession of his two bags, and when he stooped to pick them up, realized he couldn't close the fingers of his left hand. Lotto had done a number on his arm. He didn't have time to assess the damage right then, his main priority was to get as far away from there as he could, before the cops showed up. He shoved the revolver back into his waistband and gathered the bags in his right hand. He then walked over to Reggie, who lay on the ground, crying and pleading and holding his crotch and contorting in the blood that gushed from the exit wound in his ass. Rooster bent over and spat in his face. "Have a nice day, dumbfuck."

He raced to the next intersection as quickly as his legs would carry him, rounded the corner of a two-story office building on the right, and ran another block. His lungs were already burning as he passed the boarded windows of a barbecue restaurant and a hair salon before crossing Houser Way into the rear parking lot of three adjacent buildings that stood along Main Avenue to the east. He heard the first police siren. It was close—perhaps it was the cop he'd seen while hitchhiking a few minutes earlier. He quickened his pace, his muscles aching in protest. Damn, he was out of shape. He thought this was probably the first time he had run since high school...twenty years ago. He didn't remember it being this difficult.

About a hundred yards to the southeast on the opposite side of Main was a wooded hillside that Rooster thought would provide good concealment while he caught his breath and checked his map. He wouldn't be able to hide there for more than a minute or two. The cops would most likely bring in a canine unit to track him, and certainly a helicopter would be joining the search before long. His only chance was to keep moving. He jogged across the four-lane street and along a chain link fence that skirted the lot of an auto body repair shop on the corner of an intersection, crossed another street, and scrambled up into the cover of the twenty-foot cedars on the hill. He had ascended no more than fifty feet up the slope when he caught sight of a highway just beyond another forty feet of trees and thick undergrowth. He didn't need to check his map to know that it was Interstate 405, the expressway which would lead him directly to his destination in Newport Hills, ten miles north. He had hoped that, once he had reached this particular highway, he could carjack a vehicle and drive the remaining ten miles, or alternatively, have the vehicle's driver chauffeur him at gunpoint, but as he stood at the top of the embankment and studied the long stretch of asphalt, he saw not a single car on the road. He was aware that most—if not all—major highways in the Seattle vicinity had been closed to regular traffic, but he had expected to at least see a few supply trucks or disaster relief vehicles, but there was...nothing. He was sure that if he waiting long enough someone would come along, but even then, he didn't have a solid plan as to how he would get them to pull over. He could feign injury, but that might cause a person to mistake him for having the damned virus with a name few people seemed able to pronounce correctly. Nobody wanted to risk catching that shit. Someone might be compelled to stop if he leaped out in front of their vehicle and pointed his gun at the driver's window, or they might be just as apt to run him over. There was no way to predict how anyone would respond to such a threat. His best bet was to stand at the edge of the highway and try to flag somebody down. There still existed a few good Samaritans even in this climate of fear and ambivalence, and though they were far between, their scarcity was compensated for with a surplus of careless idiots. None of it mattered now anyway, because Rooster could hear the wail of multiple sirens closing in on the area, and from somewhere above distant rooftops, the *chop-chop-chopping* of rotor blades.

On the other side of the highway was a twenty-foot retaining wall that gradually tapered to ground level at a point about a hundred yards to the south. Past that was another steep embankment, which appeared to level out in a dense copse of timber forty or fifty feet up. He took a deep breath, then bolted across the southbound lanes, hopped a Jersey barrier, crossed the northbound width and ran southward in the shadow of the retaining wall. When the wall height had tapered to about four feet, he hoisted himself onto it and climbed the embankment.

Beneath the trees at the top of the hill was a six-foot chain link fence that lined a narrow street in a residential neighborhood. Directly across the street was an empty lot, overgrown with green foliage, and on either side of that were rows of three- and four-deck condominiums. Houses of varying styles overlooked the street farther down. Parked along the curb in front of the houses were several cars, pickup trucks, and SUVs.

Rooster sat against a tree and unfolded his map. The street he was on was Mill Avenue. About a half a mile to the northeast was a dog park. He didn't know anything about the scenting ability of a police tracking dog, but he figured if one could track him as far as the dog park, the smells of a thousand other mutts might be enough of a distraction to buy him some time, or perhaps even cause the canine to lose his scent entirely. Only one way to find out, but he had to move his ass because now he could see the helicopter circling the area where he'd shot Reggie's dick off.

Due to his aching muscles and the diminished function in his left arm, he had a hard time scaling the chain link fence, but he finally managed to get over it, and then fought his way through the overgrowth of the vacant lot until he came to an alleyway. Parked in the alley next to a tarpaulin-covered boat was a black Kawasaki motorcycle. He checked to see if its owner was dumb enough to have left the key in the ignition, but no such luck. He continued down the alley a little way, cut across a yard onto the next street over, crossed two more yards to the intersection of Renton Avenue and Beacon Way, then ducked into the forest behind the houses on Beacon. From there, the dog park was only another hundred yards.

When he got there, he was surprised to find an elderly couple walking their little black and white mixed breed. He hadn't considered that there might be people using the park. While such a thing had been perfectly normal before the plague struck, it somehow seemed so astoundingly peculiar now. After he scanned the area to make sure no one else was present, he approached the couple and said, "Hello there. Lovely day, ain't it?" Then he cut their throats with the same butcher knife he had used to kill Timbo, stuffed their bodies into a portable toilet, and drove away in their white Chrysler PT Cruiser.

He followed the street to where it intersected with Houser Way, less than three blocks from where a dumb thug named Reggie was probably being loaded into the back of a coroner's van, and then turned right and headed north.

"I'll be there soon, preacher man," he whispered. "I'm a comin'."

8.

Ross had known Miss Wallace for almost four years. She was a short woman in her fifties, heavyset with a bad leg that required her to use a cane when she walked. Her leg didn't seem to be bothering her today as she came at Ross like an NFL linebacker. Not knowing what else to do, he kicked her hard in the center of her chest and sent her sprawling back onto the narrow concrete walkway beneath the window.

"What the fuck are you *doing*, man?" Andre protested. Ross didn't recall ever hearing the kid swear before. The kid's mother quickly struggled back to her feet, screaming furiously as blood flowed steadily from her mouth. Her left shoulder hitched spasmodically a few times, and then she rushed forward again. Ross let go another explosive kick, and dropped to his knees when a crushing weight fell upon his shoulders. For a moment, he thought the woman was upon him, but he had felt his foot impact her breastbone and knew it was sufficient to knock her back to the ground. It was Andre who had tackled him, and Ross cursed himself for not seeing it coming. He had schooled his boxing students on the importance of situational awareness, and now he was about to pay for not practicing what he preached. He saw Miss Wallace begin to rise again, and knew that if he didn't get up quickly, she was going to infect him and Andre both. But Andre wasn't letting go. He clung to Ross's back like a spider, his forearms clamped around Ross's throat, cutting off the oxygen. Ross did a half-roll and drove his elbow into Andre's ribcage. Andre released his grip instantly, and Ross leaped up just in time to fend off the woman once more, his kick lower and weaker this time, forcing her back only a few steps. The crazy bitch wouldn't stop coming. Another kick. Another. She fell, and then Ross kicked her in the head as if he was punting a football. She grabbed at his legs but Ross was too quick for her. When she sat up, Ross delivered one more wallop to her left temple, and finally she lay on the cold ground and convulsed like a condemned prisoner in an electric chair.

Ross immediately peeled off his jacket and shirt and slathered his face, throat, and upper body with hand sanitizer lotion. Andre had gotten his mother's blood on him when she had grasped his arm through the window, and Ross didn't know if any of it had been transferred to *him* after Dre had jumped onto his back. Before he finished applying the lotion, Miss Wallace had managed to raise to her knees, her body still twitching uncontrollably. She had lost her prior vigor but was nonetheless trying to stand as a police car pulled up alongside the curb. When a pair of officers—a man and a woman—got out of the car, Andre, who had been sitting on the lawn, crying like an hysterical child, pointed to Ross and bawled, "He hurt my momma!"

The female officer drew her sidearm and ordered Ross to get on the ground. Ross refused. "This woman is infected with the Qilu virus. She just attacked me. I don't intend to be lying in the yard when she does it again."

The male cop drew his weapon and muttered something into a handheld radio microphone that was clipped to the breast of his coat, then shouted, "Sir, get on the ground and put your hands behind your head."

Rooster glanced in the direction of Miss Wallace, who was slowly rising to her feet. "With all due respect, officer, I don't think I can comply with your request."

"Get on the fucking ground. Now!" screamed the female.

"You're not listening to me, officers. This woman is *infected*. If you have to shoot me, then do what you have to do, but I will *not* get on the ground until she has been dealt with."

Miss Wallace began to limp forward, her bad leg apparently affecting her movement now. "Stay where you are, ma'am," the male officer said. Another police cruiser pulled in behind the first.

Its single occupant jumped out with gun in hand and took position behind his car. Miss Wallace continued, this time toward Andre, who watched with wide, teary eyes.

The first male cop said, "Ma'am, *stop!*"

A third police car arrived. Ross saw neighbors watching the action from their doorsteps. Andre's mother increased her pace, closing the distance between her and her son. Ross heard one of the male officers say, "Alright, tase her."

"Momma, stop," Andre begged. "They gonna shoot you."

But his momma didn't stop. One of the cops came forward and fired a pair of electrical probes which struck Miss Wallace in the midsection and upper left thigh. She clenched and jerked to the rapid clicking sound of the Taser, but after the initial five-second burst of electricity, she turned to the officer to whom she was tethered by twenty-one feet of wire and started in his direction.

"Hit her again!"

The cop delivered another five-second burst of high voltage current, after which Miss Wallace resumed her advance. The officer held the Taser in his left hand and unholstered his sidearm with his right. *Oh fuck, they're going to kill her*, Ross thought. Ignoring the commands of the police to stay where he was, he went over to Andre and knelt on the grass in front of him.

"Look at me, Dre."

Andre raised his tear-streaked face, and in his eyes, Ross saw fear and shock and confusion and utter heartbreak. "They gonna shoot my momma."

"She is sick, you understand that don't you? There's no cure, and she's suffering. She only wants to stop suffering." Ross spoke quickly—he knew the bullets were going to start flying any second now.

Andre gazed back toward his mother. "Momma." His voice was weak, childlike.

"Dre, *look* at me dammit. Don't look at them, look right here in my eyes, man to man. It's just you and me out here right now. Remember how I taught you to block out everything but your opponent when you're in the boxing ring?"

Andre nodded.

"Well, I want you to do that now. Look me in the eyes and focus, son. It's just you and me. Shut everything else out of your mind and keep looking right here in my eyes, no matter what. Everything's going to be okay. I promise."

In his peripheral vision, Ross saw a fourth police car pull up and park on the far side of the street, saw Mickey Rivera get out and raise his gun. He heard the clicking of the Taser and the shouts of police officers ordering Miss Wallace to stop, and the pounding of his own heartbeat. He placed his hands gently on Andre's shoulders. "Cover your ears, son."

Andre flinched when the gunfire erupted but he didn't look away from Ross's eyes. One shot, two, then a barrage. Twenty, perhaps thirty rounds fired in a space of about five seconds. Some of them came even after Miss Wallace was down. As the sound was still echoing off the neighboring houses, officers forced Ross's face against the ground and slapped handcuffs on his wrists. They cuffed Andre as well, who offered no resistance, and, in fact, had to be carried to the police car after he was unable to stand on his own. Through the ringing in his ears, Ross heard him say, "You killed my momma. You killed my momma."

Two officers wearing latex gloves placed Ross in the back of one of the vehicles and lowered the window when Mickey came over to ask some questions.

"You okay, Coach?"

"Not really. Are you?"

"What I'm trying to ask is, do you have any injuries."

Ross shook his head.

"Did she get any blood or anything on you? Any body fluids at all?"

"No. I'm good."

"Did you know her? Tell me what happened here, Ross."

Ross began to tell the story, when a commotion broke out among the three officers who were standing around Miss Wallace's body. The cops dispersed in different directions and once again drew their sidearms as...*what the fuck*? Miss Wallace stood up on the lawn. Her left arm hung limply at her side, and her head bobbed as if it were attached by a loose spring. Her floral dress was soaked in blood from the numerous bullet holes in her body, and yet she stumbled toward the line of police cars on the street like a toddler learning its first steps.

Ross waited for the second fusillade of gunfire, but it never came. Instead, there was a single, deafening *Boom!* as Miss Wallace closed within a few feet of the curb. Through the front windshield of the car in which he sat, Ross saw an officer aiming a shotgun, smoke drifting from the end of its long barrel. The blast had done little more than ruffle the front of the woman's bloody dress. She paused only momentarily before moving forward again. Ross thought the officer's gun must be loaded with rubber bullets, but that notion was dispelled when the second shot took a sizeable chunk out of Miss Wallace's left shoulder. The third shot removed the lower half of her face, and only then did she go down. This time the police wasted no time in cuffing her hands behind her back. They retreated to a safe distance afterward, but Ross didn't think it was necessary at that point; the hole in the back of Miss Wallace's head was the approximate diameter of a football, and he doubted there were enough brains left in her skull to enable her to do anything more than just lie there dead.

He sat in the back of the police cruiser and stared at the bullet-riddled body of Andre's mother until the world began to spin, and then Ross leaned forward and spread his knees and vomited on the floorboard.

9.

Rooster parked the stolen Chrysler along the curb and quietly observed the pandemonium in the streets ahead in a shopping area of Renton known as The Landing. There were people everywhere— hundreds, screaming and chanting and pumping their fists into the air like fans at an outdoor rock concert. Some carried homemade signs sporting slogans such as LET THEM GO and NO TO HUMAN EUTHANASIA and random nonsense such as I LIKE TURTLES. Others danced among rows of burning tires, threw objects at the military Humvees that lined the far side of the parking lot of a Target store on Rooster's left, or taunted the police officers who formed shoulder-to-shoulder phalanxes behind a wall of polycarbonate riot shields and metal barricades.

Rooster had driven as far north as he was able. He couldn't go any further without abandoning the car. The entrance ramps to I-405 were blocked by police, as were the routes that led to the residential areas east of the interstate. It was clear that government officials wanted people to stay home. The only way that someone could travel beyond city limits was by foot, through gaps in security. Rooster was sick of walking, and even sicker of running. He had barely had a chance to catch his breath.

The bite wounds on his arm ached with a ferocity. He opened his coat and pulled his arm from the sleeve, wincing in pain from the movement. There were jagged tears in his skin just above the wrist, but they were shallow. The thick fabric of his coat had provided at least *some* protection against Lotto's powerful grip, but his entire forearm was swollen and bruised nearly black. Fucking dog. "I hope you weren't infected with that damn

Quaalude virus, or whatever the hell it's called, Mr. Lotto." He didn't know if it was possible for dogs to carry the virus, but since the symptoms of infection so closely resembled rabies, he wasn't ruling out anything.

He leaned over to the passenger seat and dug through the plastic bag until he found one of the bottles of Pepsi he had taken from Timbo's refrigerator. He chugged all of it, then tossed the empty bottle into the back seat. He considered that he had taken no precautions against leaving evidence that would tie him to the crimes he had committed since being released from jail. Within the past twelve hours, he had murdered ten people and left behind such a trail of fingerprints and DNA that he might as well have videotaped himself and dropped off the recording at the front desk of a police station. Before the virus outbreak, he would have been more careful, but now it was clear that law enforcement had bigger things to worry about than some redneck junkie with a chip on his shoulder. All he had to do was evade capture until society completely fell apart, and then nobody would give two shits about what he had done. They would be too concerned with simply staying alive. If it so happened that society managed to keep itself together, then the authorities would still be faced with the problem of finding him, and he had no intention of making it easy for them.

He sunk back into the car seat and closed his eyes. His mind drifted to the previous night's incident on Beacon Hill, when he had beaten Jared Kroeger to death with a golf club. Rooster had known Jared for ten years, but he had never considered the man a real friend. The two of them had gotten high together on occasion, that was about the extent of their relationship. Rooster had sold Jared a couple grams of meth seven months ago. He'd had no idea Jared was wearing a hidden microphone which broadcasted the transaction to the police van in the alley behind Jared's house.

After being released from jail, Rooster had made his way through the Downtown riots, walked two and a half miles to Jared's house, and entered without knocking through the unlocked front door. He had found Jared asleep on the living room sofa, and beat him for over an hour with the 3-iron he had taken from the golf bag in a corner of the room. Just before Jared had finally died,

Rooster had carved the word SNITCH in the man's chest with a serrated steak knife.

When Jared's girlfriend, Jenny, had come home in the early evening. Rooster had shot her between the eyes with Jared's gun, the same SIG P238 that he now concealed in his coat pocket. The woman was dead before her body had hit the floor.

Rooster's eyes snapped open when the crowd noise began to intensify. There was a distinct pop-pop-popping sound immediately followed by a series of loud bangs. Many of the protesters screamed and ran as white clouds of tear gas engulfed them, but most stood fast, chanting "We're still here!" after the barrage ended. Several people broke from the crowd and made their way to a sward of grass on the right of the street on which Rooster was parked. Some of them lay on their backs in the grass while others poured bottled water into their eyes. Somebody, somewhere, was calling for a medic. From a loudspeaker, a voice declared, "Disperse, or we will use force." The message was repeated about every thirty seconds; each time, the protesters became more agitated but showed no sign of giving in.

Rooster watched it all in wonder for a few minutes, then, with his arm throbbing, decided to ask someone for some water to clean his wounds. He got out of the Chrysler and approached the people on the grass. "So what exactly are you all rioting about?" he asked a group of college-age kids nearest to him.

A wild-eyed guy wearing a black beanie and a gray hooded sweatshirt with a large, purple 'W' emblazoned on the chest answered matter-of-factly, "Who the hell says we're rioting? This isn't a riot. We're exercising our right to free speech by holding a peaceful protest."

"Doesn't look all that peaceful to me." Rooster said with a smirk.

"Hey, if it doesn't seem peaceful, it's because *they* aren't allowing it to be peaceful. We aren't the ones lobbing tear gas grenades and threatening people with machine guns. A lot of bad shit is happening, but this is still America, you know, the country that is supposed to be the greatest in the world. We are still Americans, and—"

"All we are trying to do is let them know we aren't just going to stand by and allow them to violate our rights as American citizens," a young, red-haired woman interrupted. "We won't let them get away with treating us like third world cattle."

"But what is it, specifically, that y'all are protesting?" Rooster asked. "And why here in the goddamn shopping center parking lot?"

"You see those tall condos over there?" The guy in the beanie asked, pointing to a group of wide, tan and gray, seven-story buildings beyond the parking lot. "A bunch of dudes in biological suits went in there yesterday and took some people out on stretchers. Word has it those people were infected with the virus. Last night, the National Guard showed up and started sealing off the doors and ground floor windows of all four buildings. This morning they've been erecting a fence around the whole lot–chain link with barb wire all across the top of it. There must be hundreds of people trapped in those buildings against their will. A few of them tried to get out through some second floor windows before the fencing went up, but the soldiers beat them down and took them away on a big police truck."

"There are little kids in there," the redhead said, "*Babies.* What's going to happen when those people run out of food?"

"This is the United States of fucking America," said a woman in a blue, twill parka. "We don't do this kind of thing here. It's like something out of Nazi Germany. I have friends who live in those buildings, and I know they must be scared shitless right now. They are in there hoping that those of us out here stand together and do something about this craziness. I mean, we have the right to bear arms specifically to prevent things like this from happening. If everybody around here who owns a gun got together and–"

"And *what*, Jessica?" said the guy in the beanie. "It's the fuckin' Army. They have armored vehicles with .50 caliber machine guns and hand grenades and tanks and fuckin' attack helicopters. You ever hear of the thunder runs in the Iraq War? A handful of American tanks and armored personnel carriers drove right down the middle of a highway to Baghdad with thousands of Iraqi soldiers firing on them with machine guns and rockets and anti-tank missiles, and, guess what? The Americans suffered hardly any casualties while the Iraqis lost almost everybody. This isn't the nineteenth century where you could hand out guns to a bunch of farmers and merchants and expect them to have a chance against the federal military. Times have changed. We've allowed our government to become way too powerful to be intimidated with the threat of force. The only thing that has kept it in check is public opinion. As long as we are able to vote, then we still have some control over the government's actions. That is why we are here today, to let them know that we, as voting citizens, won't tolerate this kind of behavior."

"I'm not sure they care too much about voters at this point," Rooster said. "If they don't contain the virus, then there won't be any voters left."

"Do you know they're euthanizing people who have been infected?" asked Jessica. "Men, women, children, it doesn't matter. They're taking the bad ones to a facility on Mercer Island and putting them down like sick animals. They've dug trenches in the ground and are bulldozing dead bodies in by the dozens. There's a field over by the Mercer Island Community Center that has been turned into a mass gravesite."

"How would you know that?" Rooster asked. "That sounds like something somebody made up to get people's panties in a wad."

"Believe what you want, but I heard it from reliable sources—*military* sources."

"Think about it," said the redhead. "The government is bending over backwards to keep people from traveling from one area to the next, yet Mercer Island residents were ordered to *evacuate*. It's the only area in the state under mandatory evacuation. There are only two ways in and out: the Lacey Murrow Bridge into Seattle, and the East Channel Bridge that connects with Bellevue. The land area is what, six square miles? So what you have is one big quarantine zone to which access can be controlled simply by securing two bridges. It's perfect, really. Kick everyone off the island, then bring in the sick people and put them out of their misery so they can't infect anyone else, and nobody has to know."

"Except you can't keep something like this a secret for very long," said Jessica. "It's too big. There are too many people involved; soldiers, doctors, engineers...people will talk. Information gets leaked to the outside world."

"If that was true, then why did they seal off these apartment buildings?" Rooster asked.

Why don't they just haul the residents off to Mercer Island?"

Jessica shrugged. "Who knows? Maybe it's because the people living in the apartments aren't actually sick yet. Maybe this is a 'wait and see' kind of thing."

"Or maybe it's just easier this way," said the guy in the beanie. "Just lock them up where they live and let them all starve to death."

The voice on the loudspeaker repeated, "This is your final warning. Disperse, or we will use force."

Rooster wiped his wet, stinging eyes as the tear gas drifted on the late morning breeze. He felt the CS particulates begin to burn at his nose and throat as if hot chili powder had been blown into his face. "Well, good luck to y'all." He nodded to the people on the grass, turned to walk back toward the Chrysler, and then paused, remembering why he had approached the people in the first place. "You think one of you might spare a little water? I tore up my arm in an accident, and if I don't clean it up soon it's gonna get infected."

"Infected?" asked the guy in the beanie, his eyes widening.

"Not *that* kind of infected," Rooster assured. He chose his next words carefully, to obviate suspicion. "I cut myself while changing a tire on my car. It's nothing serious...just don't want to take any chances."

Jessica fished an unopened bottle of Aquafina from a duffel bag on the ground and tossed it to Rooster. "You should join us. There is power in unity."

"I appreciate what you're doing here, but I have other matters to tend to. Besides, I have a feeling things are about to get ugly for all of you." As he spoke, a long, yellow, eight-wheeled truck with US NAVY painted on the side moved slowly down the street that separated the Target parking lot from the apartment complex and blasted the protesters with a pair of high-pressure water cannons.

Rooster returned to the Chrysler, where he cleaned his wounds the best he could and took a couple of draws from the meth pipe. After consulting his map, he drank what was left of the bottled water, gathered his bags, and left the vehicle where it was parked, walking two blocks east back to I-405. Through the woods that lined the freeway, he resumed his northward grind toward the church in Newport Hills, now only three miles away.

10.

On the top floor of the four-story Valley Hospital building, Ross gazed through the thick glass window of the negative pressure isolation room and watched the comers and goers on the street below. His eyes followed a woman on the sidewalk as she carried an infant child bundled in a blanket, with two additional young children hurrying along at her side. He wondered if any of them would still be alive a month from now.

He stood at the window for a long time, until his bad knees began to ache, then he sat on the wheeled hospital bed and clicked the remote for the 22" flat screen TV mounted on the wall. He flicked through the channels abstractedly, his mind not registering the images on the screen. His head was filled with thoughts of Miss Wallace and her motherless son, and of a sweeping plague that transformed its victims into mindless, screaming, suffering shells of who they once were–rabid, like the St. Bernard from the Stephen King novel. Yes, exactly like that.

A heavyset woman dressed in a green, plastic medical gown entered the room and introduced herself as Dr. Lana Grant, from the Department of Health. She wore a surgical mask and plastic goggles on her face, a blue, plastic hair cap on her head, and she held a laptop computer in her gloved hands. A tall man in matching garb stood silently near the door while Dr. Grant instructed Ross to remain as he was and took a seat at a rolling tray table in the center of the room.

"Mr. Ross, I'd like to ask you some questions if you don't mind," the doctor said.

Ross clicked the 'mute' button on the TV remote. "Should I have my attorney present?"

"I don't think that's necessary. This isn't that kind of questioning."

"I think I will be the judge of that."

"By all means, Mr. Ross. I only want to ask you about your health. I'm not a police officer."

"I have a few questions for you first." Ross swung his legs over the edge of the bed and tightened the twill ribbons on the back of his hospital gown. "Andre Wallace, the young man who was brought into the hospital with me, where is he now?"

"Mr. Wallace is right next door, in a room just like this one. I haven't spoken with him yet, but I understand he's being somewhat combative."

"The kid's mother just had her brains blown out right in front of him. He's bound to have some issues about that."

"I certainly wouldn't argue with that, Mr. Ross," Dr. Grant said flatly. "What happened was very tragic and unfortunate."

"His mother...I don't understand how she could have gotten up after having so many bullets pumped into her. Those cops shot her more than twenty times. How does a person keep going after that? Someone took me to a dogfight in the Philippines once, years ago, when I was a teenager. There were these two dogs, Presa Canarios, I think they were. Their handlers took them into a fifteen-foot fenced square with a referee and everything, just like a boxing match or something. Those two big, beautiful dogs fought in that square for what must have been nearly two hours. Every so often, the ref would order the handlers to break them up and take each dog to an opposite corner of the square, then release them to fight again. They called it a 'scratch.' The dogs had ten seconds to fight after they were released. Each one had to cross a line—a scratch line, I don't know why it was called that—and then bite the other dog before the ten seconds ran out. If one didn't, it lost. If both didn't, it was a draw. Well, those two dogs kept scratching, despite the fact that, after almost two hours, both of them could hardly even walk anymore. They kept crossing that line and sinking their teeth into each other's flesh and entwining their bodies together there on that tarpaulin-covered floor despite the blood and the pain they must have been experiencing. They just kept going until one finally died, but not before crawling across that scratch line one more time.

"Miss Wallace was like that. She had the same fire in her eyes that those dogs had, and it wasn't to be dimmed until that shotgun blast took her head off. They shot her more than twenty times, Doc. How is it that she kept on going?"

Dr. Grant sat and quietly stared at Ross for an uncomfortable length of time before finally clearing her throat and lowering her eyes to her open laptop. "I don't yet know all the details of the incident, Mr. Ross, but I assure you it's being thoroughly investigated. I will tell you that it isn't at all unusual for a person to survive multiple gunshot wounds. I recall a situation in New York in 2010 in which a man survived being shot at least twenty-one times. This sort of thing can and does happen."

Ross shook his head. "I will guarantee you that the guy in New York didn't get up from the ground and continue to aggressively confront armed police officers after he was shot. I will bet you anything that he stayed on his back until a couple of burly paramedics hauled his ass off in an ambulance. I'll also point out that Miss Wallace was a fifty-something year-old woman with a physical disability."

"Moving on, Mr. Ross. I'm going to read off a list of symptoms you may or may not be experiencing, and you just tell me yes or no to each one."

She read through the list, typing Ross's responses into her laptop. Ross truthfully answered 'no' to every one. She continued with some additional questions, and when she asked Ross if he had recently been in contact with anyone who might have been ill, Ross replied, "You mean other than the old African-American woman who just tried to kill me?"

Without missing a beat, Dr. Grant said, "I understand your wife recently died after contracting the Qilu pathogen."

Ross's breath caught in his throat, and his heart strained beneath his ribcage, as if grasped by a strong man's fist. His neck and face grew hot as his grief threatened to burst from that place deep within him in which he constantly struggled to contain it. For the briefest of moments flashed the image of her face, contorted and screaming as the madness consumed her. Then he banished the thought from his head, vowing never to allow it to return.

He was unable to speak at first, but after numerous prompts from Dr. Grant, he licked his dry lips and forced a reply. "She was in Paris when news of the outbreak in Europe started being announced on TV. She had gone over to spend a week with her college friend, Marcy. She had practically begged me to go with her, but I had a business to run and I didn't trust anyone to look after things for that long...so she went alone."

"I'm sorry for your loss," said Dr. Grant. "The records I have indicate she died on January 28, one week ago. I have to ask you, how much time elapsed between your last physical contact with her and the date of her death?"

Ross closed his eyes and remembered. He remembered the way she had felt in his arms as he said goodbye at the airport–her body, electric with excitement. He remembered the subtle scent of L'Oreal shampoo on her hair, and the sweetness of her voice when she had told him she loved him endlessly and that she would be home before he even had a chance to miss her. He remembered how she had hurried off to catch her flight with the exuberance of a little girl at Disneyland. Monica had always dreamed of going to Paris.

"She was gone for six days before things started getting bad over there. She was sitting on the plane that was supposed to bring her home a day early when the French government gave the order to shut down the airports in Paris and Marseille. She called me two days later and told me she was really sick. Told me not to worry, and then we cried together on the phone. That was the last time I talked to her."

"What date was that?" asked the doctor.

"That would have been the twenty-sixth. Two days later, I got word that she didn't make it. I didn't believe it at first. I'm still not entirely convinced."

"So...she departed for Paris on January 20?"

"It was the evening of the nineteenth actually." Ross stared at the floor and rubbed his forehead. "My god...everything happened so fast. How did such a thing come to be, Doc? This virus, is it man-made?"

"I don't know the answer to that."

"Well, what *do* you know? I mean, to hell with the clueless rumormongers on the news channels, what are we really dealing with here? I've heard so many different stories I don't know what to believe. Most people can't even agree on what to call this damned thing. I want to hear what you, Doc, a professional, have to say about it."

"To be strictly honest with you, Mr. Ross, even the professionals can't seem to agree on what to call it. The first reported outbreak came from a rural village near Jinan, China. Jinan is the capital of the province of Shandong, otherwise known as Qilu, hence the name you're most likely to hear in the news. This is also currently how most health professionals are referring to it, but names such as Yellow River Virus, Chinese Plague, Chinese Flu, and even E.V. are thrown around almost as frequently."

"E.V.?"

"E.V. stands for 'Extinction Virus,' Mr. Ross."

"*Jesus Christ.*"

"Even the health industry has its share of pessimists."

"How pessimistic are *you*, Doc?"

"Not as pessimistic as some. So far, the virus has a case fatality rate of a hundred percent, which means that it kills everyone it infects. Compare that to the Spanish Flu of 1918, or the Bubonic Plague, with respective CFRs of two and a half and five percent, and then it seems pretty scary. On the other hand, diseases such as AIDS and hemorrhagic Smallpox have CFRs around ninety percent, while Rabies and pneumonic Plague, if untreated, will have CFRs that approach a hundred. Am I going too fast for you?"

Ross shook his head. "No. Case fatality rate. Gotcha."

"Even if a disease kills everyone it infects, it still has to infect you before it can kill you. I won't lie, Mr. Ross, a lot of people will die before this virus has run its course, but when all is said and done, the death toll will be limited to a very small percentage of the population. Between twenty and fifty million people lost their lives to the Spanish Flu in 1918 to 1920. It was one of the worst natural catastrophes in human history. But while fifty million people certainly is a tremendous death toll, it nonetheless amounted to only three percent of the world's population. Death on a massive scale, absolutely, but far from an extinction-level event."

"But didn't you just say the Spanish Flu had a mortality rate of two and a half percent? If it infected two hundred people, only five would die from it. If Qilu infects two hundred people, then somebody has to dig two hundred graves."

"Qilu isn't transmitted in exactly the same way as an influenza virus," said the doc. "There are some differences, mainly regarding symptoms of illness. The flu will often cause a person to cough and sneeze, potentially spraying an infectious aerosol over everything and everyone within six feet or so. It was initially believed that the Qilu virus causes similar symptoms, but we've recently learned that it just isn't so. It's true that the contagion can be spread via aerosolized droplets, but the illness itself doesn't appear to cause excessive coughing or sneezing. However, we are currently at the height of common cold and flu season, and therefore we have the usual millions of flu sufferers walking around on the planet blasting everything with contaminates. It turns out some of these flu sufferers also happen to be infected with the Qilu virus. The flu causes them to sneeze, ejecting droplets that contain not only the flu virus, but Qilu as well. Does that make sense to you, Mr. Ross? Once the flu season has ended, we will see a significant drop in transmission rates."

"So you're saying that the Qilu virus will just die out after the flu season?"

"Not immediately, no. But it should become easier to contain until a vaccine is developed."

"What if a vaccine can't be developed?"

"It's the top priority of all the best epidemiologists in the world. I'm confident it's only a matter of time."

"And what if we're all extinct before the end of the flu season?"

"I would say there's very little chance of that happening, Mr. Ross."

Ross searched the doctor's eyes for a hint of deception or uncertainty, but all he saw was calm, clinical stoicism. "So the doomsayers can stop screaming about the end of the world?"

"They can, but they won't. Now, if we could move on. I have a few more things to ask you."

Ross was cooperative, and when the doctor finished, he asked her when he would be allowed to leave the hospital.

"You're under a mandatory five-day quarantine. If your blood work is normal after a hundred and twenty hours, then you will be good to go," answered Dr. Grant. "In the interim, make yourself comfortable."

When she stood up from the table, Ross said, "One more thing, Doc. Why does this virus turn people into stark raving lunatics?"

"It infects the brain...rewires it somehow. We don't know enough about that yet, but we're working on it. All I can tell you is that you shouldn't believe everything you hear on the news. Get some rest, Mr. Ro–" The doctor froze in place, her wide eyes locked on the television screen.

Ross turned to the source of Dr. Grant's tension. The muted TV displayed a grim-looking news reporter speaking into a handheld microphone. In the background was the White House, and on the bottom of the screen was a banner which read: BREAKING NEWS: NUCLEAR BLASTS OVER JINAN, ZIBO, CHINA.

11.

The boy watches his brother, Johnny, blow out the four candles on the birthday cake, and is annoyed that it takes the little creep three tries. I bet I could blow out twenty candles in one breath, the boy thinks. His mom removes the candles from the white frosting and cuts three slices: one each for the brothers and one for Lyle. She doesn't have any for herself. When the boy is done, he asks for another piece. His mom says no, but Lyle carves him a second slice anyway.

After they eat, it's time to open presents. Johnny opens his, and it's a Fisher-Price toy movie viewer with four movies: three of them are cartoons but one is Planet of the Apes, probably the neatest movie ever besides Star Wars. The boy also gets to open a present. His mom always gets both brothers a present, even if it was only the birthday of one of them. The boy's gift is a Merlin electronic puzzle game. Neato! Thanks, Mom!

The boy and his brother spend some time playing with their new toys while their mother gets ready for work. Later, after she is gone, they watch a cartoon about a mongoose named Rikki-Tikki-Tavi who protects his human family from evil cobra snakes. They boy sits with Lyle on the couch while Johnny lies on the floor like always with his chin propped up on his hands. Johnny is wearing shorts, and there are bruises on his legs. Lyle says come here. Where did you get the bruises from? Johnny doesn't answer, so Lyle swats him on the butt and asks him again. This time, Johnny says he got the bruises from Lyle. You didn't get them bruises from me, Lyle says, then spanks Johnny hard. Johnny cries, and Lyle asks him again where he got the bruises. Johnny says, I got them from you. Lyle spanks him even worse than before, and the boy is thinking in his head, Shut up shut up shut up, Johnny, or Lyle will keep on hitting you. Lyle asks about the bruises one more time, and Johnny doesn't answer, so Lyle grabs him up and takes him to the kitchen sink and holds his face under the running water faucet until Johnny says he don't know where he got the bruises from. That's what I thought, Lyle says.

The boy thinks about getting his baseball bat and whopping Lyle good with it, but he doesn't. He only sits on the couch and keeps his eyes on the TV, terrified that Lyle might give him the same treatment as his brother if he should move a muscle.

***

The marquee sign on the manicured front lawn of the Newport Hills First Baptist Church in Bellevue read, WHOSOEVER SHALL CALL UPON THE NAME OF THE LORD SHALL BE SAVED. Rooster patted the .357 beneath his coat and didn't feel the slightest need to call on the Lord for his salvation. He walked toward the front steps of the church building, taking note of the dozen or so vehicles in the parking lot. From inside the church came the faint sound of music. A piano. Singing. A hymn he thought he might have heard once or twice long ago. It surprised him, church service on a weekday, but he was quickly learning to expect the unexpected in this world that had changed so much since he had been incarcerated seven months ago.

He paused at the door, trying to recall if he had reloaded his guns after firing them. He couldn't remember. After more than thirty-three hours without sleep, his mind was as exhausted as his body; clarity of thought eluded him. He had fired one round from the Magnum at the thug in Renton. Five rounds left in the cylinder. How many shots from the SIG? Had he replaced the magazine? No. Maybe. Fuck. His carelessness was unacceptable. He needed rest. He would get some...after he burned the church down with everyone in it.

He stepped through the door into a narrow hallway which ran perpendicular to the entrance, terminating at an office door just past a pair of restrooms to his left and at a descending staircase to his right. Directly ahead was a well-worn set of wooden double doors beneath an arched stained glass window. Beyond those doors, the collective voice of the congregation belted out its melodious praise for a god that didn't exist.

Rooster slipped into the men's bathroom and locked the door behind him. It was a small room with a single toilet and a wall-mounted sink and an eight-inch wooden crucifix hung next to an oval mirror. He removed his coat and splashed some water on his face, then scrubbed the wounds on his arm with soap from a dispenser on the back of the sink. After rinsing the soap, he sat on the toilet and dug through the pillowcase that contained various contents he had stolen from Timbo. He removed the box of .357 cartridges and placed it on the edge of the sink while he collected a handful of pills from the bottom of the pillowcase. He downed two tabs of OxyContin to dull the pain in his arm, and stuffed the rest of the pills into his pocket.

He inspected the ammo in his handguns and was relieved to find that he had indeed replaced the magazine in the SIG with a full one after firing off several shots back at Timbo's place. He pulled the slide back and placed an extra round in the chamber, then reattached the sound suppressor. The silencer added four inches to the length of the weapon, forcing Rooster to stow the gun in his inside coat pocket with the barrel pointing upward. He double-checked the safety to assure that he wouldn't accidentally shoot himself in the head.

He traded the spent Magnum casing for a fresh hollow-point, splashed some more water on his face, and then drank from the tap. He stared at his reflection in the mirror and barely recognized himself. Dark bags of skin sagged beneath his bloodshot eyes, which seemed to have sunk in their sockets. His high, gaunt cheekbones overemphasized his nose, flat and crooked from being broken more times than he could count. His lips were cracked from the cold, and his two-day growth of facial hair was speckled with a dusting of dry skin flakes.

"When did you get to be such an ugly fucker?" he asked his reflection. Not that it mattered much; he never was big on appearances. It was a dog-eat-dog world, and he didn't have to be pretty to be the baddest puppy on the block.

Before he left the restroom, he took the crucifix from its nail beside the mirror and hung it back on the wall upside down.

He entered through the double doors and took a seat in an empty pew on the back wall. The worshippers had stopped singing and now sat quiet and still with their eyes forward, as if awaiting a sermon from Jesus himself. A few of them shot Rooster a glance as he came in, then turned their attention back to the massive man with a thick beard who spoke from the pulpit in a voice as deep as a grave.

"I would like to remind everyone that refreshments will be served downstairs following this evening's sermon. Sisters Andrea and Chloe really went out of their way to provide us with plenty of delicious food and drink, and we thank them for that."

A series of enthusiastic amens resounded from the congregation, and the big man continued, "For those of you who may not be aware, the city of Bellevue has extended its dusk to dawn curfew to include all areas north of I-90 and south of SR-520, so please don't be in those areas after dark. The 6 a.m. to 9 p.m. curfew for our area hasn't changed, and unless it does, we will continue to hold worship services every evening from five to eight. Of course, that is in addition to our normal Sunday service. We understand the need for comfort and community during this tribulation. God has blessed us with this fine sanctuary where we can all come to pray together, and there is no excuse not to take advantage of it now, when we need our father more than ever."

The man straightened and cleared his throat, and Rooster thought he bore a striking resemblance to the NFL lineman turned actor, Merlin Olsen. The Merlin look-alike stared at his notes for a few seconds, and his voice boomed again. "Another thing I'd like to mention is that the Health Department has set up a walk-in clinic at the YMCA over on 56th Street. Beginning tomorrow, they'll be offering free flu vaccinations as well as brief physicals every day between the hours of 10 a.m. and 5 p.m. Now keep in mind this is a regular flu vaccination. It won't protect you against the Qilu virus, but they're hoping to minimize its spread. If you go to the clinic, you're asked to behave in an orderly manner, and, of course, if you're showing any signs of being sick at all, especially if you're running a fever, you should remain at home and call 2-1-

1 for assistance. You all know this already, but I'm going to say it anyway: Do not call 9-1-1 unless it's a real emergency. The system is overloaded with all the non-emergency calls, and it only puts people's lives in jeopardy when they can't get through during an actual emergency. So again, if you're sick, call 2-1-1.

"Okay then, that's all the announcements I have for today. Now I ask everyone to bow their heads as we pray for Pastor Gene Anderson, who is again unable to be with us today while he continues to grieve the death of his son, Justin.

"Dear Heavenly Father...."

Rooster clenched his fists and sank back into his seat as fury and frustration infused itself into his weary mind. Pastor Gene...unable to be with us. *Well, where exactly the fuck is he?* He closed his eyes tightly and considered everything he had put himself through in order to reach this church, the trail of death he had left along the way, all so that he might conduct his business with the preacher man...who wasn't even here. "*Godammit*," he whispered.

The big man with the bigger voice concluded his prayer with a thunderous "Amen," then announced that Pastor Matthew would deliver the evening sermon.

At one end of a row of upholstered blue chairs behind the pulpit sat a second bearded man in a loose-fitting, navy blue suit. He stood and replaced the larger man at the pulpit and said, "Thank you, Brother Norman." The pastor's voice flowed like honey, and his broad smile displayed a set of teeth that were beyond perfect. Rooster planned to take a hammer and chisel to those teeth before he killed the man.

"Brothers and sisters," Pastor Matthew began, "it's a blessing to see you all here today. On my way home from service last night, my daughter, Venice–bless her little heart–pointed out to me a man who sat on a cold sidewalk, rummaging through a trash bag between his legs. Venice asked me, 'Daddy, why is that man going through the garbage like he is?' I said it was because he was looking for something to eat. Venice then asked me why we couldn't stop and get the man some food so he wouldn't have to look for it in the trash. I said, 'Honey, if we gave food to every homeless person we saw on the street, we wouldn't have enough to feed ourselves.' Venice thought about that for a little bit, and then she said, in that sweet, five-year-old voice of hers, 'Daddy, that man looks like Jesus.'

"Well, I got to looking in my rearview mirror, and I saw that Venice was right. There in the glow of the streetlights, that man *did* look a little like Jesus Christ. I thought about that. I thought, 'what if Jesus was sitting there on the ground, so hungry that he was reduced to looking for table scraps in a filthy garbage bag, and I just went on by and left him there? What would I say to him later when I saw him in Heaven? How would I explain my selfish behavior?' Brothers and sisters, can you imagine seeing Christ in Heaven and he asks you why you left him there cold and starving in the street like a stray dog? So right then I felt ashamed. I went back. I pulled up along the sidewalk where that man sat, shivering, and I rolled down the window and I said, 'Brother, my name is Matthew Corley and I'm a Baptist minister. I would like to know if there is anything I can offer you that might provide some peace and comfort on this cold, dark night?' And the man stopped digging through his trash bag and looked up at me, and do you know what he told me, brothers and sisters? He told me to go to Hell."

Pastor Matthew paused to await the dramatic gasps and groans from his listeners, and Rooster stifled a laugh.

"Fellow Christians, how many more signs must God show us? How many more warnings must he give before we finally accept the truth that we are living in the end times? The Good Book tells us clearly that in the last days men will have become Godless. *Haters* of God. Haters of *good*. Now, I don't know about you, but when a person who is starving and freezing to death in the street would rather curse a man of God in front of his family than accept a helping hand from him, all I can think is that God told me this was coming."

The pastor droned on about riots and war, earthquakes and hurricanes, plagues and famine. Rooster felt his eyelids growing heavier with each word. The effects of the OxyContin combined with his exhaustion were nullifying the short-term stimulation of the cheap methamphetamine in his bloodstream. His head drooped steadily forward as the tender caress of sleep slipped over his shoulders and up the back of his neck.

"...and every living fish in the sea shall die. And all the birds in the sky shall fall to the ground–all the sparrows and all the crows and all the roosters and all the...."

Roosters. Did he just say *roosters*? When Rooster opened his eyes, he was startled to find Pastor Matthew staring directly at him.

"And the earth shall open up, and from it shall come a beast with seven heads and nine tails, disgorging fire and brimstone from his mouth. And with him shall rise the demon souls of all those who have died at the hands of the unholy one." The voice of the young, bearded minister had increased in pitch and fervor, and there was an intensity in the man's face that contrasted sharply with his previously calm and gentle demeanor.

"...and the angel said *woe* unto the murderers and the drug users and the haters of God, for the wrath of judgment shall be poured down upon you until you are *drowned*." Now Pastor Matthew was practically screaming his words. He thrust his arm out emphatically, over and over, pointing his finger...pointing his finger at Rooster. "And you shall be stricken with *disease*, which shall blacken your vile skin and cause your eyes to cry blood. And you shall *scream* for God to have mercy on you, but he will turn his back on you as you have turned your back on HIM."

Every man, woman, and child in the congregation turned and held an accusatory gaze on Rooster as he stood from his seat in the back pew, and then Rooster saw that the pastor's mouth was no longer brimming with perfect pearly whites, but with jagged fangs.

"And the demons shall tear you open with razor claws and rip your organs from you while you beg the Lord to make it stop, but he won't, *he won't*, HE WON'T."

Rooster pulled the .357 Magnum from his waistband and shot Pastor Matthew in the head. The man's brains splattered over the huge, wooden cross that adorned the wall behind the pulpit, but the preacher didn't fall. Instead, he smiled his jagged smile, and through the blood that gushed from his mouth, said in a voice that flowed like honey, "Welcome to Armageddon, brother."

12.

"Brother? Brother? Hey, brother."

Rooster felt a hand gripping his shoulder. A voice. Rich baritone. Far away.

"Brother?"

He jumped to his feet and jerked away from the Merlin Olsen look-alike.

"Whoa, take it easy, friend," the big man said. "I'm sorry to wake you, but I wanted to ask if you would care to join us for some refreshments downstairs."

Rooster shook his head to clear the cobwebs from behind his eyes. His heart was racing; he took a few deep breaths through his nose to try to slow it. "How long was I out?"

Norman grinned benevolently. "I couldn't tell you that, brother. I saw you come in just before the sermon, not quite an hour ago." He held out a huge hand. "I'm Norman. Welcome to our church."

Rooster ignored the gesture. "I'm looking for the preacher man."

"Pastor Matthew? He's just out in the hall." Norman withdrew his hand but his kind face remained steady. "I'll let him know you'd like to see him. Do you have a name, friend?"

"No, not him. I'm looking for...Gene."

"Oh, I'm sorry, Gene isn't here. His son passed away recently and–"

"Where does he live?"

Norman's expression hardened, and Rooster saw a hint of suspicion in his eyes. "I didn't catch your name, brother."

My name is I'm gonna gut you like a fish if you don't tell me what I want to fucking know, church boy. "Jason. Jason Krueger."

"Are you injured, Jason Krueger?"

"What?"

"Your arm. I noticed your sleeve is torn, and it looks like there's some blood on it."

"I had a little mishap while I was changing a car tire. It's not a big deal."

"Well, it just so happens that there is a doctor in the house. Brother Charles. I believe he's downstairs having refreshments. I'm sure he would be happy to take a look at your arm if you'd like."

Rooster considered that for a moment. He knew it could mean the death of him if his arm was to become infected. Hospitals were overflowing, medical supplies were low, and, according to the news, people were robbing pharmacies at gunpoint to obtain such simple things as cough syrup and allergy pills. It was likely that in the near future a doctor's care would be the most sought after thing on the planet, and Rooster had never been one to look a gift horse in the mouth. "You know, Merlin, I think I'd really appreciate having Dr. Charles have a look at me if it's not much of an inconvenience."

The big man's easy grin returned. "Norman. The name is Norman. If you want to wait right here, I'll go see if I can't round up the doc for you."

Norman left, and Rooster heard him say something to someone in the hall but he couldn't make out the words. A minute later, Pastor Matthew came in.

"Good evening, brother. How are you?" The minister offered a handshake, which Rooster refused. "That's okay if you don't want to shake my hand. You can't be too careful about personal contact, I suppose. I assure you you're safe though...no Qilu virus here."

"I ain't too worried about no virus," Rooster said, "I'm just not much for shaking hands."

"I understand. Anyway, I'm Pastor Matthew. Brother Norman mentioned you had an injury. Is there anything I can do for you?"

"You could tell me how to get in contact with Preacher Gene."

"Oh, well, uh, Pastor Gene is currently going through a personal tribulation. I imagine it's going to be a while before he is back with us. Are you a relative?"

"Nope."

"Oh. Well, I personally wouldn't know how to contact Gene presently. We're all respecting his wishes for privacy right now."

"But you must have an address for him. That's all I need, just an address."

Before Matthew could respond, Norman came in with a middle-aged man with graying hair and wire-rimmed glasses and a suit that looked like it cost an arm, a leg, and possibly a couple of heads. "Brother Jason, this is Brother Charles, the doctor I was telling you about."

"Hello," the doctor said with a nod. He extended his hand, and, to the bafflement of Norman and Matthew, Rooster reached out and gave it a firm grasp.

"So how come you're not at a hospital like all the other doctors?" Rooster asked. "Last I heard, they were bringing in MDs from out of state because there wasn't enough here to take care of all the sick people."

"I'm a plastic surgeon, actually," the doctor responded. "The demand for that type of work isn't as pressing at the moment."

"A plastic surgeon, huh? Are you good at it? Could you put horns on a guy's head if he wanted you to?"

The doctor laughed heartily. "That would be a pretty unusual request, but I suppose something like that could be done, yes."

"How about a third arm? Could you do a third arm, Doc?"

"Ha, probably not, but that would be a multi-tasker's dream, wouldn't it?"

"Yessir. I could clap and pick my nose at the same time."

"Well," said Pastor Matthew, "if you all will excuse me, I believe I'm going to head on downstairs and make sure that little girl of mine is behaving herself. If you need anything, you'll know where to find me."

"Sure thing, Pastor," Norman said. "Great sermon this evening, by the way."

"Oh, well, thank you."

After the minister had stepped out, the doctor asked Rooster to remove his coat in order to access the injured arm.

"I don't think that'll be necessary, Doc," Rooster said. "How about I just roll up my sleeve?"

"Whatever you're comfortable with."

Rooster rolled up his coat sleeve with some difficulty, and the doctor sat beside him in the pew and examined the wound without touching it.

"These look like bite wounds," the doctor said. "How did this happen?"

"I thought you said you hurt yourself changing a tire," Norman interrupted.

"That's right. I was changing a car tire and some dog run up on me and clamped down on my arm. I yelled at the damn cur and swung my tire iron at him until he let go."

"You have a pretty nasty injury here," said the doctor. "It needs suturing, which I'm not equipped to give you outside of a hospital environment. There's extensive bruising...it's possible you could have a bone fracture. We can't know for sure without x-rays. You really need to go to a hospital."

"Yeah, I don't think that's gonna happen," Rooster said, "so if there's nothing you can do for me then I'll just deal with it on my own."

"I can clean it up for you and give you a topical antibiotic, dress it with some gauze, but really that's about it."

"That's better than nothing, ain't it?"

"Alright, I'll have to go out to my car and get my medical bag. I'll only be a couple of minutes, then we'll get you patched up."

"Sounds good."

Rooster waited for the doctor to leave, then said to Norman, "So I think you were gonna tell me where Pastor Gene lives."

"I don't think I was."

"And why not?"

"Because I don't think Brother Gene would like me giving out his personal information to strangers."

"Just because I'm a stranger to you doesn't mean I'm a stranger to the preacher man. We got business, me and him."

"I'm afraid I won't be able to help you, brother."

"Ain't no need to be afraid...brother. Not just yet anyway." Rooster was losing his patience with the big man. He wondered if Norman would give him the preacher's address if he started cutting his sausage-sized fingers off with a dull blade. There was something about the man–something in his eyes–that led Rooster to suspect he might be a tough nut to crack.

"Look, Norm, I appreciate your loyalty. The guy is your pastor and all, and I'm just some dude off the street. I understand your reluctance to help me out, but the fact remains, I need his address, and you're gonna give it to me one way or the other."

"Friend, that sounds like a threat."

"Take it any way you see fit."

Norman raised his chin and gazed up at the ceiling as if God were speaking to him from the rafters, then stepped toward Rooster with a look as cold and vicious as an Arctic wind. "Let me tell you something Mr. Krueger–if that's even your real name: I may be a servant of Christ, but I was also a police officer for several years. Before that, I was a machine gunner in the United States Army Rangers. If you think I'm intimidated by you in the very least, then you've got another thing coming. Now, I'm going to be a good Christian and allow you to remain in this house of God until Brother Charles treats your injury, but after that, I will have to insist that you leave and not come back. Am I clear?"

Rooster stroked the stubble on his chin and smiled. "Settle down now, Stormin' Norman. Is that what they called you in the Marines, or Army, or whatever it was you said you were in? I bet that's what they called you...Stormin' Norman. I tell you what, Norm, I'm gonna get out of your hair now. You're a pretty big dude, and I got no particular beef with you. There are other ways to skin a cat."

He pushed his coat sleeve down and gathered his bags, and when Doctor Charles returned, he said, "There you are, Doc. I decided to just take the bandages and antibiotic and treat the wound myself, if it's all the same to you."

"I really think it would be better if–"

"No, trust me on this. It would be better if I treated myself, so I'll just take the supplies and be on my way."

The doctor only stood and stared at Rooster in confusion.

"Are you gonna make me say please, Doc?"

"Give him the supplies and let him go, Charles," Norman said.

The doctor handed Rooster a roll of gauze and a small tube of Neosporin without saying a word. Rooster dropped the items into his pillowcase, and as he exited the church, he howled, "*Whoohoo! Stormin' Norman!*" He stepped out into the cold blackness of the night, and for a fleeting moment, he thought he saw Pastor Matthew standing in the parking lot, his mouth stretched wide in a fanged smile.

13.

"The White House is urging everyone to stay calm. U.S. forces *have* been placed on high alert, but officials here in Washington are telling us that the nuclear explosions in Shandong are *not* a result of terrorism, nor is there any indication that China is under attack by a foreign power. We are told the president will be holding a press conference any minute now and hopefully he'll be able to shed some light on this very grave situation. Until then, all we can do is speculate."

The segment cut back to the news studio where a suitably worried-looking Paula Banks and Joshua Holland sat behind a glass-topped anchor desk. "Thanks for that helpful information, Greg," Paula said. "Once again for those of you who are just joining us, our top story tonight: nuclear explosions in China. It has been confirmed that at least three nuclear blasts have rocked the province of Shandong, China. We are hearing reports that the cities of Jinan, Zibo, and Qingdao might possibly have been destroyed in these explosions. Now, we have no information regarding casualties, but these are major cities with populations between two and three million people. To give you some perspective, we are talking about cities the size of *Chicago*."

Joshua shook his head in genuine astonishment. "It's hard to imagine that kind of devastation, Paula. We don't have any information on precisely how powerful these explosions were, but even the smaller, tactical-style nuclear weapons like those used in Japan at the end of World War II will cause *untold* destruction in such densely-populated cities."

"Right," Paula said, "and as we all know, some of the nuclear weapons that exist today are far more powerful than what we had way back in the 1940s. If these explosions were the result of large *strategic* nukes–what some military officials refer to as 'city killers'–then we could be seeing destruction of an unprecedented magnitude."

Joshua nodded emphatically. "I guess the big question at this hour is why have these explosions occurred? As Greg Farrell, our correspondent in Washington, reported moments ago, sources are saying that this isn't a case of terrorism or any sort of foreign attack, so what other explanation are we left with?"

"That is indeed a very good question, Joshua. We have so *many* questions tonight as the world waits for–" Paula paused and glanced to her right to receive instructions from someone off screen. "Okay," she continued, "we're being told the president is now making a statement from the White House. Let's hear what he has to say."

The video feed cut to the president of the United States slightly hunched over a podium in a press briefing room. The lines in his face appeared deeper than usual, and his shoulders sagged wearily. His head, normally held proudly high, hung low with the weight of the burden of leadership in a time of extreme crisis.

The president spoke slowly, "Earlier this evening, in a desperate attempt to control a massive outbreak of Qilu virus in the Chinese Province of Shandong, leaders of the People's Republic of China ordered nuclear weapons to be detonated over the cities of Jinan, Zibo, and Qingdao, in Shandong. At this time, we don't know the exact yield of the weapons used to carry out these orders, nor do we know the extent of the casualties, although I've been informed that every effort was made to evacuate these areas prior to the detonations.

"On behalf of the United States of America, I condemn these irresponsible and reprehensible acts by China, as well as any other nation who would resort to the employment of weapons of mass destruction against its own people. There can be no justification for such measures, and the international community will not tolerate them. I hereby wish to make it known that further behavior of this nature will not be without consequences.

"As a precaution, I've placed our military forces, both at home and abroad, on heightened alert. Let me emphasize that I've done this as a necessary *precaution*. This is a very unique situation, and we must anticipate and be prepared to respond promptly to any difficulties that could potentially arise from it.

"I'd like to assure the American people that we are monitoring these events very carefully, and as we receive more information, we will make sure to keep you posted. Thank you very much."

As the president left the podium under a barrage of questions and camera flashes, Ross stared up at the tiled ceiling of his quarantine room and was incredulous that the world could go to shit as quickly and easily as it had over the course of the last few weeks. Dr. Grant had said the Qilu virus would, in time, die out naturally, but it seemed China wasn't willing to wait for that to happen.

My God. Nukes.

A phone rang on the wooden bookshelf next to his bed.

"Yeah?"

"Hey, Ross, it's Mickey."

"Mickey, it's good to hear from you, man. What's going on out there?"

"Lots. I'm not sure where to begin. How are you holding up?"

"I'm okay. I was bored as fuck until I heard China nuked its own cities."

"Crazy shit, right?"

"It gets crazier by the minute. Where did you all take my van?"

"It's at the impound lot over on Mission. You can pick it up when the hospital releases you. Listen, I thought you might want to know, Wenatchee is getting locked down."

"What?"

"Both the bridges have been blocked off. Nobody is getting in or out. Essential traffic only, as per state protocol. That Wallace lady, turns out she's been in contact with a lot of people recently. Avid church goer."

"Oh shit. How many people?"

"Not sure. Thirty...forty...maybe more. Maybe a lot more. I have a feeling things are going to start getting bad over the next few days."

"Damn, Mickey, if she infected thirty or forty people, and each of them infected others, who infected others...there's no telling how many are running around out there spreading that shit. Jeez, there could be *hundreds*."

"And let's not forget that somebody had to infect *her*."

"So why aren't we seeing dozens of people screaming in the street and puking blood all over everything? How come the hospital isn't overrun with the infected?"

"I just don't know, Coach. The emergency room is packed right now, but nobody is acting crazy. Maybe individuals react differently to the virus. Maybe it doesn't affect everybody like it did the Wallace lady. That would make sense. Or maybe there are different incubation times. I'm not a doctor, I really have no idea. We're preparing for the worst though."

"Great, and I'm stuck here in this hospital room."

"Might be the safest place to be."

"I might be safer in a cage full of lions," Ross said with a chuckle. "The hospital will be the first place people will go."

"Hopefully you'll be out of there before the shit hits the fan. Hey, do you want to hear something crazy?"

"Dude, I'm living under an umbrella of perpetual craziness. I doubt there is anything you could say that would surprise me at this point."

"Well, do you remember that white shit that was all around that Wallace lady's mouth?"

Ross thought of the powdery substance caked on Miss Wallace's mouth, the wood splinters jutting from her lips, her broken teeth. "Yeah, I remember. Did you find out what that was all about?"

"Yeah, she had chewed through some of the walls in her house. The drywall, the framing studs, she ate through that shit like a trapped dog. She must have spent hours just gnawing away; there were huge holes everywhere."

"What the hell?"

"I know! Crazy huh?"

"I suppose it's no crazier than when she tried to eat her own son, or when you guys shot her a couple dozen times before she finally died... except she didn't. She got right back up again as if nothing had happened."

"Would it make you feel better if I told you she was wearing body armor?"

"As a matter of fact, it *would*."

"Well, she wasn't. She might have been on some type of narcotic or something, or–"

"Or maybe she was a fucking zombie," Ross said.

Mickey chuckled. "A zombie...okay, sure. Or she might have been a robot sent back from the future."

"Oh come on, Mickey, let's call a duck a duck. I don't know why nobody wants to say it, but if this is what the Qilu virus does to people, then we are dealing with a full-on zombie apocalypse. It sounds funny, right? Like something you might hear from some whack job conspiracy theorist hunkered in his mom's basement with one hand on his 'bug-out bag' and the other jackin' his dick to a Guns and Ammo magazine. But it isn't funny, because it turns out those fuckers had the right idea all along. You *saw* her, Mickey. She was like something straight out of World War Z."

After a brief silence, Mickey said, "I hear what you're saying, Coach. It was some eerie shit, no doubt. But this is real life. Nobody is crawling up out of their graves and eating people."

"She tried to bite Andre. She was snapping at him like a piranha."

Mickey didn't say anything.

"Look, man," Ross said, "zombies or not, the world is getting really crazy. Six million people just got *nuked*, for godsake. Grocery shelves are empty, gas pumps are running dry, and folks are going to be getting seriously desperate. This hospital is probably going to be overflowing in the next few days. You say this town is prepared for what may come, but are we really? Look at L.A., Chicago, *Seattle*; they thought they were prepared too. There are less than forty thousand people here in Wenatchee. If there are a hundred people infected right now, how long before there are a thousand? And when there are a thousand, how long before there are ten? How long before the whole damn city is zombiefied? I wouldn't be surprised if that's exactly what happened in China. What other possible reason would they have to nuke themselves?"

"I think you've seen too many movies, Coach."

"Like I said, Mickey, zombies or not, the world is going to shit. If I were you, I'd take my family and get out of Dodge, find a little place in the mountains and wait this out. My uncle owns a cabin in the woods near Eatonville. Safe, secluded. I could take you there."

"You know I can't do that, I have a job to do. The county depends on me."

"Your *family* depends on you."

"Ross, don't go there."

"How many more people are you going to have to shoot, Mickey?"

"I appreciate your concern, but don't waste energy worrying about me or my family. I know how to handle myself, and I'll do whatever I have to do to protect my own. Everything is going to be okay, Ross. We've locked down the city, and we're tracking down everyone we think that Wallace lady might have been in contact with."

"What will you do when you find them?"

"We will do what we are trained to do."

Ross remembered the scene with Miss Wallace: the screaming cops, their confusion, the ineffectiveness of their bullets. He shook his head in apprehension. "I hope you have plenty of shotgun shells."

"Trust me, Coach. We got this. Shit, man, what zombie is gonna want to fuck with *me*?"

Ross managed a half-hearted laugh. "Spoken like a true badass."

"You know it. Take care, Ross. I'll check back with you in a couple days."

"Watch yourself out there, Mickey."

"Will do. And, Coach, this still might turn out to be no big deal."

"You don't really believe that."

After a lengthy pause, Mickey said, "You never know, man."

"Take care, Mickey." Ross hung up the phone and gazed at the TV screen, on which archived footage of a nuclear explosion looped to the voice of some expert in something or other as he babbled about the global danger of radioactive fallout.

I gotta get the fuck out of here.

14.

Rooster awoke to the sound of voices, laughter. He looked around, unsure of where he was, then saw people descending the front steps of the church and remembered. He felt nearly paralyzed with exhaustion and cold, and had it not been for the fervor of his hatred, he would have gone right back to sleep there in the shadows of the dense woods beyond the edge of the church parking lot.

He shook the cobwebs from behind his eyes and watched the churchgoers shake the hand of Pastor Matthew just inside the open front doorway as they left the building in sporadic twos and threes. A few lingered in the well-lit parking lot, engaging in small talk, but the cold was bitter, and no one wanted to waste precious gasoline warming their vehicles, so none of them hung around for long. After about fifteen minutes, there were only two vehicles left in the lot: a dark red minivan and a gray Ford Taurus, which Rooster thought must have belonged to the pastor and Norman.

As he lay shivering in the tree shadows, he considered going back into the church and killing anyone who remained inside one by one until someone gave up the address of the preacher man, but he didn't know how many people were still in the building. One of them might be able to call the police before he could get everyone rounded up. He decided to wait a little while longer before making a move. In the meantime, he dug the bag of meth from his coat pocket, scooped out a pinch of the finer granules and snorted it off his fingers. A fierce, hot pain shot through his nose and the left side of his head, causing him to wince and moan. For relief, he took out his water bottle and poured a little water into the palm of his hand and snorted that as well.

A few more minutes passed before Pastor Matthew appeared in the doorway with Norman, a woman, and two young girls. After some more talk, laughter, and handshaking, the pastor followed the woman and the girls down the steps, and the four of them hurried to the gray Ford. Norman boomed at them to be safe, then disappeared back into the church.

After the pastor and his family had piled into the Ford and driven away, Rooster tied his two bags together so that they would be easier to carry in one hand, then removed the silenced SIG from his coat and clicked off the safety. He couldn't wait any longer, with each passing moment the cold, combined with his pain and fatigue, further robbed him of his ability to function.

His plan was to go into the church and shoot Norman in the kneecaps and kill anyone else in the building as quickly as possible, and then carve on Norman with the butcher knife until the son of a bitch told him what he wanted to know. To show that he wasn't fucking around, he would start with Norman's testicles.

He stood up in the shadows and swung his arms to increase circulation, hefted his bags, and then saw the lights go out inside the church. He ducked behind a tree when Norman came out moments later with a tall, slender woman and a girl who looked to be around ten or twelve. Rooster waited until Norman locked the door behind them and started down the steps, then took a deep breath and moved briskly onto the parking lot.

Norman spotted him immediately. He handed a set of keys to the woman and said something Rooster couldn't hear, and the woman placed a hand on the back of the child and increased her pace toward the minivan, keeping her eyes on Rooster as she went. Rooster didn't need the headache of having to deal with them once they were locked inside the van, but at a distance of about sixty feet they were too far away for an accurate one-handed shot from the SIG. Nevertheless, he raised the gun and fired without breaking stride.

The round missed and struck the wall of the church building with a crack that was louder than the discharge of the weapon itself. The woman screamed and positioned herself between

Rooster and the child, who screamed herself when Rooster fired two more rounds from fifty feet. Norman lunged into the line of fire, threw his hands up and yelled, "No! Stop! I'll give you anything you want. You don't have to hurt anyone here."

"Shut the fuck up, Norman," Rooster said, continuing to close the distance. "You had your chance to make things easy on yourself earlier, but you blew it. Now I'm done being nice." He moved to within fifteen feet of the family and stopped and examined the three of them for any visible bullet holes or splotches of blood. "Is anybody hit?"

The woman frantically looked the little girl over and shook her head. "No. No, I think we're okay." She tightened her arms around the girl and stared at Rooster with eyes glassy with shock and terror. "Please, *please* don't hurt us."

"We are people of God," Norman said. "We don't want any trouble here."

"Just do what I tell you, and there won't be no trouble," Rooster said. "I want all three of you to slowly walk back inside the church. We're gonna go in and have a little talk."

"Look, whatever it is you—"

"Don't make me tell you twice, Norman. I'll gut all of you right here in the parking lot. It makes no difference to me."

"Are you going to kill us?" the young girl asked. Her voice was steady, despite her lower jaw quivering like a plucked guitar string.

"I guess that depends mostly on your daddy. Now get movin'."

Rooster made Norman lead the way while Rooster hung back a little with the sound suppressor on his gun pressed against the back of the woman's head. Once they were inside the building, he ordered Norman to lock the door, then made the woman and child lay down on the floor with their hands behind their heads.

"Duct tape."

"What?"

"I need some fucking duct tape, Norman. There's gotta be a roll around here somewhere."

Norman shrugged. "I don't...um, I'm not sure we have any duct tape."

"Let me make this simple for you, Norm. I need to secure this wife and kid of yours while you and me conduct some business. Since I'm not very good at tying knots, and I sure as fuck can't rely on *you* to do it, I gotta duct tape them. If I can't duct tape them, I gotta kill 'em. You understand what I'm saying?"

"I understand. There might be some in the maintenance closet downstairs."

"You better fuckin' hope so."

They went downstairs to an open kitchen and a large dining area that contained three rows of folding tables with plastic chairs on all sides. The walls were adorned with crosses and crucifixes and various framed prints depicting scenes from the Holy Bible, as well as Jesus himself in all manner of poses.

There were three wooden doors spaced apart by ten feet along the wall to the left. Norman opened the leftmost door, switched on an interior light, and rummaged frantically through the tiny room for about a minute, then switched off the light and stepped out. "Just let me check the kitchen drawers," he said.

Rooster sensed panic rising in the big man's voice. He trained his gun carefully on Norman's head as Norman strode into the kitchen area and searched the cabinet drawers. After a few moments, Norman stopped and hung his head and brought his massive hands up to his face. His back was to Rooster, but Rooster could hear the man's slow, deep breaths. Was he praying? More likely, he had found a knife in the drawer and was getting up the nerve to use it in a last-ditch effort to save his family.

"Step back away from the counter, Norman. Turn around so I can see your hands."

Norman didn't respond.

"Turn around, or I will shoot this kid of yours in the face." Rooster heard both the woman and the girl whimper, but he didn't dare take his eyes off Norman.

Norman glanced slowly over his shoulder, then raised his head and reached for the cabinet door above him.

"What are you doing, Norm?" Rooster's finger tightened on the gun trigger. He didn't want to kill the man until after he knew where to find Pastor Gene, but if Norman had a gun stashed in the cabinet, he might be able to turn and fire before Rooster could get a shot off.

Rooster couldn't risk it. He pulled the trigger, intending to shoot Norman in his reaching arm, but the round missed and tore through the drywall below the cabinet. Norman cried out and spun wildly. There was a flash of silver gray. Before Rooster could fire another round–this time at Norman's head–he saw an object drop and bounce on the carpeted floor and roll toward him until it came to rest at his feet.

Duct tape.

"Dammit, Norman. Either you're the luckiest sumbitch on this planet, or there really *is* a god looking out for you."

The young girl ran to her father and threw her arms around his neck while the woman fell to her knees and began to weep. Rooster wiped a few beads of sweat from his forehead with the back of his sleeve. "I think you better come on out of the kitchen, Norm."

Rooster ordered the woman and the child to lie prone on the floor with their wrists crossed behind their backs. He tossed the roll of duct tape to Norman. "Okay then, you know what to do."

"I don't think I can do this."

"It's okay, Norman," sobbed the woman, "just do what he tells you."

"That's right, Normie," Rooster said, "Do what I tell you and nobody will get their throats cut here on this pretty carpet. I need you to tape their wrists together, and their ankles. Do it tight, because I'll be checking after you're done. If you don't do it proper, I'll have to hobble them with my knife. Got it?"

"What do you want from us?" Norman asked, curling his upper lip in contempt.

"I want to cook you and eat you. Food is a little scarce out there these days. Or so I hear." Rooster smiled at the satisfying gasp from the girl. "Look, y'all, if I wanted you dead, I'd have already killed you. Now get these bitches bound up, Norman, before I change my *fuckin' mind*." He screamed the last two words so loudly that both the woman and child jerked in recoil.

As Norman wrapped the tape around his wife's and daughter' limbs, Rooster dumped the contents of the woman's purse onto the floor. He was astonished when a holstered .32 caliber Taurus revolver tumbled out.

"Well I'll be buttfucked." He pulled the gun from its holster and studied it, saw that it was fully loaded. "Ain't that some shit? You had this the whole time. It had to have been eating you alive, waiting and waiting for that brief chance to use it, *knowing* that this whole situation could be averted if you could only get up the guts to pull this little baby out of your damn purse and shoot me with it. You probably could have done it when I had my eyes glued to Norman while he was rummaging through the kitchen. It must be pretty hard knowing that what stopped you–the *only* thing that stopped you–was fear." He shook his head in amazement. "Did it ever once occur to any of y'all that maybe God is on my side instead of yours?"

Rooster dropped the gun into his coat pocket, removed a ballpoint pen and a pack of chewing gum from the items on the floor, took a seat in a plastic chair, and waited for Norman to finish with the duct tape. It felt good to sit. However uncomfortable the cheap, polypropylene chair might have normally been, here and now it felt almost luxurious. His body seemed to melt into it, and he thought if he sat too long, he would be unable to get up again.

When he was satisfied with the tape job, Rooster told Norman to strip down to his underwear.

"I'd rather not," Norman replied.

"You're starting to piss me off with your bullheadedness, Norman. What with your old lady packin' heat in her handbag, I can't take the chance you might be hiding something yourself underneath all them quadruple-X-sized clothes you're wearing."

"You can frisk me."

Rooster laughed. "I don't think I want to get that close to you just yet. Come on, let's get this over with. I don't like it any more than you do."

"I think I have to refuse."

"This is the last time I'm gonna ask you more than once, Norman. The next time you refuse, the next time you even *hesitate*, I'm gonna do something bad to either your wife or your little girl, and you won't know which one until I do it. So what's it gonna be?"

Norman stripped off his clothes. Rooster tossed him the ballpoint pen and a wadded paper receipt and told him to write the home address of Pastor Gene without saying the address aloud. "Remember, Norm, your wife and kid are going to pay for your fuckups from now on...so don't fuck up."

Norman scribbled on the paper without saying a word, and then threw it and the pen back to Rooster. Rooster was annoyed when he had to get up from his chair after the wad of paper fell short. He picked it up, sat back down, and read it to himself. "What's your wife's name, Norman? Ah, nevermind." He spotted the woman's wallet among the purse items on the floor. He opened it and took out her driver's license, along with several credit cards and forty-three dollars in cash. "Andrea Phillips. Okay then, Andrea, I'm gonna ask you the home address of Pastor Gene, and you can expect there to be consequences if you lie to me."

"I don't know the house number off the top of my head," she answered, "but it's in my address book...the little blue binder there on the floor."

Rooster smiled when he found the address written on the first page. He compared it to what Norman had written on the back of the receipt. The addresses matched. "Well, I'll be damned. Just so you know, Andrea, if your old man here had given me this address when I asked for it politely earlier this evening, none of this would have happened."

He ordered Norman to lie facedown on the floor while he went through the man's clothes. After he'd emptied all the pockets and found nothing of interest aside from a cell phone and a few dollars in cash, he told Norman to duct tape his wife's and daughter's mouths closed.

"But they won't be able to breathe," came Norman's response.

"Dammit, Norm, what did I tell you?" Rooster walked over to where Andrea lay and brought his foot down hard on her head. She screamed and spat blood, and Rooster could see that some of her teeth were broken.

"God damn you!" Norman roared. "God *damn* you!" He jumped to his feet, but froze when Rooster placed the SIG to the young girl's head.

"Get the tape, Norman. *Now*."

Norman picked up what was left of the roll of duct tape, then took his white undershirt from his clothes on the floor and used it to wipe the blood from Andrea's mouth. For the first time, Rooster saw tears in the big man's eyes. Norman tore a strip of fabric from the shirt and placed it gently in his wife's mouth. "This will soak up some of the blood," he told her, "so you won't choke on it. Everything is going to be okay."

He placed a strip of tape over her lips and told her he loved her, then moved to his daughter. "You stay calm, Nancy, no more crying. This will all be over soon and we'll go home." He stroked her blonde hair and kissed her forehead. "Everything will be alright. God is with you. I love you, angel." He taped her mouth and stood to face Rooster with his head held defiantly high and said, "What now?"

"Put your clothes on," Rooster said. "You and me are goin' for a little ride."

15.

Rooster sat behind the passenger seat in the minivan and aimed his gun at Norman's head as the big man buckled himself in at the steering wheel and turned on the ignition. He glanced at the digital clock on the dashboard and noted the time was 9:07 p.m. Seven minutes past curfew.

"How far we gotta go, Norman?"

"Not even five minutes. We could walk from here."

"We're not walking. You're gonna drive without drawing any attention. If anything goes down, you're gonna be the first to die. You get us there without any trouble, and you'll get to see your family again."

"You got the address. Why do you need me?"

"Because I know Pastor Gene will answer the door for you. It will save me the trouble of having to break it down."

Norman pulled the sleeve of his jacket down over his hand and wiped a section of condensation from the windshield. "I have to ask," he said, "what are you planning to do to Pastor Gene?"

"I don't rightly figure that's any of your damn business, Norm. The only thing you gotta worry about right now is getting me face to face with the man. Whatever happens after that has got nothin' to do with you."

"I can't help but to think you're not just going to let me go after I take you to Gene. You plan to kill me?"

"You got no reason to believe me if I tell you no, so what's the point of asking?"

"If you're going to kill me, then I need to make my peace with God."

"Don't stress about it, Norm. If you make things easy for me, I imagine I'll duct tape you up and leave you in the back of this here minivan. You'll be cold for a few hours, but somebody will find you in the mornin'. I ain't got no beef with you. If you plan on trying something stupid though, you might as well go ahead and say your prayers right now, because I won't hesitate to put a bullet in the back of your big-ass head."

"I won't give you any trouble. I'd like to be around to see my daughter grow up."

"Smart man," Rooster said. "Now let's get goin'."

As they pulled out onto the street, a light snow began to fall. Rooster leaned back in his seat and watched the flakes dance lazily in the headlights and listened to the soft rush of air from the van's heater. He didn't see any point in telling Norman he planned to cut his throat once they were inside the preacher's house. As long as Norman believed he was going to live, he would remain fairly cooperative. If he knew he was going to die gasping like a fish and squirting blood on his pastor's pretty white walls within the next ten or fifteen minutes, he would fight. Rooster was confident of that.

"So what did he do?" Norman asked.

"What did *who* do?"

"Pastor Gene. I was wondering what he could have possibly done to warrant the attention of a lunatic such as yourself. The Gene I know is one of the kindest, most generous souls I've ever met. He never has a bad word to say about anyone. His congregation loves him."

"Fucking spare me, Norman. If you want to suck his greasy cock, that's your business; I have a differin' perspective of the sumbitch. And if you call me a lunatic again, I'm liable to bash your head in."

Norman laughed under his breath. "I rest my case."

"Dammit, boy, you're pushin' your lu–"

Norman slammed on the brakes, and Rooster was thrown forward into the back of the front passenger seat. The SIG fell from Rooster's hand. He heard it tumble across the carpeted floorboard, but in the dark interior of the van, he couldn't see where it went. He didn't waste time looking for it. He reached beneath his jacket and drew the .357 from his waistband and pointed the barrel at Norman's head and started to pull the trigger.

Norman made no attempt to escape. He sat with both hands on the wheel and stared straight ahead into the snowy night with a puzzled expression on his face. Rooster hesitated long enough to glance through the windshield, and that's when he saw the man standing in the middle of the street, only fifteen feet in front of them, dressed in blue jeans and a gray tee shirt that read MARINERS BASEBALL on the front. Rooster was astounded to see that the man was barefoot.

"I thought I was going to hit him," Norman said. "He just appeared out of nowhere."

"You should have ran over his ass. Damn junkie. He don't even have any shoes on."

The man gazed directly into the headlights and slowly cocked his head until it was nearly resting on his left shoulder, held that pose for a moment, then jerked his head upright again and rushed forward a few steps, as if he were trying to frighten away a wild animal.

"What the hell is this bozo doing?" Rooster said. "Go around him, Norm. What are you waiting for?"

Norman hit the gas and eased the van into the left lane. The man in the street opened his mouth wide and let out a high-pitched scream before charging the vehicle and striking the sliding cargo door with his fists.

"People have gone absolutely crazy," Norman said as they sped away.

"People have always been crazy, Norman. Ain't nothing new."

"I'm worried he might go to the church."

"He didn't exactly seem like the prayin' type," Rooster said. "Now keep your eyes on the road while I find my other gun. You don't know how close I came to killing you back there. Do *not* hit the brakes like that again. If you come across anyone else roaming around in the middle of the road, run 'em over."

Rooster found the SIG beneath the front passenger seat and tucked the Magnum back into his waistband. He remained on his knees, bracing himself against the back of the seat in case Norman got wise and decided to hit the brakes again. After a couple of minutes, Norman turned left onto a short, downward sloped driveway and came to a stop at the door of a sub-level garage.

"Is this the place?" Rooster asked, his guts churning with excitement.

Norman nodded and switched off the headlights. "This is the place."

Rooster looked through the side window but couldn't see anything other than a cinder block retaining wall. "Back on up to the street, Norman. I want to check this place out. Can't see shit down here."

Norman did as he was instructed, backing the van out of the driveway and parking along the opposite side of the street. Rooster moved over to the seat behind Norman and studied the house through the window. It was a cheap, 70s style ranch home with an added room over the garage, with tan siding and an old wooden privacy fence around most of the yard. The fence was warped and leaning in some sections. There were neighboring homes on both sides and across the street. Rooster told Norman to kill the van engine so as to not attract unnecessary attention.

"Okay, Norman," he said, "this is how we're gonna play this. You're gonna casually walk up to the front door and knock just like you would on any normal evening. I'll be right behind you with my finger on the trigger of this here SIG Sauer, so be cool."

"What am I supposed to say when he answers the door?"

"You can say 'jumped up Jesus Christ on a saddled tadpole' for all I care. Don't matter, because as soon as he opens that door, we're goin' in. If you gotta push him out of your way, you better do it. Your life depends on this, Norman. Do not fuck it up."

"What happens when we're inside?"

"Once we're in, you just do what I tell you and don't try to be no hero. This ain't no television show, this is real life. In real life, heroes usually end up in a body bag. Now, I know you must've seen a lot of dead bodies, being an ex-cop and soldier and all. You think about those bodies, Norm, and decide right now if you want to end up like that, or if you want to go back to that church and see your wife and daughter again. It can go either way. It depends on *you*."

"I just want this to be over."

"Alright then. Let's do it."

Rooster took the van keys from Norman and climbed out through the side cargo door. He went around the front of the van and told Norman to get out nice and easy. Norman did. Rooster followed him across the street, maintaining enough of a distance that Norman, with his police and military background, wouldn't be able to pull some fancy hand-to-hand combat move and try to take the gun away.

There were curtains drawn over the windows, but Rooster could see lights on inside the house. "How many people live here, Norman?"

"Just Gene and his wife, to my knowledge."

"Is there a back door?"

"I believe there is a glass sliding door in the dining room...opens into the backyard."

"Any dogs?"

"Not that I know of."

"Okay then. Do your thing."

Rooster pressed himself against the wall to the right of the door as Norman rang the doorbell. Seconds ticked by. No one answered. Norman pressed the button again, and still nobody came to the door.

"I don't think anyone is home," Norman said after ringing the bell a third time.

Frustrated, Rooster leaned over and pounded on the door, then pulled back to the wall and listened for any movement inside. "Where else would they be?" he whispered. "There's a curfew in effect."

Norman shrugged.

"Knock again. Call his name."

Norman did. No one answered. "I don't think they're here."

Rooster clenched his teeth against the rage that brewed inside him. He was growing tired of the hunt. Tired of the cold, the fatigue, the pain. Tired of Norman's ugly, bearded face. What if this was *not* the preacher's house? Or it was, but Norman knew all along that Gene wouldn't be here. Maybe Gene was at Norman's place right now, drinking hot cocoa and listening to Johnny Cash sing *He Turned Water into Wine* on the stereo as Rooster stood here freezing his ass off like a damned fool. Perhaps Norman's wife or daughter had dialed 911 on a cell phone while Rooster wasn't paying attention. He hadn't searched either one of them. Both likely had phones in their pockets. They could have reached in and pressed the numbers without even looking. Did Norman just crack a smile? *Smug fucking bastard.*

"You think you're pretty clever, don't you, Norman?"

"What?"

"You think you're buying yourself some time until the cops can get here, but guess what...you ain't bought *shit*."

"I honestly have no idea what you're talking about."

"Get back in the van."

Norman didn't argue. Rooster followed him back to the van. They climbed back into their seats, and Rooster told Norman to drive to the next block and park on the side of the street. Rooster topped off the magazine of his SIG as Norman drove, and after they parked, he dropped a rock of meth into his pipe, melted it with a cigarette lighter, and took a long draw from the pipe stem. He leaned forward and blew the smoke into Norman's face.

Norman snapped. He twisted in his seat, and in a voice that sounded like thunder, shouted, "Why are you doing this to me? I have done nothing but cooperate with you. I tied up my family and left them frightened and alone in the church, and you sit back there like some tough guy, blowing your dope shit in my face. You're no tough guy. You're as weak as they come. If you didn't have that gun, I would come back there and rip you apart with my bare hands, and you *know* it. You are shit. You are *nothing*."

Rooster studied Norman's wide, hateful eyes and caressed the trigger of the handgun. He held his stare long enough to show the big man he wasn't intimidated, then he took another hit of meth and let out the smoke and calmly said, "Shut the fuck up, Norman."

Norman exhaled a deep breath which sounded almost like a growl and settled back into his seat to gaze out through the foggy windshield. With the slumped shoulders of a man defeated, and with his body swaying to the rhythm of his pounding heart, he lowered his head and closed his eyes. Rooster knew he was praying.

"No time for that," Rooster said, gathering his bags. "What we're going to do now is get out of the van and walk back to the house across the street from the preacher's house."

Norman raised his head and said, almost absent-mindedly, "And what are we going to do there?"

"We're gonna watch the preacher's house to make sure your wife or daughter didn't call the cops while I wasn't lookin'."

"I assure you they did not."

"You ain't assuring me of nothin'. Now hand over the keys and wait for me to come around to you, just like we did before."

Norman removed the keys from the ignition and tossed them over his shoulder. "If those people across the street see us sneaking around in their yard, they'll call the police themselves."

"We ain't gonna be sneakin' around the yard." Rooster scooped the van keys up off the floor and dropped them into his coat pocket. "We're gonna go right up to the front door and ask them to invite us in."

Norman gripped the steering wheel as if he were clinging to the safety bar of a carnival ride and shook his head in refusal. "I-I can't be a part of this."

"You got no choice, partner." Rooster got out of the van and went around to the driver side and locked the doors with the remote on the key ring once Norman was out.

They walked along the shoulder of the lightless street, through the snow, which had begun to fall more heavily, until they reached the house directly across the street from Pastor Gene's. It was a small, simple house with pine green wood siding. The front yard was separated from the street with a six-foot wooden privacy fence–nicer than the fence around the preacher's yard, but still old and shoddy. A narrow, paved driveway ran through a gap in the fence, terminating at the front of the house, and parked in the driveway was a dark blue Honda CRV. To the left of the windowless front door of the house was a glass sliding door, shaded by white vertical strip blinds. The lights were on inside the house.

"They're not going to just let us in," Norman said, hugging himself against the cold.

"Tell them we're FBI."

"Don't be ridiculous."

"I'm fuckin' serious, Norman. You used to be a cop, so act like a cop."

"What are you going to do to the people inside?"

"I still got almost half a roll of duct tape left. We'll tape them up just like we did your wife and kid and be out of their hair as soon as I'm sure the cops ain't onto us."

Norman cupped his hands and blew into them and rubbed them together vigorously. "You're being paranoid. It's that *shit* you're putting in your body. It's messing with your mind."

"I'm covering my ass is what I'm doin'. Now get up there and ring the doorbell."

"They'll never believe we're FBI."

"Convince them."

They crossed the snow-dusted yard to the front door. Norman rang the buzzer while Rooster hugged the wall to the right, out of view of the peephole. No one answered, but Rooster heard movement inside. Norman hit the button again. Blinding white light blossomed from a halogen bulb above the door, but the door remained closed.

"This is Detective...Detective Peterson with the Bellevue Police Department," Norman lied. "Open the door please."

There came the metallic clink of a deadbolt being disengaged, and then the door opened. "Can I see some ID?" It was a man's voice.

"Here's your ID," Rooster said as he stepped away from the wall and aimed his pistol at the man's face.

The man looked to be in his late thirties, with curly brown hair that was just starting to gray. He wore sweatpants and slippers and a white thermal top that didn't fully cover his sagging beer belly. He opened his mouth to say something, but before he could get the words out, Rooster shot him through the left eye.

16.

The boy sits at the kitchen table and eats chicken-noodle soup and crackers with Lyle and little Johnny. He asks his mom if he and Johnny can have ice cream for dessert. Yes, you can both have some ice cream if you finish all your soup. Lyle throws his spoon down hard on the table and says the boy don't need no damn ice cream. Look how fat he's getting. Why do you want to have a fat ass for a son, Melina? The boy's mom makes an annoyed face and tells Lyle the boy isn't fat, he's just a little chubby is all. It's baby fat and it will go away when the boy does some more growing. Lyle cocks his head and slams his fist on the table. Bitch, you best not be giving me dirty looks or I'll knock your face right off your head. That ain't no baby fat. The boy's mom doesn't say anything else, but the boy can see that Lyle's breathing is getting heavier and he keeps opening and closing his hands like he does every time before he blows up. Lyle starts staring at Johnny, then at the floor underneath Johnny's chair. Sonuva bitch! You're dropping cracker crumbs all over the damn floor, he screams. What the hell is wrong with you? You want to live in a damn pigsty? Johnny says he's sorry for dropping crumbs on the floor. Says he can't help it and starts to cry. There you go crying like a little girl again, you little sissy. I'll give you something to cry about. Lyle jumps up and grabs one of his dirty, steel-toed work boots from over by the front door and starts beating Johnny on the head with it. The boot makes a horrible sound every time it hits Johnny's head, but after a few seconds, the boy can't hear it over Johnny's screams. Johnny pisses himself. It runs down his legs and pools on the linoleum, and then Lyle makes him eat the cracker crumbs out of the piss.

You stop that, says the boy's mom. Her voice is shaky. Scared. Lyle throws his boot across the room and grabs the boy's mom by her hair and slams her head into the wall hard enough to break through the sheetrock. He beats her in the face and body until she falls to the floor, and then kicks her as she tries to crawl away. Lyle turns to Johnny. Did I tell you to stop eating those cracker crumbs? You better eat every damn one or I'm gonna give you some more of that boot. While Lyle's attention is on Johnny, the boy's mom makes a run for the front door. Lyle tries to catch her but she gets through the door and takes off running down the street screaming for somebody to call the police. Go ahead and call the cops, bitch, Lyle yells from the doorway. I'll kill them and you and your kids and everybody else.

The cops come a few minutes later. They make Lyle sit in a chair while the boy's mom throws some clothes in a suitcase and takes the boy and his brother to the car and drives away. Please don't go back, Mom, pleads the boy. You won't go back, will you? No son, we aren't going back.

But the boy knows she will. She always does.

***

Wenatchee, Washington, is a small city nestled in the eastern shadows of the Cascade Mountains, at the conflux of the Wenatchee River, which flows southeast along the northern border of the city, and the Mighty Columbia, which flows south and separates the city of Wenatchee from the smaller town of East Wenatchee. Because the city is bordered on the north and east by rivers, and on the south and west by steep mountains, only two ways exist to go in or out of the city by passenger vehicle. Those are the North Wenatchee Avenue Bridge, crossing the Wenatchee River to the north, and the Senator George Sellar Bridge at the south end of town, which spans the Columbia River into East Wenatchee. To keep people from entering or exiting the city, all the police would have to do is close off the bridges. It looked easy on paper, but Ross knew that once word got around that zombies— he didn't know how else to refer to them—were running around chewing through walls and shrugging off bullets and attacking people, folks would naturally freak out. They weren't going to want to hang around and wait to become infected...or eaten. Especially eaten. They would drown themselves in the rivers trying to get out of town. They would freeze to death when they took to the snowy mountains on foot. They would put up a fight when the police refused to let them pass beyond the city's borders. They would turn on each other out of fear and thirst and starvation and just plain meanness.

Then there were the street gangs: Surenos, Padrinos, Locos, Brick City, Colonia Chiques, and various affiliates who kept the police busy on the best of days. Ross had worked with a number of gang members as part of a "Gloves Not Guns" campaign he had been involved with over the past five years. He knew the gangs were well armed and organized and would exercise whatever violent means necessary to preserve themselves and their interests.

It was going to be a bloodbath.

Ross slid out of bed and slipped his feet into a pair of white disposable slippers and walked to the door of his room. He turned the knob and was surprised to find it unlocked. It occurred to him then that, even though he was being held prisoner, this was still a hospital, not a jail. It wasn't designed to hold people against their will. When he opened the door, there was the brief sigh of air being sucked into the room by the negative pressure ventilation system, the purpose of which was to prevent airborne contagions from escaping and entering other areas of the hospital. Ross half-expected some kind of alarm to sound at that point, but nothing happened. He stuck his head into the corridor and immediately noticed the large security guard sitting on a plastic chair a ways down the hall, fully engrossed in the screen of his smart phone. The butt of a semi-automatic handgun jutted from a black leather holster on the guard's right hip. The guard never looked up.

Ross quietly closed the door and stood there on the cold, polished floor tiles and thought about how he might escape the hospital. He envisioned calling the guard over and knocking him out cold with a left hook to the chin and dragging him into the room out of sight of anyone who might wander into the corridor. The guard wouldn't be out for long, however. In the movies, people who get knocked unconscious remain that way for several minutes, or *hours* sometimes. But reality was quite different. When a real person gets knocked unconscious by a punch to the face or a whack on the head, rarely is he out for more than a few seconds. All too often, he'll be awake even before he hits the floor. Ross knew he could probably knock the guy out, but he would have to somehow tie his hands and legs, and figure out a way to keep him from screaming long enough for Ross to make his way out of the hospital, which was another problem altogether.

Tie him up with the phone cord, or maybe the ribbon ties from the hospital gown–do hospital security guards carry handcuffs? Stuff a washrag in his mouth, put a pillowcase over his head, and hide him in the bathroom. Then what?

Ross would have to find his way to the stairs without being noticed. Which way to the stairs? He had been brought up to the fourth floor by elevator, the door of which was near a large, circular nurse's station at the intersection of two perpendicular hallways. He thought he remembered seeing the stairway sign near the elevators. There was no way he was going to get past the nurses station without being seen.

So what? Just keep on going. Down the stairs and follow the exit signs until you're out of the building. If anyone tries to stop you, run. If they catch you, fight.

Or stay and wait for the hospital to be overrun with the infected. Screaming and puking and tearing with bloodstained teeth.

But once he was out of the hospital, where was there to go? The keys to his house, his gym, his van had been confiscated along with his wallet, money, identification, his *shoes* for godsake. He couldn't go to his home or gym because the police would look for him at those places first. In his mind he heard Bill Paxton's character in the film, *Weird Science*, say, *You're stewed, buttwad!*

He walked to the window and looked out at the quiet street below. It was snowing. He placed his hands against the window glass and felt the cold. He thought of the bum he had discovered down by the railroad tracks a few winters back. It had been only a couple of days after Christmas that year. Ross had gone for a morning run along the tracks when he had found the man curled in a fetal position naked in the snow beneath a tree. Eyes closed, mouth open, arms folded tightly across his chest. Frozen solid and stuck to the ground. His pants had been pushed down around the tops of his boots, and his coat, sweater, and dirty white undershirt had been peeled off and tossed aside like old rags–paradoxical undressing, physicians called it–apparently because freezing to death feels a little bit like being burned alive.

Ross wondered what might have been going through that bum's mind as he spent his final hours tormented by the piercing cold. The fear. The desperation. The *loneliness*. In a city of more than thirty thousand people, there hadn't been *one* to whom the bum had felt he could turn for a warm place to sleep. No one to care enough to spare him from his suffering and death. If Ross had learned one thing from the dead man by the railroad tracks, it was that he did not want to die that way.

But he didn't want to die like Miss Wallace either.

He figured he was on his own, regardless of whether he stayed or went. He had friends, sure, but he was fairly certain that none of them would be much help once they learned he had escaped from Qilu virus quarantine. It wasn't something he would be able to hide. The police were taking the situation very seriously and would spare no effort in raising public awareness about his escape, should he decide to take that action. If he did *not* decide to take that action, who was going to come to his aid when the hospital was swarming with Miss Wallaces? The security guard in the hallway? Yeah, right...that guy wouldn't know it if a zombie crawled right up his ass.

Ross considered that he might be overreacting, but he knew the virus had a history of causing catastrophic turmoil in a short amount of time. It had taken only a couple of weeks for the entire city of Los Angeles, the second most populous city in the United States, to descend into chaos. Paris had collapsed in little more than half that length of time. A little town like Wenatchee, with its thirty-five thousand residents packed into an area of less than eight square miles, would fall apart faster than you could say "martial law."

He sat on the edge of his bed and pressed 0 on the number pad of his hospital phone, and when an operator answered, asked to be connected to Andre Wallace's room.

Andre answered on the third ring. "Hello?"

"Hey, Andre, this is Coach Ross. How are you holding up?"

"They got me on somethin' that's supposed to make me relax, but I don't feel too relaxed. They shot my momma down in cold blood right there in the front yard of her house. I can't get that out of my head, man."

"She wasn't your momma anymore, Dre. She was infected with something that had already destroyed her mind. She wasn't going to come back from that."

"It just don't seem right, man."

"No, Dre, it doesn't seem right, but she tried to kill us—*both* of us. Your mother was a good woman. She wouldn't have acted the way she did if she had been in control of herself. You know what rabies is, don't you, Dre? Your mom had a disease that was like rabies, but worse maybe."

"That's why she was foaming at the mouth and stuff?"

The memory of Miss Wallace's white-caked lips flashed in Ross's mind. *She had chewed through some of the walls in her house*, Mickey had said. *The drywall, the framing studs, she ate through that shit like a trapped dog.* "Yes, that's why she was foaming at the mouth...and trying to bite you. You understand that if she *had* bitten you, you would be dying right now. There is no cure for what the virus does to people. You get sick, you go crazy, and you suffer until you finally die. What your momma was going through, it would be like...it would be worse than being in Hell." Ross thought of Monica and bit hard into his lower lip and knew that if he allowed the image of her suffering to remain in his mind for another moment, he would be unable to stop himself from diving headfirst through the hospital window onto the sidewalk forty feet below. *Focus, motherfucker.*

"Listen, Andre," he said after letting out a slow breath, "I think I want to try to get out of here."

"Outta the hospital?"

"Out of the hospital first, then out of Wenatchee. What happened with your momma today, I think it was only the beginning of a lot worse to come. I don't want to be here when people start killing one another in the streets."

"I don't know what you mean, Ross. What's goin' on? Why would people start killin' each other?"

Ross tried to think of a way to explain the predicament in terms that Andre could process. "Because the sickness that took over your momma, made her turn all crazy, is going to do the same thing to a whole bunch of other people in this town. You've heard about the riots, right? The ones in Los Angeles, Seattle, other places?"

"Uh huh."

"Well, that's going to happen here. Let me put it this way. I know you go to church, read the Bible and all that, so I'm sure you're familiar with the four horsemen of the apocalypse."

"Yeah, man, the horsemen. One is war, one is hunger, the other one is, uh...death. I forgot what the last one is."

"Let's just say that the four horsemen are riding across the earth right now, and they're headed straight for Wenatchee. Do you understand what I'm telling you?"

Andre was silent for a few moments, then he said, "Man, that's kinda scary."

"It's *very* scary," Ross affirmed. "That's why I'm getting out of here. The doctor said your room is right next to mine, so I wanted to give you the choice to go with me. I want you to think about it before you decide though. If you choose to go, you need to understand that it won't be easy for us. Getting out of this hospital is going to be tough. They don't want us to leave, and they'll try to stop us. We might have to fight our way out. If we do manage to get away, the cops will be looking for us. We will have to keep moving, and it's cold out there, Dre."

"I can handle the cold, but they's cops out in the hallway, how we gonna get past 'em?"

"What, you mean that security guard? I'll deal with him. But he's not the only sheriff in town, and if we get caught, we will be sent to jail, which is about the worst place we could possibly be when things get bad. There's also the possibility that we'll be shot before we even make it out of the hospital. I can't guarantee that everything will turn out okay. We have no vehicle, no weapons, nobody to count on other than ourselves. We don't even have any shoes. We could both die trying to pull this off, Dre. You need to keep that in mind. Don't trust that I know what's best for you. If you stay here, there's a chance nothing will happen. You'll have food and warmth, and in five days you'll be a free man. You won't be able to go back to your momma's place, but you can go to my house, break in through a window or something. You have my permission."

"But how will I eat? How will I pay the 'lectricity bill? I don't want to be by myself when them four horsemen come ridin' in. I want to go with you, Ross...wherever you're goin'. I got nobody else."

"That's why I'm giving you the option to come along." Ross thought about that, wondered how much truth there was to it. He wondered how much his decision to invite Andre to risk his life was influenced by his own fear of dying alone like that bum by the railroad tracks. "You just think about it, Dre. Once we start down this path, there's no turning back."

"I already made up my mind. I'm coming with you, man."

17.

Ross peeled the blanket back on his bed and grasped the underlying sheet and made a small tear in the end with his teeth. He then tore a three-inch strip down the length of the sheet. He tore a second strip and wrapped his hands with the fabric the same way he would wrap them prior to putting on a pair of boxing gloves before a fight. He was a hard hitter, and the last thing he wanted to do was break his hand when he punched out the security guard in the hallway.

As he was wrapping his hands, the idea occurred to him that he might be able to weave a rope from the bed sheets and blanket, smash a window, and rappel down to the street, bypassing hospital security altogether. There were, however, a number of problems inherent with this idea. First, he was unsure he would be able to fashion enough cordage to support the descent of his two hundred thirty-pound weight. He thought it was possible, but he doubted he would be able to weave more than twenty feet of length, and if he dangled from a knot at the end, it would still leave him with about a fifteen-foot drop into the shrubbery below. The shrubs would help cushion his impact, especially if he waited for the snow to build up on them, but there remained a chance that he could break his leg...or perhaps even his neck.

He would have to shatter the thick, double-paned glass in the window. Looking around the room, he saw nothing he could use for that task. There was a wood-framed chair in one corner, but when Ross hefted it, he found its weight insubstantial. He could perhaps use the rolling bed as a battering ram. It was probably his best shot, but he still wasn't certain it would work. If he did manage to break the glass, the sound of it would most likely be enough to compel the guard in the hallway to take his attention away from his smart phone long enough to investigate, and when he discovered Ross hanging from the makeshift rope, he could simply pull him back up into the room. Or untie the rope from its anchor point and let Ross fall to his death, if he wanted to be a dick.

Then there was Andre. Ross was torn on whether to leave Andre behind to fend for himself or take the kid along and look after him as best he could. Either scenario could end in disaster, but Ross didn't think Andre would last long on his own, not with a general learning capacity approximately equal to that of a ten-year-old child.

He sat on the edge of the bed and wrapped his hands and thought about these things for a while longer. When he committed to the plan of taking out the guard and making a run for the stairs with Andre alongside, his focus turned to figuring out where the two of them might go once they had escaped the hospital. Ross had developed numerous relationships throughout the years since he had opened his gym, but he knew he couldn't just show up on somebody's doorstep in the middle of the night and ask for a place to hide. To open your door to *anyone* was to risk infection with the Qilu virus. To harbor a couple of fugitives who were suspected by the medical community of carrying the virus was a different matter entirely. The only way that was going to happen was if Ross could think of someone who owed him enough of a favor to take that risk.

But who?

There was one name that came to mind: Joe Diaz. Diaz, the twenty-one-year-old gangbanger who had joined Ross's gym five years earlier mainly to help him develop a reputation as a "tough guy." At fifteen, he had already outweighed Ross by ten pounds, and stood two inches taller, giving Ross the hope that he might be able to make a solid heavyweight boxer out of the kid, show him there was a better existence than street gangs and all the pitfalls that go along with that way of life.

Diaz had showed tremendous potential in the boxing ring, and over the next three years, he and Ross had developed a bond that was almost familial. Shortly after Diaz's eighteenth birthday, Ross had approached him and said, "I think you're ready for your first amateur fight." Diaz had seemed excited about the idea, and after another month of hard training, Ross had driven him to Olympia for the annual Golden Gloves competition, convinced he would win in spectacular fashion.

However, Diaz choked. As soon as the first bell sounded, he went into defensive mode, hiding behind his gloves and backpedalling around the ring, stricken by fear to the point of being unable to throw a single punch. His opponent picked up on the fear and hammered him relentlessly until the referee stopped the fight just over a minute into the first round.

Diaz never fought again after that. At Ross's urging, he hung around the gym for a few more months, but the periods of his absence steadily grew until he stopped coming at all. He was later arrested for selling stolen firearms, and was facing a lengthy prison sentence, but after Ross vigorously petitioned the court for leniency, a judge deferred the sentence in exchange for supervised probation and community service. Diaz still spent six months in jail, but that was a good deal less than the years he would have spent in prison had Ross not gone to bat for him.

Diaz owed Ross big.

Ross got on the phone and once again requested a connection with Andre's room. "Get ready," he told Andre. "We're going to be getting out of here soon. Keep your hospital slippers on and stay by the door. Listen for me to knock twice. Come out as soon as you hear me knock. I don't know which room is yours exactly, so if you don't come out immediately, I'll move on to another door. Do you understand?"

"Yes, sir."

"We're going to stroll right out of this building like a couple of cucumbers. And what are cucumbers, Andre?"

"Green."

"They're *cool*, Dre. Cucumbers are also cool. We're gonna waltz out of here as cool as a couple of cucumbers. We don't want to draw any attention to ourselves. If anyone asks us to stop, we're going to keep on walking, unless they have a gun pointed at us. Do what I say, and maybe we'll get out of here, okay?"

"Yes sir."

"And Dre, if we get separated somehow, go to Joe Diaz's apartment over on Maple Street and tell him you're meeting me there."

"Joe Diaz? Man, that dude always be fuckin' with me. Why we gotta go there?"

"Because there's nowhere else to go. Don't argue with me about this, Dre."

"But he don't like me, man."

"That doesn't matter. He owes me a favor. You tell him that. You tell him that if he gives you any shit, he'll have to answer to me. Understand?"

"Yes sir."

"Alright then, be ready when I knock. I'll see you soon."

Ross placed the phone back in its cradle, took a few deep breaths, and walked to the door. He started to open it, but hesitated. An idea occurred to him. He turned and went into the bathroom, took a plastic drinking cup from the edge of the sink, and pissed in it, filling the cup about three quarters full. With the cup in hand, he went back and opened the door.

The security guard sat with his head leaned back against the wall, his face raised upward toward the ceiling. His eyes were closed. Ross thought he could creep up to the guard and knock him unconscious before the guy ever opened his eyes, but he didn't want to have to drag the fat bastard back to his room to tie him up. "Excuse me," Ross said.

The guard jerked upright and stared at Ross with a puzzled expression.

"Can you help me with something?" Ross asked, holding the cup of urine inside the doorway out of sight.

The guard stood from his chair and slowly came forward. "You're not supposed to be out here. You need to go back in your room."

"I understand, sir," Ross answered. "I only need you to take a look at something if you could, please."

"Look, I can't help you. If you need a doctor, go back into your room and push the call button." The guard continued to make his way forward. His left hand dropped to the handheld radio clipped to his belt.

"I don't need a doctor, it isn't that kind of a problem. You see, there's this strange liquid pouring in from the ceiling." Ross held the cup of urine up for the guard to see.

"I can't help you," the guard said. "Call the desk and ask them to send a maintenance man or something."

"I don't think you understand. Could you please just poke your head in and have a look at this? I don't know what to do here. I'm not sure it's safe to go back in my room." Ross stood outside the doorway and stared into the room, feigning bewilderment.

"Stand back," the guard said, increasing his stride. "I'll look from out here in the hallway, but I can't go in your room."

Ross took a few steps backward as the guard sauntered up to the doorway. The guard wrinkled his face in annoyance, then looked into the room.

"I'm really sorry about this, man," Ross said.

"Sorry about what?" asked the guard. "I don't see what you're talking about."

"I'm sorry about *this*." Ross threw the urine in the guard's face, blinding him long enough for Ross to close the distance between them and smash the guard on the chin with a left hook. He torqued his body, putting his full weight behind the punch, and the guard dropped like a sack of potatoes.

He wasted no time dragging the heavy guard into the room and closing the door behind them. He swiftly yanked the sheet strips from his hands and began to tie the guard's wrists behind his back when he noticed the handcuff pouch on the guard's belt.

Bingo!

He cuffed the guard, then stuffed one of the sheet strips into the guard's mouth and bound his ankles with the other strip. He removed the guard's belt and shoes, rolled him over onto his back, pulled him up into a semi-sitting position and gripped him beneath the armpits and tugged him backwards across the floor. Christ, he was heavy.

Halfway across the room, the guard began to struggle: lightly at first, but then flopping and jerking like a trout on a riverbank.

"Settle down," Ross demanded, "or I'm going to have to hit you again, and I don't want to do that."

The guard snapped his head backward, narrowly missing Ross's testicles, and shouted something that was muffled and incoherent due to the ball of fabric in his mouth. Ross took him in a chokehold, compressing the arteries of his neck until he went limp after about ten seconds. The guard regained consciousness only five seconds later and recommenced his struggling. Ross choked him out again, dragged him a few feet, and repeated the process once more until the guard finally settled down. Ross left him in a fetal position on the floor of the tiny bathroom as he went to get the guard's belt and a pillowcase from the bed. From the belt, Ross removed the holstered handgun along with a pouch containing two magazines for the weapon, the radio, and the handcuff pouch. He dropped all of the items into the toilet water tank, and then he placed the pillowcase over the guard's head and secured it by knotting the belt loosely around the guard's neck. He apologized to the guard before closing the bathroom door, and then he went into the main room and tried on the guard's shoes. The shoes were a couple of sizes too big, but they would keep his feet warm outside in the snow.

He started to leave, but then the idea occurred to him to go back into the bathroom and search the guard's pockets for his car keys. If the guard's vehicle had an alarm system, Ross could find the vehicle in the parking lot by pressing either the door unlock button or panic button on the key fob. He found the keys in the guard's pants pocket, apologized once again, and then went out to the corridor.

He moved quickly to the left, rapped his knuckles twice on the door adjacent to his room, waited five seconds, and, after there was no answer, hurried to the door adjacent to the opposite side of his room. He knocked twice, and Andre opened the door immediately. "Let's go," Ross said.

Just beyond where the security guard had been sitting, was a set of red-painted double doors with an illuminated exit sign hanging overhead. Ross led Andre through those doors, then further down the corridor to another pair of doors, these painted gray. Beyond them, the corridor branched off to the left, with signs indicating both the exit and elevators in that direction. When they rounded the corner, Ross spotted the nurses station ahead on the right, the brushed metal elevator doors on the left, directly across the hall from the nurses station. The door to the stairway was on the same wall as the elevators, a bit further down the corridor. "Almost there," Ross said. "Stay cool, Dre."

There were three women in various colored scrubs at the nurse's station. One worked at a computer with her back to Ross and Andre as they approached. The other two–a pretty blonde with a stethoscope draped across her neck and a heavyset brunette with dark circles around her eyes–were engaged in conversation but acknowledged the men with smiles when they passed by. As Ross opened the door to the stairway, he thought he heard one of the women say, "Wait a minute, aren't those guys supposed to be in quarantine?"

Here we go.

"Excuse me," the woman said, raising her voice, "aren't you guys under quarantine?"

Ross shook his head. "No, ma'am. I don't know anything about any quarantine." He ushered Andre onto the landing and followed right behind him.

"Wait, sir," the woman called. "Wait just a minute."

Ross pushed the door closed. "Move your ass, Dre. They're onto us."

They bolted down the stairs as fast as they could go. When they were about halfway to ground level, Ross heard a voice blare over a public address system: "CODE GRAY, CODE GRAY, LEVEL FOUR STAIRS."

"Faster, Dre!"

They reached the ground floor in seconds, flung open the door, and burst into the hallway. Ross glanced right, then left, looking for an exit sign. He saw it on the left at a hallway that branched right. "This way!"

Ross had taken only a few steps when a security guard appeared from around the corner. Ross froze in place, but when he saw the guard drop his hand to the pistol on his hip, he exploded forward and drove his fist into the man's nose as he raised the firearm to take aim. The guard tumbled backwards onto his ass, blood spurting from his face. The gun clattered across the floor. Andre scrambled after it.

"No, Dre!" Ross shouted. "Leave it!"

They sprinted down the hallway past an orderly, then a nurse, both of whom flattened themselves against the wall and made no attempt to intervene. They came to a single gray door with thick, narrow windows that ran vertically on either side of the doorframe. Ross grasped the door handle and pulled, then pushed, then pulled again. The door wouldn't open. "Fuck!" he screamed.

"Stop right there!" A voice called from behind them. Ross didn't look back. He studied the door for a moment and noticed the large, green button to the right of the frame. A sign posted above the button read, PUSH BUTTON TO OPEN DOOR. *You damned idiot!* his mind screamed as he slammed his palm against the button. A loud buzzer sounded. The clack of a magnetic lock being disengaged. Ross yanked the door open and he and Andre ran through with the bloody-nosed security guard in close pursuit.

The hallway narrowed, then opened up into an area that was packed with people, dozens of them. Most were seated in rows of plastic chairs, but several were standing, and some were sitting on the polished tile floor. All of them had their eyes on Ross and Andre. Ross realized he was in the emergency room. He had been there before, numerous times. He knew exactly where the exit door was; he headed in that direction. *Almost there. Just a little further.*

He heard the crackle of a radio. Saw movement on the right, not a security guard this time, but a police officer. The cop was grabbing at a holster on his belt.

"Stop those guys," yelled the bloody-nosed security guard from behind.

There it was, the exit door. A few more strides, and Ross and Andre would be free, at least from the confines of the hospital.

"Freeze, motherfuckers!" screamed the cop.

From the corner of his eye, Ross saw the officer raise his weapon. From the public address speakers came: "CODE GRAY, CODE GRAY, E.R."

Ross gave Andre a push, urging him to pick up his pace. The automatic sliding doors opened, and Ross felt frigid air on his face. He breathed it in, savored the relief of it. Snow fell in thick sheets over the hospital parking lot, brightening the night with its reflective whiteness. It was beautiful, and yet terrifying.

Ross opened his mouth to tell Andre to bear right, and then his breath caught in his lungs, and he felt claws tearing at his back. His legs froze up. He fell facedown onto the sidewalk, screaming as lightning pain flared throughout his body. It was as if his insides were being sucked out through his skin in a tremendous vacuum. Then, as suddenly as the pain had seized him, it stopped completely. *Dammit! They tasered me. The bastards tasered me.*

He looked up and saw that Andre had stopped and was watching in horror and bewilderment. The kid threw his hands up in a gesture of "What do I do?"

"Go," Ross said. He pushed himself up onto his knees, and then the pain hit him again.

18.

The man in the doorway turned to run back into his house, then dropped as if his bones had liquefied in his body. Behind him, a blonde, heavyset woman in a red button blouse stood from a sofa in the living room. Her mouth fell open, and Rooster shot her in the chest. She screamed, "Oh God!" and Rooster shot her again.

Then Rooster felt an explosion of pain in his head. He saw a bright flash of light, and as he was stumbling backward, realized that Norman had struck him in the nose. He swung his pistol toward Norman, but the big man was swift. He grasped Rooster's wrists and brought them down hard against his knee, knocking the gun from Rooster's hands. He then struck Rooster in the chest with an open palm, sending him to the ground. The two of them stared at each other for a moment, both of them breathing heavily, and then Norman went for the gun.

Rooster tore the .357 from his waistband and had the barrel trained on Norman before Norman had a chance to aim. He pulled the hammer back. "My gun is bigger than yours, Norm. Don't make your daughter grow up without a daddy."

"You said you were only going to tie those people up. You said you weren't going to hurt them." Norman stared absent-mindedly at the silenced .380 in his hand, then back at Rooster.

"You didn't have to do this."

"You put that gun down right now, Norman. This is a three-fifty-seven fuckin' Magnum pointed at your head. One shot kill."

"You're a lousy damn shot."

"Not from this distance."

Norman looked up into the snowy sky as if he were asking advice from God. After a few seconds, he dropped his head in defeat and tossed the gun away.

"Good move," Rooster said as he got back to his feet. "The only reason I didn't shoot you is because the blast from this cannon would draw attention from the whole damn neighborhood." He wiped his bloody nose with the back of his sleeve as he moved cautiously to where Norman had tossed the .380. "But make no mistake: If you hadn't dropped this here SIG when you did, you'd be about as dead as dead can be."

He picked up the weapon and wiped snow from it, then grabbed his bags and told Norman to go into the house. The two of them went in and Rooster locked the door behind them. After he checked the pulse of the man on the floor to assure he was dead, he ushered Norman into the living room and made him lie on the floor with his hands behind his back.

The woman sat on the floor with her back against the sofa. Her eyes were wide open, glossy, and the front of her red blouse had darkened with blood. Rooster saw she was still breathing. He moved close to her and snapped his fingers in front of her eyes. She blinked.

"Hello there," Rooster said with a grin. He went back to Norman, straddled him, duct taped his hands, then his ankles. He returned to the woman and squatted beside her. "Can you talk, lady?"

The woman made a whining-groaning sound but didn't speak.

"Anybody else in the house? Just nod or shake your head."

She did neither.

Rooster took a seat on the couch behind her and rested the back of her head against his crotch. He drew his butcher knife and pressed the blade against the soft, white flesh of her throat and sliced deeply, carving in short strokes, working his way from left to right. The woman let out a thin cry, which became a gurgle as the blade slid across her windpipe. Her whole body trembled, and blood sprayed and cascaded over her breasts and Rooster's legs, warm and viscous—the metallic scent of it permeating the air. Rooster cut until the blade met bone, and then he pushed her shuddering body sideways onto the floor and watched her bleed.

He could hear Norman praying softly...desperately. On the widescreen TV opposite the sofa, John Travolta and Uma Thurman danced merrily to Chuck Berry's *You Never Can Tell*.

He stood and crossed the living room to a short hallway in which there was a bedroom at each end and a bathroom in the center. He went into the bathroom first, where he checked the shower to be sure no one was hiding, wiped his hands and knife on a white towel, and took a piss without flushing. He then went to explore the bedrooms.

The first room seemed to be an office of some sort. There was a desktop computer, a four-drawer file cabinet, some office supplies in a small closet, and little else.

In the second room was a queen-sized bed with a wrought iron headboard, matching nightstands on either side, a vintage armoire packed with women's clothes, a long dresser with a small flat screen television monitor atop, books and framed photos and jewelry boxes full of cheap jewelry, and a walk-in closet crammed with hanging clothes and boxes containing who-knows-what. Beneath the bed, Rooster discovered an empty, black duffel bag. He slipped the shoulder strap over his head and left the room.

He went back into the living room and plopped down in a faux-leather recliner perpendicular to the sofa. Sleep began to pull at him immediately. His vision blurred, and the weight of his body seemed to diminish until he was left with an airy floating sensation. The walls of the living room pulsed and shimmered, and then Rooster was in the woods of Oklahoma, standing beneath a giant maple tree. Hanging by its neck from a lower limb of the tree was a ten-point whitetail buck, its pink tongue hanging almost comically from its mouth, and in the lifeless deer's big, black eyes, Rooster could see the reflection of a young boy.

"Take this," said a familiar voice.

Rooster looked up into the deeply lined face of an old man. The sun was at the man's back, and it cast a brilliant halo around his balding head, giving him a saintly appearance.

"Take it," the man demanded.

Rooster dropped his gaze to the man's outstretched hand. The hunting knife, its blade polished and pristine and sharp as a razor.

Rooster took it gently in both hands, studied it. He relished the way it felt in his small hand. It made him feel like a man.

"What ye wanna do is make a shallow cut right here," the old man said, tapping a spot high on the deer's belly. "Ye don't wanna go too deep, but just enough to get through the skin."

Rooster did as the old man instructed, careful and precise.

"Atta boy. Now you're gonna cut all the way down, just like you're unzipping a coat. Not too deep just yet. Ye only need to get through those first few layers of skin."

Rooster made the cut, and then the old man told him to go ahead and go deeper, but not so deep as to puncture the stomach. Again, Rooster did as he was instructed, and when the deer's guts finally pushed through its skin like a birthing infant, he felt his hands begin to tremble with a strange and unexpected excitement.

"You'll have to answer for this, you know," said a voice that sounded like Norman.

Rooster stopped cutting and looked around to see where the voice had come from. There was no one present aside from himself and the old man.

And the deer.

Rooster looked up to see the deer staring down at him with its shiny, black, judgmental eyes.

"You will have to answer to God," the deer said.

Rooster jerked upright in the recliner, his hand already gripping the handle of his Magnum. He slapped himself hard in the face, both to wake himself, and as punishment for falling asleep. He gave Norman a once-over to assure that the man hadn't worked his bonds loose, then he dropped a yellow rock into his meth pipe, melted it with his cigarette lighter, and sucked a long draw of smoke into his lungs. Instantly he felt more alert. He knew he couldn't keep going much longer, however. He needed to deal with the preacher man soon, so he could get some rest.

He sat for about ten more minutes, placing a second rock of crank into his pipe and smoking that one after the first had burned away. Then he went to the sliding glass door at the front of the house and peered through the vertical blinds, looking for any sign of a police presence. All clear so far.

Grasping the dead woman by her ankles, he dragged her aside so that he could prop Norman up against the sofa. Norman protested when Rooster tried to move him.

"I don't think I can take the smell of all this blood," he said. "The air is rank with the stench of it."

"Stop being such a pussy, Norm."

Rooster hefted him into a sitting position with his back to the couch, then returned to the recliner and lit a cigarette. He offered one to Norman, and Norman told him to go to Hell.

They sat without speaking for a couple of minutes, then Rooster asked, "Why did you stop being a cop, Norman?"

"Why did you start being a Satan-loving, vicious killer?" Norman spat the words out as if he had just been force-fed a cupful of shit.

Rooster laughed. "Is that what you think I am? A Satan-lover?"

"There is no doubt in my mind."

"I got no love for Satan. In fact, if Satan was real, I think he'd be scared to death of me." Rooster thought about that as he blew out a cloud of cigarette smoke. "Hell, maybe I'm the devil himself, and just don't know it."

"What is it, Mister?" Norman asked. "What is it that made you who you are? What could damage a man's mind so severely that he would do the things you've done?"

Rooster didn't answer. He finished his cigarette and extinguished it on the glass top table next to his chair, and went and knelt on the floor beside Norman. He put his hand gently on the man's shoulder. "I'm gonna kill you now, Norman."

Norman snapped his head up and looked pleadingly into Rooster's eyes. "No." The strength had left his voice, his rich baritone transformed to a frail whimper. In that moment, the big man seemed to Rooster like a small, scared little boy.

"It has to be done. Don't fight it. That'll only make it worse. A *lot* worse."

"No. You don't have to do this. I cooperated with you. You said...you said I could go home with my family when this was over." Tears welled in his eyes, streamed down one of his cheeks into his thick beard.

"What can I say, Norman? I'm a liar." Rooster drew the butcher knife from his coat.

"Please. Please don't do this. My family...I...no...*please*. I can still help you."

Rooster shook his head. "There's nothing you can say. It's over."

Norman began to thrash wildly and scream for help. Rooster had never heard a man scream so piteously.

"Stop it, Norman."

Norman didn't stop. He fell over onto his side and bucked like a shark on a fishing line. Then he tried to roll away from Rooster, screaming, "HELP ME," at the top of his lungs.

"Norman, listen to me. If you don't stop this, I'm going to go back to the church and rape your wife and daughter. Then I'm going to kill your wife in front of your daughter, just like I did the bitch over there on the floor..."

Norman stopped screaming and lay still.

"And then I'm going to get nasty." The last word came out of Rooster's mouth in a hiss. "Now sit up and take this like a fucking man."

Rooster grasped Norman's beard and pulled him back up against the sofa.

Norman hung his head and began to pray in a rapid flow of words: "Dear Heavenly Father, please forgive me for my–"

Rooster plunged the butcher knife into Norman's chest. Norman made a startled sucking sound, and then began to breathe in quick, shallow gasps.

"Shhhh...look at me, Norm," Rooster said gently. He pulled Norman's face toward his own and tried to look into the dying man's eyes.

Norman squeezed his eyes tightly shut and began to sob. Rooster stabbed him again.

"It's almost over, Norm." Again, he thrust the knife.

Norman let out a despairing cry, then opened his eyes wide and clenched his teeth and twisted his face into an expression of pure rage. Breathing like a woman in labor, he locked his eyes on Rooster's and held his gaze as the long blade of the butcher knife entered his body over and over again until death finally took him.

"So long, Stormin' Norman."

Rooster took a long shower, then rummaged through the clothes in the dead couple's bedroom until he found some baggy blue jeans that would stay up with a belt and a fleece sweatshirt that was three sizes too big, but comfortable if he rolled up the sleeves some. After that, he once again settled into the faux-leather recliner, and, despite the stimulating methamphetamine in his system, he soon found himself dreaming of swaying deer carcasses and fang-toothed pastors and bearded giants with voices like thunder.

19.

When Rooster awoke, he didn't immediately know where he was. At first, he thought he was still in jail, but when he saw the bodies on the floor and smelled the sickly sweet funk of decaying blood, his memories came flooding back. The house was lit up with daylight; a clock on the wall near the kitchen indicated that it was a quarter past noon. He cursed himself for sleeping so long, even though he was aware of how much he had needed it. His muscles ached worse than he thought they had ever before. His left arm was swollen and throbbing with a deep, dull pain, and he found it difficult to move the fingers of his left hand. His nose hurt worst of all. He wondered if it was broken. When he squeezed the bridge of it with his fingers and a sharp bolt of pain shot through his skull, he knew it was.

He stood and stretched, his eyes lingering on Norman's body. *You're looking a little pale today, Norm.* He went into the bathroom and took a leak, then stared at his gaunt reflection in the mirror for a minute. He was surprised to see dark bruising around both his eyes, and figured it must be a result of his broken nose. In the medicine cabinet behind the mirror was a tube of topical antibiotic ointment. He rubbed some into his bite wound, then went back into the living room and wrapped the wound in gauze that he'd taken from the doctor at the church.

The church. Norman's wife and daughter. Rooster wondered if they were still taped up in the basement or if they had somehow managed to escape. If they had escaped, they certainly would have sent the police to the preacher man's house, but when Rooster peered through the blinds over the sliding glass door, he saw nothing out of the ordinary. It wasn't to say that the cops hadn't come while he was sleeping, but he was pretty sure they would have found Norman's van parked up the street and conducted a thorough search of the neighborhood, likely going door to door, asking residents if they had seen a skinny dude in an olive drab coat or a huge guy with a beard. No, mama had probably choked to death on her own blood, and the little girl was still lying scared on the floor, wishing she had a drink of water right about now.

I should have killed both of them, Rooster thought as he stood watching the preacher's house. He knew that people would be arriving at the church for the daily service in only a few hours. Norman's wife and daughter were going to be discovered, and then this whole neighborhood was going to be crawling with cops. *Dammit!*

He rummaged through the house until he found the keys to the Honda CRV parked outside, then he put on a black leather jacket and a Seattle Mariners baseball cap he found in the bedroom closet, and stuffed his guns and spare ammunition into the pockets of the jacket. He drove up the street to see if Norman's van was still there, and when he saw that it was, he turned around and drove back to the church.

He parked as close to the front door as he could get, and without wasting any time, went up the steps and tried the keys on Norman's key ring until he found one that fit the door lock. As soon as he went inside, he heard the little girl call out, "Help us! We're down *here*. Please help us!" Her voice was shaky, weak, but full of hope.

Rooster went downstairs and put two bullets into her head, then did the same to her mother. He dragged their bodies into the maintenance closet, went back up and relocked the front door, and drove back to the house across the street from the preacher man's home.

He made himself breakfast–two eggs, toast, four strips of bacon, and a big glass of orange juice–and ate it slowly at the dining room table. For dessert, he smoked a bowl of methamphetamine. Afterward, he transferred his belongings from the garbage bag and pillowcase he had been carrying to the duffel bag he had found beneath the dead couple's bed. He gathered his bloody clothes from the bathroom floor and stuffed them into a washing machine in the kitchen area. He got the washer going, then carried a dining room chair to the sliding glass door at the front of the house, where he sat and smoked meth and watched the preacher's house through the blinds.

It wasn't long before a police car raced by with its lights flashing, followed moments later by a second one. There were sirens–lots of them. They were close by, to the east, heading north. Others to the west, those too heading north. Adrenaline coursed through Rooster's body, but he didn't see any indication that the commotion had anything to do with him. If the sirens shifted back in his direction, then he would allow himself to worry, otherwise he was content to stay right where he was and keep an eye on the house across the street.

Shortly before 4 p.m., a cell phone rang somewhere in the house. Rooster traced the sound to the dead woman's purse and dug out the phone just as it stopped ringing. The display screen indicated the call was from someone named Janette. A "New Voicemail" tone chimed, and Rooster listened to the message.

"Oh my god, Karen, I can't believe I got through. I must have tried twenty times, but the circuits were busy as usual." The woman's voice was loud, excited. "Something is happening on the East Channel Bridge–I think there may have been an *explosion*. There are cops everywhere. We're going down to 34th to see if we can get a better look. I hope you and Doug are safe. Please call me if you can."

Rooster set the phone on the dining room table and transferred his freshly washed clothes into the dryer. As he was walking back to the sliding door, he caught a strong whiff of feces and wondered which of the three corpses had shit itself. "Was it you, Norman? I bet it was. Even death can't stop you from trying to get on my nerves."

He sat in the chair by the door and unfolded his crumpled map and saw that the East Channel Bridge was only about a mile to the north. Rooster had been across the bridge numerous times but had not known the name of it. It was a steel box girder design that spanned the East Channel of Lake Washington, connecting Bellevue and Mercer Island by way of Interstate 90. The protesters in Renton had mentioned something the day before about Mercer being a home for mass gravesites and facilities where people infected with the Qilu virus were taken and euthanized like animals. Maybe it was true, or maybe not, but with the police activity and reports of an explosion, it seemed possible that the protests had evolved into blowing up bridges.

Keep it up, diehards. Anything to distract the cops from my *doings.*

At five-thirty, as night was just beginning to paint the outside world in darkness, Rooster took his clothes from the dryer and changed into them. Then he found a tee shirt in the bedroom and tied it around his face to block out the stench of blood and body waste. It didn't help much.

At a little past seven, there was the faint, mechanical sound of a voice amplified through a loudspeaker. Rooster couldn't make out the words. Red and blue flashes of police strobe lights approached from the north. A black and white Bellevue Police cruiser appeared on the street, and from the vehicle-mounted megaphone came: "A state of emergency is in effect until further notice. Stay in your homes and do not answer the door for anyone other than a properly identified police officer. This is for your own safety. Tune to radio station seven-one-zero AM for further information." The car continued down the street, repeating the message as it went.

Rooster went room-to-room until he found a radio alarm clock on a table next to the dead couple's bed. He switched it on and tuned to 710 AM and listened to the recorded announcement.

"This is a FEMA emergency announcement. A manhunt is underway for suspects involved in possible terrorist attacks on police and National Guard units stationed at checkpoints near the I-90 Lacy V. Murrow Memorial Bridge and the East Channel Bridge. The identity of these suspects remains unknown at this time. Be advised that these suspects are armed and dangerous. There also exists the possibility of a Qilu virus quarantine breach in areas near the Lacy V. Murrow Memorial Bridge and the East Channel Bridge. Residents in and around these areas should shelter in place. Lock your doors and do not answer to anyone unless it is a properly identified law enforcement officer. Anyone found outside in these areas is subject to immediate arrest and prosecution. These areas include the neighborhoods of Mt. Baker, Judkins Park, Atlantic, and Leschi in Seattle; Beaux Arts, West Bellevue, and Newport in Bellevue, and the entire area of Mercer Island. If you live in these areas, stay in your homes and await further instructions. Residents of all areas of King County are hereby ordered to stay off the streets until otherwise notified."

Rooster took the radio clock into the living room and plugged it into an electrical socket near the sliding door so that he could listen for updates while he sat. The stench in the room was overwhelming; he struggled to keep from vomiting. He toked up another rock of meth, partly to mask the fetor.

For the next few hours, Rooster didn't get up from the chair. He smoked cigarettes and methamphetamine and listened to the occasional helicopter coming and going overhead and imagined how things would play out once he finally met up with the preacher man. At around midnight, he got up and turned off all the lights in the house, as well as the exterior light, slung his duffel bag over his shoulder, and walked out through the front door.

The night air was ambrosial in contrast to the stink inside the house. Rooster breathed it deeply into his lungs and relished the freshness of it for a full minute before he walked to the edge of the yard, squatted, and studied his surroundings. When he was certain there were no cops lurking nearby, he crossed the street and made his way down the preacher man's descending driveway. He peered in through the narrow windows of the sublevel garage door, but it was too dark to see inside. He went around to the side of the house and found another window that opened into the garage at just above ground level. It was a two-pane sliding window with a PVC frame, small, but Rooster thought he might be able to squeeze through. He checked to see if it was locked. It was.

He knelt next to the window and took what was left of the duct tape from his bag. He placed strips of tape in the shape of an X, from corner to corner on one pane of glass. Then he placed two more strips that intersected in a cross on the center of the pane, from edge to edge, and then taped around the border of the glass. When he broke the glass with the barrel of his .357, it was held in place by the tape instead of falling inward and shattering noisily on the garage floor. He removed the glass, shard by shard, pushed himself through the window feet first, and then pulled his duffel bag in after him.

Inside the garage was as dark as the Devil's heart. Rooster cursed himself for not bringing a flashlight, but he was able to see by the flame of his cigarette lighter for short periods at a time. There was an eighties model, red Volkswagen Rabbit parked amongst strewn piles of junk, a work table along one wall, some tools scattered here and there, and at one end of the wall opposite the window, a set of rickety steps that went up to the door of the living quarters. Rooster treaded softly up the steps and placed his ear against the door and listened.

He heard no sound from inside. He twisted the door handle and found it locked. In one hand, he gripped his silenced SIG, and in the other, he slid the blade of his butcher knife between the door and its frame and jimmied the latch. The door popped open in only a few seconds. He put the knife in his coat pocket, and with both hands on the SIG, entered the house.

The door opened into a narrow kitchen, which was lit by a weak night light above the stovetop. Just past the kitchen was a small dining area with a sliding glass door that opened to the backyard. On the right was a living room with an old couch, a chair, a coffee table, television, too dark to see much else. To the left of the living room was a hallway, dimly lit by a small, shrouded bulb on an electrical outlet near the floor. With the SIG held at arm's length, Rooster stepped silently into the hallway.

He came to an open door on the left, peered inside. Bathroom. Dark, empty. Directly across from it was another door. Clearly some kind of closet. He kept moving toward the room at the far end of the hall, the bedroom. When he reached it and placed his hand on the doorknob, he had to pause and try to gain some control over his excitement. His heart raced, and his hands trembled. He sucked air in rapid, shallow breaths. *Slow down, Rooster. Nice and easy.*

He pushed open the door and flicked a light switch on the wall. What he saw on the bed in front of him caused his blood to run cold in his veins. It was a woman. Heavy. Dark hair streaked with gray. Her arms were spread wide and tied to the black metal head frame with what appeared to be paracord. Her legs were bound to the footboard posts in the same manner. There was a gag in her mouth. She opened her eyes, the sclerae of which were Venetian red, and began to thrash like a trapped animal and scream through her gag. The headboard thumped against the wall like a bass drum.

If Rooster hadn't told himself to breathe, he might have passed out from lack of oxygen. He wondered if he was dreaming again. Deciding that it didn't really matter whether he was dreaming or not, he aimed the SIG at the woman's head with the intention of emptying the entire magazine into her face, and that was when the voice behind him said, "Drop that gun *now*, or I will blow ya in half."

The voice made his knees feel like gelatin, made his stomach churn, his head reel. Just as it always had.

It was the voice of the preacher man.

20.

Rooster had no awareness of the butt of the shotgun colliding with the back of his skull. One minute he was standing with his gun trained on the woman in the bed, the next, he was face-down on the floor with his hands tied behind his back and his tongue bleeding from where he had involuntarily bitten it. His head felt as if it were being squeezed between a giant's fingers. The preacher man was speaking, but Rooster couldn't make out the words over the ringing in his ears.

"Broke in...drugs...God...Norman..."

"*Wha–?*"

"I said, where's Norman?" The preacher man tightened the paracord around Rooster's ankles. "I saw the both of ya together when ya were poundin' on my door last night. You two know each other?"

Rooster closed his eyes and willed the pain in his head to subside, but it only seemed to worsen.

"Ya gonna answer me, boy?"

"No. Yes. Yeah, Norman went home."

"Just what the hell was he doing with *you*?"

Rooster took a deep breath through his nose, exhaled it through pursed lips. He tasted hot bile in his throat. "He showed me where you live. Then he left."

"I saw ya leave together."

"Yeah...that's right, we did leave together. He let me stay at the church. I walked back here tonight."

The preacher man bent Rooster's legs at the knees and attached his ankles to his wrists with another length of paracord.

Then he rummaged through Rooster's pockets and removed everything and placed it on a dresser. He paid no attention to the woman on the bed, who was still bucking and screaming and snarling through the material tied over her mouth. "So what are ya doin' breaking into my house with all these guns, boy?"

Rooster dug deep inside his mind for a clever lie, but he could think of nothing to say.

"Alrighty, then," said the preacher man. "If that's how ya want to play it." He tore a strip from Rooster's roll of duct tape and stuck it over Rooster's mouth, then grabbed Rooster by the legs and dragged him into the hallway and closed the bedroom door. He knelt and leaned in close to Rooster's face. He looked old, haggard. His face was deeply lined, with a red, bulbous nose that one might associate with alcoholism. His light red facial hair was peppered with gray and grew in all directions. The hair on his head was almost completely gray and started way back on his scalp. In his green eyes were secrets, deep and dark.

"Here's the situation," he said. "I don't know what your relationship is to Norman, and I sure as hell don't know what you're doin' in my house, but now that you're here and have seen what's in my bedroom, there's no way I can let ya leave. Normally I would just call the cops and have them haul your ass off to jail, but this here predicament is anything but normal, wouldn't you agree? Now, since I can't call the cops, that doesn't leave me with too many options. In fact, I think my only option is to kill ya and find a good hidin' place for your body."

Rooster snorted through his nose. Panic flooded his mind, and he felt the urge to buck and scream like the woman on the bed. But there came the image of Norman begging for his life, and Rooster thought he would rather suffer an eternity in Hell than beg anyone for anything, especially the preacher man. He forced himself to stay calm and focus on finding a way out of his situation.

"Now, I don't want to kill ya, boy, but I just don't know what else to do here." There seemed to be genuine anguish in the preacher's voice, in his eyes. Rooster was startled by it. "If I take your weapons and send ya on your way, then I got to worry about ya gettin' a hold of another gun and comin' right back here, or doin' the same thing to someone else. Or maybe ya wind up gettin' picked up by the police and tell them what ya saw here. I can't risk it, son. You're a drug addict. I can tell that from all the dope you were carryin' on ya. I've dealt with my share of drug addicts. Ya all are unpredictable. Desperate. Ya don't care to hurt other people for your own selfish gains, even if it's only a dimebag of marijuana. I'm pretty sure what this is all about. Ya prob'ly went to my church lookin' for a handout. Norman, the kind soul that he is, woulda taken ya under his wing and tried to help ya best he could. I'm sure he brung ya here last night to see if I might give ya a warm place to stay, maybe a home cooked meal. And when ya knocked and I didn't answer, you reckoned I wasn't home, so ya came back later to burgle my house. Ya can't take advantage of the kindness of the Lord, son, and expect there won't be consequences."

Rooster shook his head rapidly. The motion made him dizzy, nauseous. He feared he might vomit, and if he did it with the tape over his mouth, he would choke to death right where he lay. The preacher man wouldn't have to put a finger on him.

The preacher again grabbed Rooster by his legs and dragged him into the kitchen, stopping every few seconds to catch his breath. "There is a bright side to this," he said, reaching into a kitchen drawer. "At least ya won't have to experience the heartbreak of gettin' old."

Thinking the preacher man was getting a knife from the drawer, Rooster lost control of his panic. He bucked and yelled and struggled against his bonds while the preacher observed him with sadness etched into the lines of his face. He ran out of energy quickly, not being able to draw enough oxygen through his nose, finally just lying on the linoleum and waiting for the preacher to cut his throat.

From the drawer, the preacher man took a large roll of shrink wrap and tucked it under his arm. "I know this is hard on ya, son, but I'll make it as painless as I can." He opened the door to the basement garage and dragged Rooster down the steps.

Stop! Stop! Rooster screamed, even though his words were incoherent through the duct tape. *You motherfucker! You can't do this to me. THIS IS NOT THE WAY IT WAS SUPPOSED TO HAPPEN.*

The preacher man took some time to catch his wind, and then, by the light of the open kitchen door, he pulled Rooster up on his knees and held him in that position and wrapped his upper body in shrink-wrap. When Rooster struggled, the preacher man took a rubber mallet from a tool chest and hit him hard in the head with it. "I'm sorry I had to do that, son, I truly am. Please don't make this harder on yourself."

After Rooster was fully encased in shrink-wrap, except for his head, the preacher man used a box cutter to remove a section of corrugated cardboard from a large box on the floor, and taped it over the window that Rooster had broken earlier. Then he taped additional cardboard panels over the two narrow windows in the garage door, so that no one would be able to see inside. "Sorry that took so long," he said. "My eyes ain't what they used to be."

He wrestled Rooster back to his knees and pulled up a folding metal chair and sat beside him. "Now listen to me," he said gently. "I'm gonna give ya a chance to make your peace with God. No matter the bad things you've done in your life, you should not be denied the opportunity to ask the Lord for forgiveness. I'll take that tape off your mouth, but if ya scream, I will be forced to go ahead and get on with what has to be done here. Okay?"

Rooster nodded. *This is your last chance. You have to say something that will stop him from killing you. Think, dammit! Convince him to let you live.* "Can I please have a cigarette?" he said after the preacher man removed the duct tape.

"No, son, I'm afraid ya can't. Now bow your head and ask the Lord to come into your heart."

"God don't want you to do this," Rooster said. "Thou shall not kill, remember?"

"God will forgive me, as he will forgive you. You only have to ask."

Rooster said nothing.

After a minute, the preacher man said a prayer on Rooster's behalf, then stood and pulled a sheet of shrink-wrap away from its cardboard tube.

"Thou shall not kill! Thou shall not kill!"

The preacher man shook his head solemnly and pressed the shrink-wrap against Rooster's face.

"Wait! Stop! Don't do this. I WAS WITH YOUR SON WHEN HE DIED."

The preacher man stopped, took a step backward. "What?"

"That's right," Rooster said. "I was with your son when he died in jail."

The preacher's lips began to quiver. "You're a liar."

"No, I was there."

"Tell me his name."

Without hesitation, Rooster said, "Justin. His name was Justin."

The preacher man's face paled. He dropped the roll of shrink-wrap to the floor and slumped into the metal chair behind him. "Tell me more."

The lie grew in Rooster's mind like a flowering weed. "I found him in the shower after those prisoners stabbed him over and over. I held him in my arms. Tried to comfort him. Before he died, he asked me to look after his daddy. He begged me to protect you from that Qilu virus and anyone who would try to hurt you. I promised him I would if it was the last thing I ever did. I *promised* him."

The preacher man's arms fell limply to his sides. His jaw moved as if he was going to speak, but he said nothing.

"I came here...to protect you," Rooster said, staring mournfully into the preacher's eyes. "I came because that is what Justin wanted, Brother Gene."

The preacher's head wobbled a bit. "How can I trust that what you're saying is true?"

"How else can you explain it? Norman trusted me. That's why he brought me here, let me stay the night in the church. He never came back for me, so I walked here myself. Justin...he was like a brother to me."

"Why didn't ya protect *him*? Why did ya let him die?"

"I tried to protect him. The guys who killed him told the jail guards I had contraband hidden in my cell. The guards detained me while they searched my cell. That's when the animals went into the shower and shanked Justin forty-something times. By the time the guards realized I had nothing hidden in my cell and let me go, it was too late for me to save your son."

"I...I just don't think I can trust ya."

"What does your heart tell you?" Rooster said. "How else would I know about Justin, and how he died? Why else would Norman, who is loyal to you, bring me here to your home? Come on, you know he wouldn't bring a random stranger here without good reason."

"Why did you break into my house?"

"I tried knocking. You didn't answer. I was afraid something was wrong."

"You pointed a gun at my wife."

The words hit Rooster like a glass of cold water. "That woman...she's your wife?"

The preacher man folded his arms across his chest and stared into the shadows and was silent for a long time. After a while, he looked up at the ceiling, then lowered his head as if in prayer. His eyes wandered dazedly. Finally, he straightened and licked his lips and said, "We been married over thirty years. She got sick about a week ago. At first, it didn't seem like much. A cold. Maybe the flu. Headache, runny nose, a bit of a fever. It got worse over the next couple days. She had a seizure. Went a little crazy after that. Seeing things that weren't there, hearing things too. Then came the cryin', the screamin'. I was scared to take her to the hospital. Scared of what they would tell me. Scared of what they would do to her. She started pullin' her hair out, big ol' hands full. I tied her up and gagged her because I couldn't take the screamin' no more. After about another day of it, she had another seizure. It was a bad one. An awful thing to watch. After it was over, she just laid there still as can be for a long time. I thought for sure she was dead. I couldn't tell that she was breathin', and when I put my head on her chest, I didn't hear a heartbeat. I kissed her on the forehead and covered her face with the blanket. I went into the livin' room and cried a little bit. I tried to call an ambulance to come get her but I never did get through. Weren't more than twenty or thirty minutes after I left her when I heard her screamin' and thumpin' again, worse than before. Turns out she weren't dead at all."

Rooster thought carefully before he spoke. The preacher man was in a highly emotional state of mind. Volatile. Unpredictable.

The wrong words could blow everything. "How long do you plan on keeping her tied up in the bed?"

The preacher man seemed to consider it for a moment, and then said, "I don't reckon I know. Part of me is hopin' she'll just go to sleep, but another part of me wants her to get better."

"Don't you think she'd be better off in a hospital?"

"A hospital? Do ya even know what's goin' on out there, boy? There ain't no room at the hospitals. What they're doin' to sick people now is takin' them over to Mercer Island and gassin' them, just like the Nazis did the Jews. There ain't nothin' else to do with them. Do ya think I'm gonna let them take my wife of thirty years away to be stuffed in some gas chamber? Hell no, I won't do that. That's about as wrong as wrong can be."

He sat quietly for a minute, lost in his own thoughts, then he looked at Rooster and said, "Listen, I ain't gonna kill ya. I believe what you're tellin' me about my son might be true, but I ain't for sure just yet. You bein' a damn drug addict don't make it easy to trust ya. I'm gonna go ahead and take this plastic off of ya, but I'm gonna leave ya hog-tied until God tells me what to do about ya. The bedroom closet should be big enough to hold ya. We can make ya a little bed in there. It might take a few days to get them drugs out of your system, then we'll see how things go."

"Wait," Rooster said. "A few *days*?"

"It won't be so bad," the preacher man said as he pressed the stubby blade of the box cutter to Rooster's shrink-wrap cocoon. "Better than dyin' ain't it?"

"But what happens if you get infected? I don't particularly want to be left to die of thirst in some closet."

The preacher flashed Rooster a smile. "Son, if I get infected, you'll have worse things to worry about than thirst. And besides...who's to say I ain't infected already?"

"But if there must be an end, let it be loud. Let it be bloody. Better to burn than to wither away in the dark." -Mike Mignola, Hellboy, Vol. 6: Strange Places

21.

The man in the adjacent room started screaming just after dawn and hadn't stopped since. It was loud, harrowing, even through the thick walls. Ross folded his pillow over his ears to block out the sound, but it didn't help much.

There had been other screams periodically throughout the past three days. A woman in the corridor, wailing as if she were being burned alive while an accompanying male voice shouted at someone to hold her still. A second woman, hours later, crying, "Make it stop. Oh, God, *please* make it stop." A male voice, higher pitched than that of the man next door, eerily rising and falling like the cries of a rutting alley cat.

Worst was the child. A little girl, or perhaps a very young boy, whose heart-rending screams of terror and torment still echoed in Ross's mind.

At about eight-thirty in the morning, Benny and Monroe came in to give Ross breakfast and change his bedpan. A third man followed them in and stood by the door and observed. As usual, the three of them were covered head to toe in standard Personal Protective Equipment.

"I would ask you guys how things are looking out there," Ross said, "but I can tell by the bags under your eyes that it's not going so well."

"Not great," Benny said as he set a breakfast tray across Ross's lap. "It gets worse every day. We're overwhelmed right now. I don't think we'll be able to take any new patients after today."

"A lot of people coming in, huh? Where are you going to send people you have to turn away?"

"FEMA is putting up surge tents in the surrounding parking lots. I heard talk of a couple of motels being converted as well. It's a bad time of year for this to be happening. There's eight inches of snow on the ground, and it's colder than a witch's titty."

Ross took a sip of milk from a glass on his tray, grimaced. "This milk tastes like shit. You sure it isn't spoiled?"

"It's powdered," said Monroe. "Supplies are running low. Be thankful you even have *that*. There are a lot of people who would give their left nut for a glass of powdered milk right now."

"Well, I certainly don't want to seem ungrateful," Ross said, "but I can't help but wonder how eager those people would be to trade their balls for milk if it meant being shackled to a hospital bed."

"You shouldn't have run," Benny said. "Your stay here could have been much more comfortable if you hadn't acted all crazy. You don't have the right to put people's lives at risk, then come back and complain about your milk."

Ross stuffed a peach slice in his mouth to cover the taste of the milk. "Don't judge me. The last thing I wanted to do was hurt anyone, but I saw an old woman get up off the ground and try to attack police officers after being shot twenty-something times. This hospital isn't exactly the most ideal place to be hanging out while this kind of stuff is going on."

"You're better off in here than you are out there," Monroe said as he attached the cuff of a Sphygmomanometer around Ross's bicep.

"Do you think?" Ross said. "How many confirmed infections have been brought in over the past three days? Out there, I have doors with locks on them. I have a gun to defend myself. I have space to run away if I need to. What I *don't* have is a zombie screaming bloody murder in the next room. *Jesus Christ,* can somebody shut that guy up?"

"Someone will take care of it soon," said Benny. "In the meantime, I need to get a blood sample from you."

Ross ran his hand through his hair and exhaled a long sigh. "Look, guys, I don't mean to be a dick. I know this whole thing is stressful for everyone. It's just that I'm having some difficulty dealing with losing my wife, *knowing* she went out screaming like the people who keep pouring into this hospital. If that wasn't enough, a sweet little old lady tried to kill me, and now I'm handcuffed to this hospital bed and can't even get up to take a shit. What am I supposed to do when the guy next door decides to come in here and eat my face?"

"If it makes you feel better," the man by the door said, "you'll most likely be transferred to the county jail once your quarantine is over."

Ross imagined the man smiling beneath his facemask. "Yeah. That makes me feel *much* better. Thanks."

Dick.

Benny drew some blood from Ross's arm, dropped the needle into a sharps container, and inserted the Vacutainer into a tube rack on the nurse's cart. "Okay, we're done here. Someone will pick up your breakfast tray in a little while."

As the men were leaving, Ross asked, "Do you know if Andre Wallace has been found yet?"

"No idea, Mr. Ross. Enjoy your breakfast."

Benny returned early in the afternoon with a soldier in full camouflage. The soldier wore a heavy tactical vest over his fatigues, latex gloves on his hands, and a gas mask. On closer inspection, Ross saw a Chelan County Sheriff badge clipped to the leg strap of the man's gun holster.

"How you doing, Coach?"

"Mickey?"

Mickey nodded and tipped his camouflaged bush hat. "Looks like you're being transferred." He leaned over Ross and removed the shackles from Ross's right ankle, then unhooked the shackles from the bed frame and stuffed them into a pouch in his vest. Then he loosed Ross's left wrist from the handcuffs that were also attached to the bed frame.

"Go ahead and get dressed," said Benny as he handed Ross a pair of vacuum-sealed bags containing the clothes and shoes Ross had been wearing when he was brought into the hospital.

Ross rubbed his wrist where the handcuff had been and swung his feet over the edge of the bed. "Where am I being transferred to?"

"You're being transferred to voluntary quarantine," Benny said. "You're going home."

"Wait, what? I don't understand?"

"The Health Department has determined that you're eligible to spend the remainder of your quarantine at home. There are certain rules you must abide by, of course. Someone will come in and explain all that to you shortly."

"I can't believe it," Ross said. "I thought I was going to jail."

"The criminal case against you is still ongoing," Mickey said, his voice thin and mechanical through the gas mask. "You'll be issued a summons to appear in court on the date specified. I believe the date on the paper was sometime in August."

"August? That's six months from now."

"Yessir."

After Ross was dressed, Benny provided him with a pair of latex gloves, a surgical mask, and a pair of plastic booties to cover his tennis shoes. "You're to put these on and leave them on until you've been released at your place of quarantine by Officer Rivera here." He handed Ross a Ziploc bag that contained his wallet and cell phone.

"What about my keys?" Ross asked. "Where are the keys to my van, my house?"

"They're most likely with your vehicle at the impound lot," Mickey answered.

"How am I supposed to get in my house?"

Mickey shrugged. "I'm sure it won't be too hard for you, Coach."

A Health Department official came in a short time later and explained to Ross that his blood work had come back negative for Qilu virus, and that he was being released to voluntary home quarantine on the condition that he stay inside his house and have no contact with anyone for at least the next thirty hours. He signed some release papers, and then Mickey handcuffed his hands behind his back and escorted him to a patrol car parked outside. Mickey removed the cuffs once they were clear of the hospital exit, and after they were in the car, he took off his gas mask and laid it in the seat beside him. "I hope you don't mind riding in the back, Coach."

"I don't care if I have to ride in the trunk," Ross answered, "as long as you get me the hell out of here."

As they were leaving the hospital grounds, Ross saw a crowd of people in all manners of distress packed around the emergency room doors, pounding on the glass, pleading to be let into the hospital.

"Look at that," Mickey said. "All those people begging to be let in, and you're trying to fight your way out. I believe that's what they call *irony*."

"Those people don't know any better," Ross said. "They're scared and desperate. They need someone to tell them what to do. People live their whole lives being *instructed*. They're told what to eat, what not to eat, how fast to drive, what phone number to call in an emergency–they wouldn't even know how much to feed their dogs if there weren't instructions on the damn dog food can. No matter where you look, signs. Everywhere, just like the song says. Push, pull, stop, turn, keep off the grass, don't slip on the wet floor and bust your ass. What happens if you take away a stop sign from a four-way intersection?"

"People kill themselves."

"Or others. Just because they don't have the basic sense to slow down and watch for oncoming traffic of their own volition. It's crazy. You take away its instructions, and modern society will collapse quicker than you can say *depopulation*. Those folks trying to get into the hospital, they're lost. They don't know what else to do. I figure most of them will be dead in a week."

"You're just a ray of sunshine, aren't you, Coach?"

Ross studied the snow-topped buildings along the street. He realized Mickey was driving west when he should have been driving south. "You taking the long way to my house?"

"FEMA is distributing emergency supplies through the drive-thru window of the Jack in the Box down on Chelan. It's a mess over there. We're going to bypass that whole area."

"How are things out here, Mickey? Honestly."

Mickey was slow to answer. "I won't bullshit you, Coach. It's like a warzone out here. We've had some shootouts over the last couple days. At the bridges. Other places too. People trying to get out of town. There was an officer killed and another wounded yesterday when some people tried to cross the Wenatchee River. A couple of guys made it across, but the State Patrol shot them down in an apple orchard up by River Edge Road."

"I heard something about that on the radio," Ross said. "Couple of Mexican guys."

"Yeah, man. I can't blame people for wanting to leave. That Wallace lady. We keep finding others just like her. Worse even. And as you might expect, we've had to shoot a couple of them."

"What do you do with the ones you don't have to shoot?"

"Well," Mickey said, "some of them are so sick that you can just strap them down on a stretcher and take them to the hospital without too much of a problem. Others, not so easy. It's sort of like dealing with wild animals. A handful of animal control officers can capture a full grown grizzly bear alive with the right tools and a little bit of ingenuity, but if it's just you, and that bear is coming at you with a big, hungry grin on its face, you're going to open fire and hope you kill it before it catches you.

"Now, if it's just me and some regular guy, I'll subdue him using a Taser or a baton or a good old-fashioned punch in the face. But these people are infected, man. You can't get near them without risking being infected yourself. It makes things tricky, but it can be done. That is, with the right tools and a little bit of ingenu–"

There was a *THUD*, and an instant later, a man in a black and white flannel shirt and blue jeans struck the windshield of the patrol car and tumbled into the street like a sack of meat. Mickey swerved to the right, ran up onto a sidewalk, stopped and switched on the strobe lights and got out of the car, talking into his radio microphone as he did. He glanced at Ross through the window and mouthed the words *You okay?* Ross gave him a thumbs up and twisted his head around to look at the guy in the street.

The man's face was ragged on the left side, his lips torn, his nose smashed flat. Blood pooled on the asphalt beneath his head. His left arm twitched spasmodically as he reached out toward Mickey, then placed his hand against the side of his bloody head and ripped out a clump of his own hair. He made a throaty cackling noise, as if he had just heard the funniest joke ever told, and then he began to push himself up off the street.

Then Mickey was slammed into the patrol car with such force that the vehicle rocked on its suspension. Ross looked up to see Mickey grappling with a stocky man with black, matted hair wearing a red button shirt flopping open over a white tee stained with what appeared to be blood. The man grasped at Mickey's face and snarled like a mad dog while Mickey thrust the palm of his hand beneath the man's chin and tried to push him away. Mickey swept the man's legs out from under him, but the man was back on his feet in an instant. He grabbed onto Mickey's tactical vest and snapped his teeth as Mickey grabbed the man by his throat and held him at bay long enough to draw his pistol from its hip holster. Mickey shoved the barrel of the gun through the man's teeth and blew his brains out the back of his head. Before the man's lifeless body even hit the ground, Mickey turned and opened fire on the first man, who was dragging himself across the pavement in Mickey's direction. Ross counted seven rounds. The man lay still.

"You okay, Mickey?" Ross yelled through the window.

Mickey didn't answer. He pressed his fingers against his left eye for a moment, then held them up in front of his face and examined them. He said something Ross couldn't understand. Louder, but Ross still was unable to make out the words. Finally, Mickey threw open the car door and shouted, his voice shaky with panic, "Is that my blood?"

Ross said nothing. There were multiple gashes down the left side of Mickey's face. Fingernail marks. Shallow, but shiny wet with blood.

"Answer me!"

"Yes," Ross said. "You're bleeding."

"Oh God!" Mickey threw his hands up and spun to his right, then to his left, as if he couldn't decide which direction he wanted to go. "*Oh God!* The bastard clawed my face. He clawed my...." His words trailed off into a sort of half laugh and half whimper.

"Take it easy, Mickey." Ross slid out of the back seat and reached to place his hand on Mickey's shoulder. He jumped when Mickey stepped back and pointed his gun at Ross's face.

"Get back in the fucking car!"

"Mickey?"

"*Back!*"

Ross did as Mickey ordered.

"Just like that," Mickey said. His breath came in short, quick gasps. "Just like that, and it's over. I can't...I can't fucking believe it."

He squatted and pressed his hands against his forehead. He still held his pistol in his right hand. "Just like that."

"Mickey, you don't know for sure, man. Go to the hospital." Ross didn't know what else to say.

Mickey shot Ross a puzzled glance, then stood and stared up at the dark gray sky. After a minute, he nodded and wiped his brow and said, "I think I'm going to go home now." He holstered his weapon, blew out a long breath, and walked off down the street.

"God, Mickey," Ross whispered, "I'm so sorry."

He sat and watched Mickey go, and tried to get his head around what had just happened. When he heard sirens in the distance, he got out of the car and started to leave the scene himself, and then his eye fell on the rifle attached by Velcro straps to a rack on the front floorboard. It was an M4 assault rifle with a vertical forward grip and an attached flashlight. Ross tore it free of the Velcro straps and shoved it up under his jacket, then grabbed Mickey's gas mask from the seat and ran down the street and ducked into a wall of snow-covered shrubbery.

He walked at a quick pace, trying not to draw attention to himself, one block through a residential neighborhood, then across a street into a large park and toward some public restrooms at the end of a winding walkway. The restroom doors were locked, but

Ross used his driver's license to slide the latch open so that he could get into the men's room.

He waited there for a long time, shivering on the restroom floor, his back against a cinderblock wall. He kept the surgical mask and latex gloves on for fear of the germs that might be lurking in the restroom. He attempted several times to use his cell phone to call someone to come pick him up, but the circuits were busy. He dialed 911 just to see if the lines were open. They were not, which meant if some random citizen spotted him walking down the street with an assault rifle, they wouldn't be able to immediately report him to the police. At least that was the hope.

He examined the assault rifle. He had never used an M4 before, but he knew enough about firearms to figure it out. He checked the magazine. Thirty rounds of .223. There was no spare, so once those thirty rounds were expended, that was it. He flicked the select fire switch to full auto, then to semi auto, then back to safe. He pressed the ON button on the EOTech sight and studied the red holographic reticle, dimmed the brightness of it to conserve battery power, and then shut it off. He chambered a round, double-checked the safety, and laid the rifle across his lap.

When the light through the tiny window high in the wall faded to black, Ross stood and pushed the rifle up beneath his fleece jacket and left the restroom. He decided to go to his gym since it was only about a mile away and a half mile closer than his house. He walked the distance quickly and stealthily, ducking behind cover at the sight of a vehicle or pedestrian. He encountered both, but infrequently enough that he had very little concern of drawing suspicion to himself.

As he approached the gym, he began to have doubts about being able to get inside without a key, but then he saw the pried and twisted metal of the roll up door and realized someone else had already found a way in.

He squatted by the door and weighed his options. His main concern was the possibility that someone was still inside the building, in which case Ross stood a reasonable chance of being murdered as soon as he entered. If someone had come and gone, it was unlikely they had left him with any of the food supplies that were there four days earlier, so it seemed like a lose-lose situation for Ross either way.

Screw it. Enjoy your spoils.

He stood and began to walk away when the thought occurred to him that perhaps Andre Wallace was the person who had broken in. Andre would have gone to Diaz's apartment as Ross had instructed him, but there was no guarantee that Diaz even lived there any more. For all Ross knew, the guy was back in prison. If he was not, he was certainly under no obligation to take Andre in. The two of them didn't even get along very well. If Andre were unable to hole up with Diaz, then he would have gone to Ross's house, or more likely, to the gym, since it was closer.

That was just the excuse Ross needed to go in and check things out.

Dammit, here goes nothing.

He held the M4 in front of him and clicked on the holographic sight and pushed the door up enough to squeeze through in a stooping position. He let gravity bring the door back down as he pressed up against a wall and listened in the dark. After a couple of minutes he called out, "Andre? Are you in here, Andre? It's me. Coach Ross."

He moved to the opposite wall and crouched and waited for a response that never came. He crept slowly along the wall, studying the darkness, his finger rested on the M4's trigger guard.

He jumped at the sound of gunshots. Eight or ten blasts in rapid succession. A couple of blocks away. Probably nothing to worry about, but he moved back to the roll up door and slid the locking lever into a slot in the bent metal frame just to be safe.

He called Andre's name a few more times, and then he passed through the lobby and went behind the service counter and made his way to the staircase that led up to his office. He clicked on the flashlight that was mounted on the M4 and ascended the stairs.

The office door was open. The cases of energy drinks, water, protein bars, tuna cans, all gone. His desktop computer was gone too. He opened the door of his half-size refrigerator. Empty. He stuck the rifle barrel out through the window that overlooked the gym floor and scanned the area with the flashlight. There was no sign of intruders.

He went back downstairs and checked the restrooms and storage closets and beneath the two boxing rings. There was nobody there. Whoever had broken in had left with everything they could carry. He shone his light over the drink cooler and knew it was empty before he got close enough to see inside. He checked for a signal on the cordless phone on a table near the cooler. The line was dead. He gave the entire floor one last lookover, then returned to his office and switched on a desk lamp and sat down to plan his next move.

Pop pop pop! More gunshots, closer this time and accompanied by screams. Ross couldn't tell whether the screams were from a man or a woman.

Time to go, Coach.

Ross focused his thoughts on his uncle's cabin near Eatonville. It was secluded, surrounded by a forest full of deer and rabbits and squirrels, enough to provide an indefinite supply of food. The cabin sat on the edge of a seven-acre fishing lake. Ross remembered fishing on that lake as a youngster, the fish biting almost as soon as his bait hit the water. There was no electricity, no running water, no phone lines or cable television. The bathroom was a tiny outhouse set twenty feet behind the cabin. But there was everything a man needed to stay alive in an apocalypse.

The problem was getting there. Two hundred miles over the Cascade Mountains in the dead of winter. Next to impossible without a vehicle. Even if it weren't, he still had to sneak out of Wenatchee without catching a bullet in his brain.

Or getting eaten by zombies.

What are you?

I'm a warrior.

Then keep your eyes on the prize.

He went downstairs and took a hot shower without getting his hair wet, then dressed in as many layers of clothes as he could fit into without overly restricting his movement. He filled a half dozen empty water bottles with hot tap water, placed two in the front pockets of the fleece hoodie closest to his skin, and the other four in a sports bag, along with the blanket off the sofa, some spare clothes, a box of latex gloves, a first-aid kit, and a map. He placed a five-pound weight on the end of a dumbbell and locked it down with an iron collar. He slipped the gas mask over his face, slung the M4 across his shoulder, hefted the dumbbell in his left hand, and exited the gym through the back door.

Now to find Andre.

22.

I don't want to go back, Mom, says the boy. Why do we have to? Hush, son. I've made up my mind. The boy's mom fumbles with the door keys but she tries the handle and discovers the door is unlocked. The house looks exactly the same as they had left it a few days ago, but it smells bad, like rotting food and beer and piss. Lyle is spread eagle on the bed in the bedroom, facedown in his underwear. He smells as if he hasn't washed in days. His red hair is sticking out in every which way and the boy thinks he looks like a drunken circus clown.

I don't reckon none of you missed me, says Lyle. I did, the boy's mom answers. What about you boys? Lyle asks. Did either of y'uns miss me? The boy only looks down at the floor without responding. I missed you, Johnny says as timid as a mouse. Lyle sits up on the bed and digs a Marlboro cigarette out of a pack on the nightstand. Sticks it in his mouth and lights it. That's okay if you don't want to talk to me right now, he tells the boy, but I just want you to know I love you, even if you don't love me back. The boy knows he's only saying it to get on his mom's good side.

What the hell did you walk out on me for, Melina? I thought you said you would always be there for me.

I was afraid.

Afraid? What the hell were you afraid of?

I was afraid of you.

Lyle shakes his head like the boy's mom does when the boy gets a bad grade in school. I'm disappointed in you, Melina. You know I'd never hurt you. If you were so damn scared, why'd you come back for?

Because I love you. And because I'm pregnant.

***

Rooster awoke to muffled screams and the sound of the headboard thumping the wall. Didn't this bitch ever sleep? He was going to relish killing her. He arched his back to try to stretch his muscles as much as possible, and pain exploded throughout his body. His legs and shoulders cramped and spasmed and his hands and feet felt as if they were being jabbed by a thousand needles simultaneously. His pants, as well as the carpet beneath him, were soaked with his urine. It was ice cold against his skin. He didn't want to give the preacher man the satisfaction of hearing him scream, but enough was enough. "*I can't take this anymore,*" he wailed.

A minute later, Gene opened the closet door. "Didn't I tell ya I'd have to gag ya if you didn't keep it down in here?"

The daylight coming in through the bedroom windows was dim, yet Rooster had to squint against the brightness of it. "I'm hurting. I'm cold. I just need to stretch a little bit. And I have to take a shit. I haven't gone in days. Don't make me go in my pants. It's bad enough I have to lie here in my own piss."

"I don't like this any more than you do," Gene said, "but I just don't know what else to do with ya right now."

"Look, you can keep my hands tied, just let me stretch my legs and use the toilet. I can't hold it too much longer."

"I want to be able to trust ya, brother, but I don't feel like I'm able to do that yet. Tell ya what, hold on."

The preacher closed the door and returned a few minutes later with a chain and a pair of padlocks. He untied the rope that bound Rooster's wrists to his ankles. He straightened Rooster's legs, and Rooster screamed with the fierce cramping of his muscles.

"Breathe, brother. Just breathe."

Gene removed the paracord from Rooster's ankles and replaced it with the chain, attaching it with the padlocks in such a way as to provide a ten-inch length between Rooster's ankles. "Now you'll be able to walk. You'll have to take small steps though."

"Can I go take a shit now?"

The preacher stepped back and reached to his left and picked up the shotgun that he had leaned against the wall. "D'ya think ya can get up on your own?"

"Yeah," Rooster said, "I think so."

It took him awhile, but Rooster managed to get to his feet and step out of the closet while Gene kept the shotgun pointed at his chest. The sight of the woman thrashing on the bed sickened him. The skin of her face and hands were mottled with deep bruises. Her lips were cracked and oozing what looked to be a mixture of pus and blood. The rag in her mouth was crusty with it. Her eyes were glazed over like dusty glass and they moved erratically in their sockets.

"She don't look so good," Rooster said.

"Don't ya worry about her. Just get on to the bathroom so I don't have to clean up after ya."

Rooster waddled to the bathroom and asked the preacher to untie his hands so he could use the toilet. He was surprised when Gene loosened the rope.

"I'm gonna give ya the chance to show me I can trust ya, but if ya try anything funny, I'll have to shoot ya with this here 12 gauge."

Rooster nodded and worked the paracord loose and let it fall to the floor. "You gonna give me some privacy?"

"You've been in jail," the preacher said. "You should be used to going in the company of others."

"Fuck it. Enjoy the show then." Rooster dropped his pants and did his business under Gene's watchful eye.

After he finished, Gene escorted him to the dining room and told him to sit on the linoleum floor.

Rooster did as he was told. "Why is it so cold in here? I'm freezing."

"The power went off sometime in the night. I don't rightly have any idea when it might come back on, or if it even will. It ain't really all that cold. It's probably just your wet breeches makin' it seem worse than it is. I'll get a blanket for ya here shortly."

Gene went into the kitchen and laid the shotgun on the counter and made three sandwiches. He gave two to Rooster on a paper plate and took a seat at the dining room table. "Ya might as well help me eat up this lunch meat before it goes bad. It's a damn shame to throw food out when it's gettin' so hard to come by."

Rooster hadn't been out of the closet since the preacher had imprisoned him there more than two days earlier. The preacher had brought him food periodically: a bowl of fruit cocktail or green beans or instant mashed potatoes, an old, dry apple, some cold cereal without milk–nothing significant enough to quell his hunger even temporarily. The sandwiches were luxurious, despite the light scent of mold on the wheat bread.

"So you gonna tell me your name, brother?" Gene asked.

"People call me Rooster."

"And why's that?"

"Because I have a big cock," Rooster said matter-of-factly.

Gene chuckled. "Is that right?"

"That's *exactly* right."

"It didn't look so big to me back there in the toilet."

"Yeah, well you can fuck off."

"Settle down, brother." Gene laughed. "I'm only giving ya shit."

"Well I'm sick of your shit."

They ate in silence for a couple of minutes, and then Rooster said, "The truth is, I used to go to chicken fights once in a while back in Oklahoma. A bunch of Mexicans and rednecks were all into it. I'd go throw some money down on a bird or two. Sometimes I'd win, sometimes not, but I'd drink and get high for free either way. Sometimes I'd make a few bucks slingin' some dope. Anyway, one night this big red rooster–his owners called him '7-Time,' because he was a seven-time winner–got loose and started flappin' and floggin' and ended up stickin' me in the hand with the gaff on his leg. I still have the scar. Pissed me off, so I yanked that bird up and tore his head right off with my teeth. The Mexicans didn't much like that I killed their prize chicken. They beat me half to death over it. Some of the people who were there and saw what happened that night started calling me *Devorador de gallos*, which means 'rooster eater' in Spanish, I guess. But it also means 'cock eater,' so I made them stop calling me that. After they got tired of gettin' punched in the face, they just shortened it to *gallo*, or plain old 'Rooster.' The name stuck."

The preacher nodded and took a big bite of his sandwich. "So you're an Oklahoma boy," he said with his mouth full. "I figured you weren't from around here, with that hillbilly accent."

"Being from Oklahoma don't make me no hillbilly."

"No, you're right. I didn't mean no offense. I once lived in Oklahoma myself for a time. Lived in several different states over the years, matter of fact."

"What made you become a preacher?"

"Weren't nothing *made* me become a man of God, brother. It just happened. The good Lord came into my heart in the same way as you would fall in love with a woman. I was at a low point in my life back then. Felt like I was in a hole I had no way of diggin' myself out of. Then Jesus came and lifted me out of that hole and set me on top of the world. I figured the least I could do to repay him was share his gospel to all who would listen. Now, I don't think God would approve of everything I do, but I try to–" He stopped and shifted his eyes and cocked his head.

"What is it?" Rooster said.

"Shhh. Listen. D'ya hear it?"

Rooster did hear it. Screams. From somewhere outside.

The preacher got up and grabbed his shotgun and went to look out the living room window. Rooster tried to stand, but the preacher turned and told him to stay put.

"What's going on out there?"

"I can't tell," the preacher answered. "The fence is in the way."

"Maybe you should go out and have a look."

"And maybe you'd like me to put ya back in the closet."

More screams. The sound of glass breaking.

"Sounds close," Rooster said.

"It's right up the block a little ways. I don't think it's somethin' we necessarily need to worry about."

"Easy for you to say with that shotgun in your hands."

"Oh don't ya worry," said the preacher. "Ain't nobody comin' in here."

"I got in easily enough," Rooster said with a smirk.

"Yeah, and look how *you* ended up."

I wouldn't let that go to your head. You caught me slippin' is all. The lady on the bed threw me off guard."

The screams intensified, and then there came a long, agonizing cry, a male voice that caused adrenaline to surge through Rooster's blood. Rooster recognized that cry. It was the sound of someone dying a horrible death.

"The Devil is risen from the abyss," said the preacher. "God help us all."

Gene watched through the curtains for a while longer, and then he returned to the dining room table to finish his sandwich.

"How about that blanket?" Rooster said.

"Whassat?"

"I'm cold. You said you were gonna get me a blanket."

"Oh. Yes."

The preacher got up and slung his shotgun over his shoulder and took a folded quilt from the hall closet and tossed it onto Rooster's legs. Rooster covered himself with it as Gene poured each of them a snifter of brandy.

"They were sayin' on the radio that a bunch of people infected with that virus escaped from a big hospital on Mercer Island and came across the bridge into Bellevue. Dozens of 'em. Overran the police checkpoint. That ain't but a mile or so from here." The preacher set one of the snifters on the floor without getting too close to Rooster, then sat back down at the table. "I've been seein' 'em out there ever so often. Walking around all twitchy and confused-like. Some of 'em ain't got no shoes on. Hell, some of 'em ain't got no clothes."

Rooster remembered the man he and Norman had encountered on the street a few nights earlier. The one who had attacked the van like a wild animal. He had been barefoot in the snow.

The preacher sipped his brandy and stared into space. "This virus. It makes people mean. Ol' Janice in there, if I was to turn her loose, I believe she'd try to kill both of us. Even if I was to put her outside and lock the door, I think she'd try her best to get back in here and kill us. I don't know why that is. I don't believe it's somethin' she can control at all, it's just some bizarre urge. I've tried to talk to her about it, but she don't hear me no more. Her mind is gone."

"They say on the news there ain't no cure. How long you think she's gonna be like this before she passes on?"

The preacher shook his head. "It's already been too long. Ever mornin' I wake up expectin' to find her dead, but she keeps clingin' to life. Don't need to be no doctor to know she's sufferin' like a person should never have to suffer, and I just don't know what to do about it, except to try to take care of her best I can."

"Have you thought about taking it upon yourself to end her misery? I mean, out of love and all."

"Ever time I look at her I think about it. I just...I just ain't sure if it's the right thing to do. I need the Lord to guide me."

"Well," Rooster said as he reached for his own glass of brandy, sniffed it, took a swallow, "while you're waitin' for the Lord to tell you what to do, your wife is layin' in there screamin' in pain and probably beggin' you in her mind to be a man about this."

The preacher stared down at the table and said nothing.

Rooster studied the man's face and weighed his next words carefully. "Do you want me to do it?"

The preacher looked up, startled. His eyes hardened.

"I can make it quick," Rooster said. "Painless. She wouldn't even–"

The preacher stood abruptly and yanked up the shotgun and aimed it at Rooster. "Get on your damned belly!"

"What? What did I do?"

"You *heard* me."

"Okay, okay, just take it easy." Rooster placed the brandy snifter aside and rolled over onto his stomach.

"Cross your hands behind your back."

Rooster did, and the preacher man walked around the table and stood over him. There was a bright flash of light behind Rooster's eyes. Then blackness.

When he came to, he was lying on the bedroom floor near the open closet door. The preacher was on the bed, straddling his wife at the waist, speaking to her as she bucked and screamed beneath him. Rooster tried to get up but realized his wrists were once again bound behind his back.

"Our Father, who art in Heaven, hallowed be thy name..." The preacher placed his hand on his wife's head, stroked her hair.

"Thy kingdom come, Thy will be done on Earth as it is in Heaven..." He kissed her forehead and lifted a thick, white pillow in one hand.

"Give us this day our daily bread..." He pressed the pillow against her face. His muscles bulged and his voice strained as he leaned forward and shifted his weight into the pillow. "And forgive us our trespasses as we forgive those who trespass against us."

The preacher finished his prayer and gripped the pillow long after his wife stopped moving. He whispered things to her as if he were comforting a child. Finally he sat upright and placed his hands on his thighs and said, "Rest now, my sweet Janice. Go be with our son."

After a couple of minutes he took a folding knife from his pocket and severed the ropes that had bound his wife's wrists and then cut the gag away from her mouth. He held her for a long time and wept. Then he got up from the bed and removed the paracord from her ankles and covered her completely with a blanket.

When it was all over, he went to Rooster and stood over him with the knife, and then he bent down and sliced the bindings on Rooster's wrists. "God's will be done. If you're gonna kill me, then I reckon that's the way God intends for me to go. If you're tellin' me the truth, and ya really are here to help me, then thank you, and thank God and my son for sending ya. Either way, I'm through worryin' about it."

He left the room, and after he was gone, Rooster saw he had left his shotgun leaning against the wall. Rooster smiled. *Okay, preacher man, let's get this party started.*

Rooster struggled to his feet, which were still shackled by the padlocked chain. He picked up the shotgun and moved into the bedroom doorway, where he saw the preacher at the opposite end of the hallway holding a framed photograph in his hands and staring down at it with teary eyes.

The preacher glanced briefly into Rooster's eyes, then at the shotgun. He carefully returned the photo to its hook on the wall, then turned and began to walk away.

"Stop," Rooster said. "You and me, we got some things we need to talk about."

The preacher did stop, but he didn't turn around. Rooster inched forward. "Why don't you go ahead and put your hands up where I can see 'em."

Pastor Gene lifted his hands and eyed Rooster over his shoulder.

Rooster continued forward in the hallway. "Turn around. Look at me."

The preacher didn't move. "What is your intention here, brother?"

Rooster thought about it for a moment. "Oh, don't you worry, Preacher Man. I'm not gonna shoot you. What I *am* gonna do is–"

He stopped. Listened. A noise from behind him. It sounded like bedsprings. He turned his head to peer over his shoulder, and there she was, standing in the doorway, her hands dangling at her sides, her head cocked like a curious little girl. She pulled her lips back in a sort of wide, grotesque smile. Then she lunged.

Rooster spun and aimed the shotgun and pulled the trigger. Nothing happened. He pumped the slide but then the woman was upon him, grasping at the collar of his coat. He could almost taste her foul breath as she screamed maniacally in his face. He gave her a push, and with one hand, shoved the shotgun barrel beneath her chin and again pulled the trigger.

Click.

The preacher man had set him up, had intentionally left the shotgun in the bedroom unloaded, as a test of Rooster's trustworthiness.

He felt the cold, clammy skin of her hands against his face. He instinctively took a step backward and tripped over his own feet and fell hard onto the floor. She came down atop him but he gripped the shotgun horizontally in both hands and pressed it into her throat. She snapped her teeth at his hand, forcing him to let go of the shotgun. He grabbed a handful of her hair and pulled her head back, and then a bomb exploded in the house, and the woman fell over onto the floor, leaving a wad of hair with part of her scalp still attached in Rooster's hand.

Rooster's ears instantly filled with a ringing that drowned out all other sound. As he pushed himself away from the preacher's wife, he saw the round hole in her forehead and the brain matter–it reminded Rooster of blackberry pie–spilled from the back of her skull. The smell of gunpowder tickled his nostrils, and he looked up to see the preacher man standing over him with the .357 Magnum he had taken from Rooster, a wisp of gray smoke curling away from the barrel.

The preacher lowered the weapon to his side and pulled a cigarette from a pack in his breast pocket and lit it and took a long drag. "Ya better get yourself cleaned up. Looks like ya got some of her blood on ya."

23.

Ross saw the guy coming from a block away, approaching at a fast walk beneath the street lamps on the opposite side of the street. He was dressed in a blue hoodie and baggy gray sweatpants and white tennis shoes. His arms swung awkwardly as he walked. As he drew closer, he began to cross the street, increasing his pace to a slow jog. He came directly toward Ross.

Ross unzipped his jacket and clicked the safety off the M4. "You better tell me something right now to let me know you aren't crazy," he called as the guy came within fifteen yards.

The guy didn't answer. He was young. Teens, early twenties. There were dark circles around his eyes and his lips were parted over teeth that glistened with a dark substance that might have been blood.

Ross let his duffel bag slide off his shoulder and gripped the dumbbell that dangled from his left hand. The guy broke into a sprint at ten yard, slipped on a patch of ice and tumbled face-first onto the sidewalk only a few feet in front of Ross. He got back up, and Ross swung the dumbbell as hard as he could. The iron weight plate connected with the guy's head with a sickening crack, causing the guy's right eyeball to be ejected from its socket. The guy remained on his feet but staggered aimlessly back into the street, stopped and held his hands in front of his face and stared at them with his one good eye, then turned and came back toward Ross, his hoodie darkening with blood.

Ross swung the dumbbell again in a wide overhead arc and struck the guy on the top of his head. The guy wobbled almost comically before dropping to the sidewalk. He let out a cry that was sheep-like, and when he rose up on his knees, Ross struck him again. Blood droplets spattered on the eye shield of Ross's gas mask, and out of fear of being infected, he dropped the dumbbell and left the guy twitching and squirming on the snow-covered sidewalk.

Ross grabbed his duffel bag and jogged half a block, and when he looked back, he was astonished to see that the guy in the hoodie had managed to get to his feet and was lurching drunkenly in pursuit. Ross intended to just keep going down the street, but he thought about the possibility of other people being infected by the guy, and decided he couldn't let that happen. He took the M4 from beneath his jacket and walked back toward the guy until he was within about twenty yards, then he placed the holographic reticle on the guy's nose and pulled the trigger. The guy dropped to the street and spasmed violently, and Ross knew he was done.

Thirty minutes later, Ross reached the doorstep of Joe Diaz's ground floor apartment on Maple Street. He removed the gas mask and held the duffel bag in front of him to cover the rifle jutting from beneath his jacket. He stood so that he could be seen clearly through the peephole and knocked on the door.

"Who is it?" a voice called from inside.

"Coach Colin Ross. I'm here to see Joe."

The door opened a few inches and a Latino man in a white sleeveless shirt stuck his face in the gap. "Yo, what do you want with Joey?"

"I need to talk to him about a personal matter," said Ross. "I'm his boxing coach."

"What's in the bag?"

"Just some bottled water and clothes mainly."

"Who is it, Chente?" Joe Diaz said, his head appearing above the guy in the doorway. "That you, Coach?"

"How you doing, Joe?"

"Yo, I heard you were infected with that Qilu virus or something. Heard you were all quarantined up in the hospital."

"Who told you that?"

"Your little pet, Dre, told me."

"Andre? Where is he? I'm looking for him."

"He's right here."

Joe pulled the door open wide and there stood Andre right beside him.

I'll be damned.

"Man, Coach, I didn't think I was ever gonna see you again," Andre said, grinning from ear to ear.

Ross shrugged and offered a smile. "Well, here I am."

"Yo, you sick or what, Coach?" Joe asked.

"I'm fine. The hospital let me go because I'm clean."

"Come on in then."

As soon as Ross stepped inside, someone yelled, "This fool's got a gun, yo!"

There was the sound of a round being chambered in a handgun, and then a man stood from a chair in the corner of the living room and aimed a small-caliber semiautomatic at Ross's head.

"You better check yourself!" Andre told the man, puffing out his chest.

"Put that shit away," Joe told the guy with the pistol. "This is my fucking boxing coach, fool." To Ross he said, "What's with the gun, Coach?"

"What do you think?"

Joe nodded. "Yeah. Yeah, I feel you. Well, pull up a seat if you can find one. Sorry about Filipe. He's a little jumpy."

"I can't blame him."

The living room was small. The seven people who occupied it made it seem a lot smaller. A guy on a sofa playing a video game on the TV, a slender Latina girl in short shorts draped across his lap. Another young man, cross-legged on the floor, he too engaged in the video game. The man with the pistol. A white guy with long blond hair on a beanbag beneath the room's only window. And Joe and Andre.

"Everything okay, Joey?" a woman called from the doorway of a bedroom.

That made eight.

"Everything's cool," Joe answered. "I'll be in in a minute."

"Don't you own that gym over by the railroad tracks?" the guy on the beanbag asked.

"Yeah, that's me," Ross said.

"Cool, bro. I thought about joining but my lungs are kinda shot. I been smoking too long, you know?"

Ross nodded.

"I mean, I'm seventeen now. I started smoking cigarettes when I was eleven. Started smoking weed when I was thirteen. It's hard to work out when you been smoking as long as I have. You know?"

Ross ignored him and turned his attention to Andre. "I'm glad you made it here safely, Dre. I was worried about you."

"I hid in a dumpster until it got dark. Man, it sure was cold in there. Then I came straight here, just like you told me too. Joe didn't want to let me in at first, but then I told him what was goin' on, and he finally said okay."

"He said you were going to pick him up here," Joe said, "but after a couple days, I didn't think you were coming. I was getting ready to tell him to hit the road."

"Well, thank you for letting him stay until I got here," Ross said.

"It's all good. I hooked him up with some clothes. They're a little too big for him, but I couldn't have him running around here with his bare ass hanging out of that hospital gown. Yo, it true what happened to his mom?"

"Yeah. It's true. It was pretty horrific."

Joe shook his head. "The whole world has gone *loco*."

"Indeed it has, Joe," Ross agreed. "Indeed it has.

"So what's your plan, Coach? You going to stick around Wenatchee or will you try to leave?"

"I think I'm going to head west if I can figure out a way. How about you?"

"I'm afraid I'm going to starve if I stay here."

"Ain't that the truth," Andre said. "I've barely ate anything in two days. You got any food in that bag, Coach?"

"Unfortunately, I don't."

"Anyway," Joe said, "some of us are going to try to make it to Bridgeport. My mom and brother are there, and there's good fishing up behind the dam. All you can eat."

"How do you think you'll get out of Wenatchee?" Ross said. "They have the bridges blocked. They're shooting people who try to cross."

Joe smiled. He flicked his head toward the bedroom. "Come on, Coach. Let me show you something."

Ross followed him into the bedroom. Joe told Andre to wait in the living room, and then he closed the door. The girl on the bed smiled at Ross. He nodded and told her hello.

"Get up off the bed a minute, Andrea," Joe said.

The girl got up, and Joe pulled the bed, which was only a mattress stacked atop a box-spring without a frame, away from the wall and pulled up a quilt that was wrapped around something heavy. He laid the quilt on the bed and spread the edges away from what was concealed beneath.

"Holy shit," Ross said.

Wrapped within the quilt were half a dozen assault rifles: three AR-15s, a pair of AK 47s, an HK-91.

"There are more in the closet," Joe said. "An SKS, an Uzi, a MAC-10, pistols, shotguns. We are going to shoot our way out of Wenatchee if that's the only choice we have."

"Where did you get all of this stuff?"

"Come on, Coach. You wouldn't be too happy with me if I told you."

"There are too many cops for you to just blast your way out, Joe. Helicopters. Armored vehicles. It's better to try to sneak through the gaps."

"There are no gaps. To get to Bridgeport, I have to cross the river. There is no other way."

"You'll never make it. Even if you were to get out of Wenatchee, you're still looking at seventy miles of highway with mountain walls on one side and the river on the other. It will be too easy for the cops to box you in. It's suicide."

Joe rewrapped the weapons in the quilt and dropped the bundle back behind the mattresses. "Staying here is suicide. Just slower. More painful. I need to try to get to my mom, *vato*."

Ross expected the girl to say something in protest, but she only stood in a corner and examined her fingernails and pretended to ignore the conversation.

"I might be able to help you figure out a better way to get you where you need to go, Joe, but right now, I need to use your bathroom. I haven't showered in days."

"Go right ahead."

Ross showered, shaved, and scrubbed the gas mask with disinfectant. He changed into a fresh set of clothes and asked Joe for a plastic garbage bag in which he stuffed the clothes he'd been wearing when he had bashed the skull of the guy in the blue hoodie. He placed a fresh pair of latex gloves on his hands for safety, and spread his map over the kitchen counter.

He studied the map for a long time as Joe's guests passed around a bong in the living room. After a while, he called Joe into the kitchen to look at the map with him. "How about this, Joe." He traced a route on the map with the blunt end of an ink pen. "You go west over the hills for a few miles and cross a section of the Wenatchee River that isn't heavily observed. You don't have to cross at a bridge. There are places shallow enough for you simply to walk from one bank to the other. Sure, it will be cold as hell, but once you've made it across, you can steal a vehicle and be almost to Bridgeport before anyone even knows it's missing."

Joe rubbed the stubble on his chin and considered Ross's idea. "A couple things, Coach. First, even if we get across the Wenatchee River, we still have to cross the Columbia at some point before we can get into Bridgeport. There is no wading across *that* bitch."

"So you drive north up 97 until you come to a bridge that isn't locked down. Maybe in Chelan Falls or Brewster, or further up in Okanogan. In the very unlikely event that all the bridges are blocked, then you steal a boat. There will be plenty along the way."

"Okay, okay, I hear you. I guess my other issue is getting over the hills to find a place to cross the Wenatchee. You're talking about going hundreds of feet up steep slopes in a foot of snow and walking for miles, Coach." Joe's eyes scanned his guests in the living room, and he lowered his voice almost to a whisper. "I could do it, yeah, but I got my girl. She's in no kind of shape for that. And some of these other fools, man, they haven't exercised a day in their lives."

"You plan on taking all these people with you, Joe?"

"Yo, what else are they going to do? *Padrinos trece*, I got obligations, *vato*."

"What are you, a gang leader now?"

"I'm no leader, but I'm loyal to my fam."

"Yo, what you fools doing in there?" called the guy with the pistol. "You ain't doing *coca* without me, are you?"

"Nah, fool," Joe said. "We're just planning how we're going to take over the world."

"*Orale*, that's what's up. Just let me know when you're ready. I'm with you, *carnal*."

"So what are *you* going to do, Coach?" Joe said. "You going to chill with us in Bridgeport?"

"Like I said, I'm heading west. There's an airfield in Cashmere. I'm gonna steal a plane."

Joe laughed. "Yo, check this out, he says he's going to steal a *pinche avión*!"

Laughter from the living room.

"I never knew you was a pilot, Coach," Joe said with a broad smile.

Ross shook his head. "I'm not, but I'm a fast learner."

"No offense," Joe said, "but I like my plan better than yours."

"I'm not really gonna try to fly it myself, smartass. I'm gonna find someone who can fly it."

"If that works out for you, you can swing by and pick us up."

"Sure thing. You all can wait on the roof. I'll drop you a rope ladder or something."

Joe laughed. "How are you going to get to Cashmere? It's like ten miles."

Ross slid his pen along the map. "There are old forest trails I can follow all the way there, essentially. All I need is a couple of snowmobiles. You know how to hotwire a snowmobile?"

"Listen to you, Coach. You're a gangster at heart. I never would have thought."

"I'm just trying to stay alive for a while longer."

"And what does your wife think of you stealing planes and snowmobiles and shit?"

Ross squeezed his eyes shut and fought back the anguish that threatened to rip his heart right out of his chest. He didn't see any point in telling Joe that Monica was gone. He didn't want to get into a conversation about it. Didn't want to think about it. Couldn't.

"She ain't even gonna know." It was Andre–*good old Andre*–who had stepped in behind Joe unnoticed. "She over there in England."

Ross couldn't help but grin. "France, Dre. She's in France." He put a hand on Andre's shoulder. "You ever driven a snowmobile, Dre?"

Andre thought about it for a moment. "I think maybe I did once, but I don't remember for sure."

"Well, if not, then now is a good time to learn how."

Andre cocked his head in perplexity. "We goin' snowmobilin', Coach?"

"Maybe," Ross said. "If one of these fine, upstanding citizens can teach me how to hotwire one."

"Any of you fools know how to hotwire a *motonieve*?" Joe asked his friends.

"*Simon*." Felipe raised a hand. "What you want to hotwire a snowmobile for, Joey?"

"Not me, *vato*," Joe said. "Coach here wants to know."

"You don't need to hotwire a snowmobile to steal it, fool. It's not like a car. Just load it up onto a truck and drive away with it."

"That's not an option," Ross said. "I need to get one started."

"Well, if it's an older one, alls you gotta do is feel around behind the key switch and unplug the wiring harness. Then pull the starter rope and it should fire right up. Easy."

"That's all there is to it?"

"*Simon*. I could do it in under ten seconds."

"Have you done it before?"

Filipe smiled. "You a fuckin' cop?"

"No," Ross answered. "I'm not a cop. I just want to be sure it's going to work before I risk getting shot by somebody who would rather I didn't steal their five-thousand-dollar sled."

"Oh, it'll work, man," Filipe said with a wink. "You can take my word for it."

Ross nodded and folded his map and tucked it into his hip pocket. "Well then, I guess my next order of business is to go out and find a snowmobile."

24.

Rooster toweled himself off and watched the preacher man wrap his wife's body in a double layer of blankets. "You sure she's dead this time?"

Gene went into the kitchen and returned with what was left of the plastic wrap he had used to encase Rooster days earlier. "Why don't ya give me a hand?"

"I don't want to touch her."

"We have to get her out of here, get her blood cleaned off the walls and the carpet."

"How you expect we do that? That shit is soaked into the subfloor by now. There's probably virus particles all over this house, floatin' around in the air. You shouldn't have kept her around screamin' and shittin' and pissin' like you did. We're probably both dying right now."

"God's will be done."

The preacher wore a pair of green rubber gloves on his hands and plastic grocery bags over his feet. The bags were secured to his ankles by rubber bands. He told Rooster it would be in his best interest to go into the kitchen and protect himself in a like fashion.

"And maybe I'll just go ahead and jump in that car out in the garage and get the hell out of here."

"Go right ahead, brother. Janice was the last to drive it. I don't know how long that virus can live outside of a human body, but if it's longer than about ten days, then that car is brimmin' with it."

Something struck the window in the living room.

"The hell was that?" Rooster asked.

The preacher drew the .357 from his waistband and then went to peer through the curtains.

"Oh sweet Jesus Christ in Heaven," he said, taking a startled step backward.

Another knocking sound on the window, then an animalistic scream.

"Fuck me," Rooster said. "You telling me there's one of them infected fuckers out there?"

Gene shook his head and checked the ammo of the revolver. "There's two of 'em."

"Huh? What the hell are they doin' *here*?"

"I dunno. Maybe they heard the shot. Maybe they can smell the blood of one of their own. Your guess is as good as mine, brother."

Another thump on the window.

"Give me my guns," Rooster demanded.

"Shhh. Just be quiet and maybe they'll go away."

Thump-thump-thump.

"I'll be damned if I'm gonna be standing here unarmed when those sonsabitches bust through that window."

"Shhh. *Quiet.*"

Rooster eyed the empty shotgun on the hallway floor but didn't want to touch it. That woman had grasped it in her clammy hands. "Keep the Magnum," he told Gene, "just give me my .380."

The preacher kept his attention on the window. He stepped forward and peeked through the curtain again. "Looks like there might be a third one comin' down the street."

"Oh fuck this," Rooster said. He went into the kitchen and rummaged through the drawers looking for a pair of rubber gloves so that he could handle the shotgun without getting the woman's body fluids on him. There were no gloves in the drawers, but there was, however, a large butcher knife. He held it while he searched the overhead cabinets.

From outside came a shrill, piercing cry that caused Rooster to shudder. Then another. Then two simultaneously.

"Shit the bed," said Pastor Gene.

"What? What is it?"

"I think they saw me."

As if to confirm the preacher's observation, the thumping on the window intensified. Two pairs of hands–possibly three– frantically pounded on the glass with increasing force.

"It's gonna be pretty damn hard to plug that window up if they break it out," Rooster said.

The preacher shot a worried glance at Rooster, and then he stepped to the front door and removed the chain lock.

"What the hell do you think you're doin'?" Rooster yelled. "Are you crazy?"

Without saying a word, Gene opened the door and stepped out and managed to get off a single shot before he was forced back inside. A man with graying skin and a torn yellow, long-sleeved shirt thrust his head and left arm into the gap before the preacher could get the door closed. He screamed and whipped his head back and forth and smacked his hand against the inside of the door, grabbing blindly at Gene as Gene resisted with every ounce of his body weight.

"Help me," Gene pleaded to Rooster, or maybe God, likely both.

Rooster hurried to the doorway. "Give me my gun."

"Under the couch cushion."

The man flailing in the doorway reached for Rooster and let out a sound like he was choking on his own vomit, and then Rooster plunged the butcher knife into the man's eye socket. The man screamed–a wet, strangled howl–but didn't let up in his efforts to get through the door.

Rooster went to the sofa and threw the cushions onto the floor and picked up the .32 revolver that he had taken from Norman's wife. "Where's the SIG?" he shouted to the preacher.

"There's no time for that." As Gene spoke, a second arm tore through the gap in the doorway, this one quite muscular with skin so pale it looked almost translucent. "Help me, Rooster."

Rooster walked forward and shot the first man in the forehead. The man's movement slowed but didn't stop. Rooster shot him again. The guy spasmed and his remaining eye rolled back in his head. Rooster couldn't get a shot at the second man because the first was in the way, so he slammed his weight against the door along with the preacher. There was the *snap-crunch* of bones breaking, and then Rooster sprang away from the door instinctively when blackish blood spurted from the first man's mouth. He raised the revolver in one hand. "Open the door, preacher."

Gene groaned, straining against the pressure on the door. "I don't think…"

"*Open* it."

The preacher hesitated only for a second, then he gave up the struggle. The door flew open, knocking Gene against the wall. The still-twitching body of the first man fell to the floor and the second guy burst in over him. Rooster emptied the revolver into the man's face.

Rooster stood in the middle of the room and watched the two bodies bleed out onto the floor and listened to the ringing in his ears and the pounding of his heart. "The cops are going to be coming."

The preacher shook his head and slid down against the wall and held the .357 Magnum in his lap. "Things ain't what they were before," he said between deep, wheezing gulps of air. "Ain't no phones. Cops are too busy to worry about this right now. Maybe later, but right now we're on our own." His shaky hand reached into his breast pocket and pulled out a cigarette.

"Let me get one of those," Rooster said.

A shadow played across the doorframe. An instant later, a man appeared in the doorway. He was dressed in orange plaid pajama bottoms and a blood-soaked white tee shirt. He didn't have any shoes on. A four-inch piece of skull flapped loosely below the hole in the side of his head. His eyes wandered sluggishly in their sockets and his mouth hung open as if his jaw was unhinged. His muscles twitched uncontrollably and he moved awkward and slow like he was a hundred years older than what his otherwise youthful features suggested. *Uhhhhhhhhhhhhhhh* came the sound from his throat.

"You got this one?" Rooster said to Gene.

Boom!

The man's head erupted in a geyser of blood, brains, and bone.

Gene lit his cigarette and mumbled something Rooster couldn't understand.

"I can't hear you, preacher. I'm deaf."

They sat and smoked and stared at the bodies piled in the doorway and said nothing, and after a little while, the preacher man got up and went into the bedroom. He came back a few minutes later with a scoped, bolt action deer rifle slung over one shoulder and a camouflaged backpack hoisted over the other. He stretched a black beanie over his balding head and tossed Rooster the duffel bag Rooster had taken from the dead couple across the street. "Here's your shit. I'm gonna hold on to the .357 if ya don't mind."

"As a matter of fact, I damn well *do* mind."

"The SIG is in the bag. So is a good count of shotgun shells. I'll trade ya the 12 gauge for the Magnum. Fair trade."

"Ain't no fair trade. The shotgun is got your wife's infected juices all over it. I ain't touchin' that shit."

"Suit ya self. I'm gettin' outta here. You can stay or come with me. Either way, I'm goin'."

"And where do you think you're goin'?"

The preacher shrugged. "I don't rightly know. I guess I'll go to the church. What better place to hole up in the end times than the House of God?"

Rooster took the SIG from the duffle bag, checked the ammo: one full seven-round magazine, three rounds in the other. He shuffled the contents around in the bag and looked up at the preacher with growing alarm. "Where are the drugs?"

"Oh, ya won't be needin' those."

He slammed a magazine into the SIG, chambered a round and stomped over to the preacher and shoved the suppressor in his face. "I will not ask you again, preacher man."

"Your dope is gone, boy. Ain't nothing you can say or do to bring it back, so you'd best deal with it."

Rooster clenched his teeth so hard he tasted blood. The pistol trembled in his hand as he placed the suppressor against the preacher's temple. "You...you son of a bitch."

The preacher's eyes were soft. Calm. "Ya think I'm afraid to die, brother? To be with my wife and son and walk with the Lord on streets of gold and leave behind all the worries of this mortal existence, why would that scare *anyone*? If ya want to kill me, then it's part of God's plan, and who am I to argue with God? So you go right ahead and pull that trigger. I will pass into the arms of the Lord without fear."

Rooster's rage ate at his guts like acid. He felt the salty burn of tears in his eyes and wanted to pull the trigger more than he had ever wanted anything. He clicked off the safety.

Wait, said a voice in his head. *This isn't the way*. It was the voice of a woman. Familiar.

He pursed his lips and pressed the gun harder against the preacher's head until the preacher squeezed his eyes closed in pain, and then he pulled the pistol away and dropped it to his side and turned his attention back to the bodies in the doorway.

"Ya have a lot of anger, brother. We make it through this, and I'll help ya with that. *God* will help ya."

"Fuck you."

The preacher walked into the kitchen and opened his backpack and began stuffing it with food from the cabinets. "There is enough food here to last us a few days if we don't go crazy with it. There's more at the church. I'd advise ya wipe that shotgun down with bleach. Should be fine. It'll make a better weapon than that pea shooter ya got."

"Give me back my Smith and Wesson. *You* take the shotgun."

"Would that make ya feel better, brother, if I gave ya back your hand cannon?"

"You stole it from me. What kind of preacher steals from someone?"

"Let me ask ya, brother, who did *you* take this gun from?"

"I took it from a sorry piece of shit. And I ain't claiming to be no man of God."

"I think I'm gonna hold on to it for the time being. Take the shotgun." Gene opened the cabinet beneath the sink and took out a pair of rubber gloves and a spray bottle of cleaner and tossed them on the floor near Rooster. "Won't take ya but a minute to disinfect it."

Rooster put the gloves on and sprayed the shotgun with the bleach cleaner and wiped it with a towel from the bathroom. He filled the five-round tube magazine with buckshot shells and racked the slide to chamber a round. "If the cops catch us out on the street, they'll arrest us, if they don't shoot us first."

"What, arrest us for goin' to church on a Sunday?"

"Is it Sunday?"

"Time flies when you're havin' fun, don't it?"

There was a brief interruption in the light of the doorway. A ripple. A passing shadow.

"Somebody outside?" Rooster said, raising the shotgun.

The preacher turned toward the door and worked the bolt of his rifle. Just then, a long-haired heavyset woman wearing a blue tee-shirt with *Moses Lake Steel* emblazoned on the front stepped through the doorway and studied the bodies for a few seconds, then looked up at the preacher, opened her mouth wide and charged, screaming.

Rooster shot her. The buckshot struck her in the chest, shoulder, and neck. She stumbled sideways and locked her blood red eyes on Rooster and came at him. He pumped another round in the chamber and blew her head off just as he came within arm's length.

"This is fucking ridiculous," Rooster said. "Why the hell do they keep pourin' in here?"

"Like I said before, maybe they're attracted by the sound of the gunshots, or maybe the smell of their own dead. Maybe the virus makes ya telepathic, or whatever they call it." Gene put his arms through the straps of his backpack and moved toward the front door. "Maybe it's the Devil hisself tellin' them where to come to. Who knows? But we'd best be goin'." He raised his rifle and stepped over the bodies in the doorway and scanned the outside. "You comin', brother?"

Rooster replaced the spent shells in the shotgun and followed the preacher into the daylight. "Don't tell me you plan on walking all the way to the church."

"I already told ya we can't take my car. Maybe ya think if we flap our arms fast enough we can fly there."

Rooster glanced at the dead couple's Honda in the driveway across the street and unzipped his duffel bag and felt around inside to see if the keys were still there. They were. "How about I steal that CRV over there?"

The preacher eyed the vehicle for a few seconds, then laughed. "Ya think the people that live in that house are just gonna sit by while you take their car?"

"Trust me," Rooster said, "they ain't gonna do shit about it."

"Oh? And why would that be?" Gene shook his head and started down the street.

"You think anybody in their right mind is gonna come outside and mess with a man with a shotgun after all this screamin' and shootin'? These neighbors around here, I guarantee every one of them are sitting behind their locked doors and shakin' in terror right now. Those of them who are still alive, that is." Rooster could see a bloody body lying in the street less than a hundred and fifty feet north.

"No," said the preacher. "I won't take from an innocent family just because I can. Those are good people. I've known 'em for quite some time."

"I ain't suggesting you take from anyone. I'll do it."

"You do what you want, Mr. Rooster. I think it's time for you and me to part ways anyhow."

"You stubborn son of a bitch! You would rather risk getting killed by crazy sickos on the street than borrow a damn vehicle without its owner's permission. We don't have to keep it forever. We can give it back later with a big old apology. Goddammit! What kind of man can smother his own wife to death but is too good to ride in a stolen car?"

The preacher man kept walking. Rooster watched him until he disappeared around a bend in the street, then went over into the dead couple's driveway and climbed into the Honda.

He caught up to Gene twenty seconds later. "The morons left their keys in it," he said through the open passenger window.

The preacher stopped and stared at Rooster in disgust. "Brother, it'd be best if ya turn around and take that vehicle right back where you got it."

"After what I just witnessed back there at your house, I don't think we need to be walkin' around out here. Now get in."

The preacher man raised his face to the winter sky and closed his eyes as if he were consulting with God. After a few moments, he looked back at Rooster with an expression of pity and sadness, and then turned and walked away.

Rooster pulled forward a few feet, then got out of the vehicle and approached the preacher from behind and raised the shotgun.

Gene stopped and turned to face him. "I told ya, brother, I ain't afraid to die. Ya don't have any power over me."

"Is that what you really think?"

The preacher nodded. "Either kill me now, or let me get on to my church."

Rooster struck him on the head with the butt of the shotgun. Gene let out a sharp cry and staggered backward a few steps. Rooster hit him again and he fell to his hands and knees.

"You wanna go to the church?" Rooster said. "I'll take you to your fucking church." He slammed the shotgun down on the preacher's back. Gene dropped to his belly with a moan, and then Rooster kicked him hard in the ribs. "Gonna keep me tied up in a dark-ass closet for two and half days?" He kicked the preacher again and again. "Make me sleep in my own piss?" He brought the shotgun down hard against Gene's head. "I don't give a damn if you ain't afraid to die." Another strike to the head. Blood spewed from the preacher's mouth, nose. "I'm gonna make you afraid to keep *living*." He cracked the preacher once more on the head, and then Gene lay still.

Rooster checked the preacher man's pulse to make sure he was still alive, then he took the Magnum and the rifle and worked Gene's backpack free and placed it all in the passenger seat of the Honda. He spread the preacher's hands out on the asphalt and smashed them with the butt of the shotgun, then he crushed the man's ankles in the same manner. When Gene cried out, Rooster beat him with the shotgun until he was quiet again. Then Rooster dragged the preacher to the rear of the Honda and hoisted him up into the cargo space.

He jumped into the CRV and started the engine but left the transmission in park. Where to go? The preacher's house was out of the question, no way was he going back to that infectious shit hole. Same for the house in which he had finished Norman and the unlucky residents. The smell of the bodies would be unbearable after days of rotting. He considered the church but only briefly. He had no idea what might have transpired there since he left Norman's family dead in the basement. It wasn't safe, of that he was certain.

Don't just sit here in the middle of the street like an idiot. Drive. Anywhere.

He drove to the next intersection and took a right, and when he did, he saw the child–a boy, eight or ten years old–kneeling over the woman on her back, motionless on the sidewalk. The child's face was pressed to the woman's, as if he was performing CPR, or as if he were a dog eating from a food bowl. The concrete beneath the woman's head was red with her blood. The boy looked up with dull, black eyes as Rooster passed. It was then that Rooster could see the ragged tears in the woman's face and throat. Her skull was exposed in places. Her lips had been torn away. The child bared his bloodstained teeth, then returned to what he had been doing before Rooster had interrupted him.

The street ended at a three-way intersection a few blocks up. Rooster turned left and drove a couple hundred yards until he spotted an approaching truck. It was a big, white utility vehicle with a large pipe strapped to an overhead rack. Rooster put the Honda directly in the truck's path and stopped and studied the driver and passenger, both in orange utility vests. The truck's air brakes clanked and hissed. The driver blared his horn. Rooster only sat and thought about what he was going to do next.

When the truck's backup bell began to chime, Rooster got out of the Honda and approached the truck on the driver's side. On the door was painted *Seattle Public Utilities*. He stepped onto the runner and ordered the driver to roll down his window.

"I don't think so, buddy," the man responded.

Rooster raised his SIG and tapped the glass with the suppressor. "Lower the fucking window."

The driver did as he was told.

"Do you guys have access to the freeway in this truck?" Rooster asked. "Will the cops let you through roadblocks?"

"Yes, sir," said the driver, "but we aren't allowed to transport unauthorized passengers. They'll get suspicious at the checkpoint if they see a third person in this cab."

"Don't worry about that. What's your name?"

"Vincenzo."

"Passenger, take off your vest and hand it to Vincenzo."

The passenger unhooked his seat belt and removed his vest and gave it to the driver.

"Now open your door," Rooster told the passenger.

The passenger opened his door, and Rooster shot him twice in the chest. The man turned and tumbled out of the cab and disappeared from Rooster's view.

Vincenzo began to cry and beg, and Rooster told him to shut up and get out of the truck.

"Please don't kill me, sir, I have two little girls."

"I ain't gonna kill you as long as you jump when I say jump. You got any duct tape on this vehicle?"

"Duct tape, electrical tape, whatever you need."

"Get me a roll of it."

Vincenzo opened a compartment on the back of the truck, searched a moment, then found a roll of duct tape and offered it to Rooster.

"You just hold on to that for now," Rooster said.

On the bed of the truck amongst traffic cones and coils of thick, black cable was a big, shiny aluminum box. "What's in there?" asked Rooster.

"Just tools and such."

"Empty it."

Vincenzo removed the contents from the box and tossed them with the miscellanea on the bed. Then Rooster ushered him around to the passenger side of the truck.

"Oh, God. *Ricky*," Vincenzo whined.

The passenger was face down and lifeless on the asphalt. His eyes were open. Blind. Dead.

Rooster took Vincenzo behind the Honda and opened the hatch.

"What are you doing, brother?" The preacher moaned. "This is the Devil's work. Brother, please, don't let yourself be victimized by the Great Deceiver."

"Slap some duct tape over this asshole's mouth," Rooster told Vincenzo.

"I'm sorry about this," Vincenzo said to Gene as he applied the tape.

"Good. Now tape his wrists and ankles so he can't get free, then carry him to the truck and drop his ass in that big metal box."

Gene screamed through his nose as Vincenzo jostled his broken hands and ankles. Once the preacher was taped up, Vincenzo hoisted him over his shoulder and took him to the box and placed him inside.

"Atta boy, Vince," Rooster said. "Now lock the lid down and let's get the hell out of here. You're driving."

"Where we headed?"

"South," Rooster said, lighting one of Gene's cigarettes. "Get us on Interstate 405 and take us south."

Vincenzo turned and studied the landscape in the direction Rooster indicated. "If you don't mind me asking, sir, what is south?"

Rooster blew out a plume of gray smoke, and as he slipped into the dead passenger's orange vest, he answered Vincenzo with a single word: "Vengeance."

25.

"It sure is cold out here, Coach. If we don't find a snowmobile real soon, I might have to go back to Joe's and get warm." Andre cupped his hands and blew into them.

"Just keep walking," Ross said. "It's not as cold as it seems. When I was younger, my friends and I used to go snowboarding up on Stevens Pass. We would stay out all day long in temperatures way colder than this. This is nothing. Harden up."

"I'm not tryin' to be no little girl, man, but this coat Joe let me wear ain't too thick."

"Don't go giving up already, Dre. Our journey is only getting started."

"I'm not givin' up. I'm just sayin' it's cold out here."

"You don't have to keep reminding me." Ross was fully aware of the biting cold on his face, the numbness in his feet. "Just stay focused on the task at hand. Maybe we can find a snowmobile that has a heater."

"Dang, I didn't know snowmobiles have heaters. Learn somethin' new every day."

"Well, it's not the same type of heater you have in a car. It only warms up the seat, but it sure feels good on a night like this. Unfortunately, not every snowmobile has one."

"I hope we find one that *does*, because I'm freezin'." Andre stopped and broke into a set of jumping jacks.

"Stop that, Dre. You're going to make yourself sweat, and then you'll *really* be cold."

They walked a few more blocks, checking every yard, every driveway of the homes that lined both sides of the street, and then

Ross spotted a pair of low-set handlebars jutting out from beneath a blue, snow-covered tarpaulin next to an outbuilding. "There, Dre!"

The house was a doublewide mobile home set only twenty-five feet from the street. The lights were on inside, and a black Jeep Wrangler was parked in the open driveway. Ross looked around to get his bearings and plan his escape route. He didn't think he could outrun the Jeep on a snowmobile, but if he was fast, he and Andre could give themselves a good head start. He knew the town well. To access the mountain trails that would lead him west to the town of Cashmere, he would have to cross a narrow irrigation canal close to his current location. The nearest crossing was about nine blocks away. Just before the crossing was a large apple orchard. If the Jeep came after him, Ross thought he might be able to lose it in the orchard. If the Jeep did manage to catch up to him, he would not hesitate to shoot out its tires.

"Okay, Dre, let's do this."

As they approached the tarpaulin, Ross winced with every step; the sound of the snow crunching beneath their feet was tremendous in the late-night silence. He expected the front door of the doublewide to fly open at any second, and was relieved when they made it across the yard without incident.

He pulled the tarp away to reveal an older model black and silver snowmobile, not large but plenty big enough to accommodate him and Andre. He checked it over to assure it was intact, then lifted the hood and unplugged the wiring harness from the ignition, just as Filipe had instructed.

"Okay, Dre, the instant I get this thing started, you jump on behind me and hold on tight, because we're going to boogie out of here in a flash."

"Yes, sir."

"Here goes nothing." Ross yanked the starter cord, which caught at mid-pull and caused his fingers to snap off the handle painfully. He cursed and drew the cord again, then again when the engine failed to ignite. After ten frantic pulls, Ross began to believe the vehicle wasn't going to start. He adjusted the choke, gave the cord a couple more yanks, and then the door of the mobile home opened and a male voice called, "Hey! What the hell are you doing out there?"

Ross turned his eyes to the figure in the doorway but continued to pull the cord. Andre mumbled something but Ross couldn't tell what. A woman joined the man in the doorway, stood there a couple of seconds, then both the man and woman disappeared back into the house.

"They gone, Coach," Andre said in obvious relief.

Yeah, gone to get a gun, Ross thought, but didn't say, because he didn't have the breath.

Then the engine came to life with a pop and a sputter. Ross and Andre jumped onto the seat and Ross pressed the throttle lever. The snowmobile lurched forward and the engine died instantly.

No! Don't do this to me, you piece of shit!

He yanked the cord again. Nothing.

"Those people are comin' back out," Andre said.

Again, Ross drew the cord, and still the engine didn't start. He got off the vehicle and brought the M4 up and aimed it at the man, who was coming down the front steps with a long object in his hand. A baseball bat.

Ross walked toward him. "Go back in the fucking house."

The man stopped where he was, and Ross could see his eyes widen even in the darkness. The woman in the doorway gasped and threw her hands up over her mouth.

"Hey, buddy, it's cool," the man said, dropping the bat and raising his hands. "Just take it. I'm not gonna fight you over it."

"Go back in the house," Ross repeated. "We'll be out of your hair in just a minute. I don't want to hurt anyone, so please don't make me."

"No problem, buddy. I'm going inside now. Don't shoot." The man backed up the stairs slowly, turned, and went back into the doublewide and closed the door behind him.

Ross grasped the handle of the starter rope once again and jerked it so forcefully he was surprised the handle didn't break off in his hand. On the next pull, the engine finally caught. Ross forced himself to wait a full minute before pressing the throttle, and when he did, he stroked it with the same tenderness one might use to clear a grain of sand from the surface of a baby's eye. The snowmobile eased forward, its engine hitching but maintaining power. A minute later, Ross and Andre were zooming across the irrigation canal.

They went west past rows of expensive homes, then south on Maiden Lane until the pavement ended. They continued on a dirt road along a barbed wire fence, its lower strands concealed by three and four foot drifts of snow, past a massive round water tank, and then finally up into the hills. They followed a crooked westward trail for perhaps three quarters of a mile until it disappeared before them, then they took the path of least resistance, picking up a second trail which took them a couple of miles before they lost that one too. After a while, they came upon an orchard populated with sparsely branched saplings supported by hundreds of feet of wire attached to eight-foot training stakes driven three feet apart. Beyond the orchard was a valley that ran north and south. Ross and Andre went north along that valley, and before long, came to a road that led west. They followed the road until they came to a hill too steep to traverse with the snowmobile. Ross left the vehicle running while he consulted his map. He took a few moments to figure out their position, and his heart sank when he realized they were only about halfway to their destination.

"We've still got a ways to go, Dre, but if we follow the road north for a mile or two it will put us near the town of Monitor. The terrain is fairly level in that area, and there are hundreds of acres of apple orchards that will keep us concealed from any police patrols. Once we leave the cover of the orchards, there shouldn't be more than a couple miles left to the Cashmere airfield. I'm guessing we can be there in under ten minutes if we go all out."

"And what do we do when we get there?" Andre asked.

"We find us a pilot to fly us out of here."

"How we gonna do that?"

"I don't know yet, but I'll figure it out when we get there."

"I trust you, Coach. Let's go. I'm freezing."

Ross pocketed his map and turned the snowmobile north and gunned the throttle. The engine produced a high-pitched, deafening whine and died with a *snap*. Ross yanked the starter rope repeatedly until his arms felt as if they might drop right out of their sleeves, but he couldn't get the vehicle going again.

"Dang, Coach," Andre said, "what you think is wrong? We out of gas?"

Ross checked the fuel gauge, tapped its plastic cover, then removed the cap from the gas tank and used the flashlight on the M4 to look inside. "We have gas. Not much, but enough. It's something else. Maybe she overheated and will start back up once we give her some time to cool off."

"Shouldn't take too long, as cold as it is. Man, that seat warmer sure did feel good."

"This sled doesn't have a seat warmer, Dre."

"Oh. I thought it did. It felt kinda warm when I was ridin'."

"Body heat maybe."

Ross lifted the hood and shined his light over the engine, but he didn't know enough about engines to tell what was wrong. "We'll give her a few minutes, and then I'll give it another try. If she doesn't start, I'm afraid we're going to have to walk."

"Didn't you just get through sayin' we still have a few miles to go? I don't think I can do it."

"Dammit, Dre, don't give me that shit. When I was your age, I could *run* that distance with snow up to my knees. You either toughen up and walk or sit here and freeze to death, because I'm sure as hell not going to carry you. What *are* you?"

"I'm a warrior."

"Good. Act like it."

They paced back and forth for the next several minutes to keep their blood circulating, then Ross went to work on the starter cord again. After twenty-eight pulls, he let Andre take over. The snowmobile still wouldn't start.

"I'm no expert on snowmobiles," Ross said, "but I heard sometimes you can lift up the back and they will be easier to start. So let's try that. I'll lift, and you pull the cord."

"Yes sir. I'll try anything."

"Ready? On three. One...two...*three*." Ross grabbed the frame beneath the seat and hefted the rear of the vehicle off the ground while Andre yanked the starter cord again and again.

"Forget it," Ross said after several tries. "It's not going to work." He set the snowmobile down and removed the blanket from his duffel bag and gave it to Andre. "Wrap this around your shoulders. I know it's cold out here, and we have a long walk ahead of us, but we'll be okay as long as we keep moving. Try to focus on how good it's going to feel when we're sitting by a nice warm fireplace in a cabin on the lake, away from this whole damned mess. Keep your eyes on the prize, Dre."

"Maybe we should wait a little bit longer. Like you said before, this piece of junk might just be overheated. If we give it some more time to cool down–"

"No. We have to go. If this bitch had overheated, don't you think she'd be cooled off by now? It's like fifteen degrees out here." Ross put his hand on Andre's shoulder. "Listen, son, it's going to be okay. You can do this. I know you can. Believe in yourself, like I believe in you."

"Okay, sir."

"Good. And stop calling me sir."

Before they left the snowmobile, Ross emptied one of his water bottles and siphoned some gas into it with a coolant hose he removed from the radiator. He tore off the seat cover and took out the underlying foam padding and gave it to Andre to place beneath his shirt for some added warmth. Then the two of them walked north along the snow-packed road.

They hadn't gone far when they came upon what appeared to be a scrapyard. Old boat hulls and junk vehicles and broken furniture and appliances scattered around a large, unmarked metal building. There was a pair of bulldozers parked in front, along with a semi truck with a trailer attached. There was writing painted on the truck's doors, but the letters were so faded it was unreadable. Snow was heaped atop both dozers and the semi, indicating that none had been driven in some time.

"Do you think there's anybody here?" Asked Andre.

"I don't think so," Ross said, scanning the area with his flashlight. "I'm not even sure anyone uses this place any more."

"What do you think is in that big building?"

"Who knows?" Ross climbed onto the aluminum steps of the truck and pulled the driver's door open. He was surprised when the interior light came on. "The battery is working. Do you know what that means, Dre?"

"What does it mean, Coach?"

"It means this truck has been run recently. I bet if we searched that building we could find the keys for it."

"You think we can drive it out of here?"

"With all this snow? No chance. But we can use the heater to warm up a little before we move on."

"That sure would be great," Andre said. "How we gonna get into that building though? I don't think there's any windows."

"Oh, there's probably a window in there somewhere. If not, we can find something around here to pry open that roll up garage door."

"You think there's a heater inside the building, Coach?"

"I think there likely is, but I doubt it will warm us up as fast as the heater in this truck."

Beneath the various switches, dials, and knobs of the truck's cracked dashboard was a plastic console with a change tray and a pair of drink holders. In the change tray was a handful of greasy-looking pennies, and in one of the drink holders was a set of keys. "We might not need to get into that building after all, Dre."

Ross examined the keys for a few seconds, then inserted one into the ignition and turned it halfway and smiled when the indicator lights illuminated. *Come on baby come on baby come on baby.* He pressed the clutch pedal and turned the key further and held it while the engine chugged. *Come on, baby!* The engine roared, then settled into a smooth idle. "Yes! Get in, Dre."

Andre ran around to the passenger side and climbed in and held his hands up to the heater vents.

Ross laughed. "You have to give it some time to warm up. It'll only take a couple of minutes."

Andre nodded but kept his hands where they were.

Ross waited until the temperature gauge needle reached the 160 mark before he switched on the cab heater. He was nearly teary-eyed with relief when the warm air enveloped him. "Oh, my god, Dre, it *works*. I was afraid it wasn't going to."

Andre lowered his head and moved his lips in silent prayer, then he and Ross sat for a long time, savoring the warmth without speaking.

Ross folded his arms across his chest and closed his eyes, and when he opened them again, he was staring out the window of the SkyCity Restaurant atop the Space Needle in Seattle. Monica was beside him in a green floral sundress, her hair pulled back in a short ponytail, revealing the sexy lines of her neck.

"This is the greatest city on Earth," she said with her stunning smile.

Ross took her hand in his and kissed her fingertips one by one. "Tell me what you find so great about it."

She pressed herself against him and looked him in the eyes–looked into his *soul*–and said, "For starters, how great is it to be standing here in this fabulous restaurant five hundred feet above the ground with the most wonderful man a woman could ever know?" She kissed him softly on his lower lip. "There is magic here in this Emerald City. Can you feel it?"

"Oh, I feel it," he said. "I feel it every time I look at you. I feel it every time you brush your hand gently across my cheek. Every time you laugh that girly little giggle of yours. Every time you crinkle your nose when you squint against the summer sun. I feel it every morning when I wake knowing you love me. I felt it the moment I first laid eyes on you. Yes. I feel the magic. I'm carried away by it."

"How far do you suppose it will carry you?"

"It will carry me into forever."

"Forever, huh? That's an awfully long way. Are you sure you want to go that far?"

"I will go that far, and back, and into forever again. As long as you are there with me."

"You kinda like me, don't you, Colin Ross?"

"Yes. Yes I do."

"That's good." She kissed him again. "Because I kinda like you too."

"Ross!"

He felt a slap on his shoulder and he snapped awake. "What is it, Dre?"

"Someone's comin'."

It was a slow-moving shadow in the darkness, approaching from twenty yards away. As it drew closer, Ross could see that it was definitely a person. Man or woman, he couldn't be sure. He killed the truck engine and laid the assault rifle across his lap. The shadow sauntered up to the front of the truck and stopped and sniffed the air and gazed at Ross and Andre through the windshield. It was a man. Gray-haired in a red flannel shirt open to reveal a massive belly that hung over the waistband of his sweat pants. The man exploded forward and flung himself into the grill of the truck, then disappeared out of sight.

"Lock your door, Dre."

Ross raised himself up in his seat as high as he could to improve his field of vision. "Where did he go? I don't see—"

Ka-thunk!

The cab rocked on its chassis. Ross looked down through the driver's window in time to see the man's fists come crashing against the door simultaneously. The man struck the metal over and over again, screaming wildly as he did. Ross noticed black patches on the man's face. Necrosis. Frostbite. One of the man's fists smacked against the window, and Ross was astonished the glass didn't shatter. Another strike on the window and the glass seemed to shimmer from the force of it.

"Fuck this." Ross turned the ignition key and pressed the window button. He brought the window down halfway, shoved the barrel of the M4 through the gap, and shot the man in the top of the head. The man dropped his hands and swayed for a moment like a tree in a strong breeze, then fell backward onto the snow.

"He dead?" Andre said.

Ross didn't answer. His ears rang from the sound of the gunshot, his nostrils burned with the smell of gunpowder, and his mind reeled from the absurdity of it all.

"Coach!"

"Yeah. Yeah, I think he's dead."

"They's more people comin'."

Andre pointed at two additional shadows moving toward the truck. The shadows transformed into a heavyset woman in her fifties dressed in pink pajamas beneath a bathrobe of the same color, and a skinny, bearded man in gray boxers and a navy blue tee shirt.

"Where the hell are they coming from?" Ross said. "We're in the middle of nowhere."

"I don't know, Coach, but they comin' from somewhere."

Ross put his window back up and restarted the truck and switched on the headlamps. When he did, he spotted another couple approaching on the road from the north. A fifth silhouette emerged from the darkness further up the road.

"They sick, ain't they?" Andre said. "Just like my momma. That's why they walkin' all funny."

Ross nodded but had no words to respond. His throat tightened and his heart thundered in his chest. His head swooned as he teetered on the edge of panic. It was like a scene from a nightmare. Trapped in an immobile vehicle in a dark mountain canyon as raging psychotics–*zombies*–closed in around him. Things like this weren't supposed to happen in the real world.

"What do they want with *us*?" Andre asked.

"I don't know, Dre. None of this makes any sense to me," were Ross's words, but his thoughts were: *They want to eat us.*

The bearded man opened his mouth and let out a cry and shambled forward with the grace of a newborn calf taking its first steps. The woman in the robe stopped for a moment, cocked her head quizzically, then broke into a wobbly sprint from ten yards away.

"Dammit!" Ross said. "Dre, watch my back, and don't open your door for anything." He leaped out of the cab and went around the front and barely had time to fire off a round at the woman before she was upon him. The bullet struck her in the right cheek and exited behind her ear in a jet of flesh and bone. She paused briefly, screamed and flailed her arms as if she were treading water, then came forward again. Ross shot her through the mouth at point blank range, and she fell to the ground in a lifeless, pink heap.

He swung the barrel toward the bearded man and put the holographic sight reticle on his forehead and pulled the trigger. The man took another couple of steps, fell, convulsed violently for a few seconds, and then began to drag himself forward through the reddening snow. Ross started to shoot him again, but the man's movement slowed, then stopped completely.

Ross turned to the three figures in the road. The two closest to him were men. One of them was dressed only in stained, white briefs and dark socks. He was a bald man in his forties with blood smeared around his mouth and across the right side of his upper body. His right arm was also streaked with blood, and he seemed to be missing part of his hand. He waddled forward on hairy, bowed legs, holding his left hand oddly above his head. His fingers plucked at the air as if they were strumming an imaginary harp. Ross shot him in the head, and the man fell backwards and thrashed wildly in the snow before getting up again. The man fell twice more and managed to get back on his feet both times, so Ross put another bullet through his head, dropping him for good.

The next man appeared to be in his seventies, toothless with thin tufts of wiry gray hair. He wore blue pajamas beneath a navy bathrobe and moved as if his limbs were rubber bands. Slow. Spasmodic. There was a ragged, bloody hole where his left ear should have been. Ross dispatched him with one shot between the eyes.

A slender young woman followed behind the men. She wore a purple tee shirt and was naked from the waist down. The skin of her legs, face, arms was blistered and scabbed with severe frostbite. Her nose and lips were black with rot. Her gait was stiff and labored, and she walked with her right ear forward, a blind woman tracking the sounds ahead of her. Ross shot her in the head, and she yelped like a struck dog and fell and didn't get back up.

When the last gunshot stopped echoing against the canyon walls and the ringing in his ears began to subside, Ross heard voices in the distance. Lamenting wails. Screams of pain and despair...and rage.

He climbed back into the semi cab and locked the door and put the heater on its maximum setting. "Enjoy the heat, Dre, because we're bugging out of here in sixty seconds."

Andre's eyes were wide and glossy with adrenaline. "I'm ashamed to admit it, but I'm scared, Coach."

Ross stared out at the road ahead and saw the shadows creeping into the furthest reaches of the headlights. "I'm scared too, son. I'm scared too."

26.

Ross left the truck engine running and the headlights on while he and Andre climbed out of the cab on the driver's side and ducked into the shadows behind the metal building on the lot. Over the next several minutes, he watched them converge on the truck. Three. Five. Nine of them eventually. They smashed out the glass and crawled into the cab through the windows, piling in on top of one another, writhing and screaming and fighting amongst themselves, then exiting the same way they had gone in without thinking to open the doors. They came out one at a time, as if birthing, wriggling out through the windows past those who waited their turn to climb inside, each of them falling headfirst onto the ground to either get back up and wander aimlessly around the truck, or lay still in the snow after breaking their necks from the impact.

"Time to go," Ross said.

He led Andre north through the scrapyard, dodging behind old semi trailers and boat hulls. He kept the barrel of the M4 pointed into the darkness ahead, ready to fire at anyone who should appear in their path. After a couple hundred yards, they came to a small, cinder block outbuilding with a red pickup truck half-buried in snow parked nearby. Beyond the outbuilding was a doublewide mobile home and a detached garage, in front of which sat a newer-model four-door car. Ross studied the windows of the house, looking for any sign of life, but found nothing but darkness.

They walked further, past more outbuildings and a pair of matching singlewide mobile homes, themselves devoid of life. There was a two-story brick home with several apple bins stacked to one side. A king cab 4x4 pickup truck in the driveway. A tarpaulin-covered motorboat on a trailer beside the truck. Another home. Then another. Every few hundred feet was a mobile home or farmhouse with barns and outbuildings scattered between. Ross and Andre kept moving through the darkness as stealthily as they were able, and then the valley widened into tens of thousands of leafless apple trees lined in perfect rows that extended across the horizon further than the eye could see.

"How are you holding up, Dre?"

"I'm cold, Coach."

"Don't focus on it. It's only temporary. You're going to feel like a badass when we finally get where we're going."

"I sure don't feel like a badass. I feel like a coward for running away."

"There is nothing cowardly about wanting to live to fight another day, son." Ross spoke in broken sentences between deep gulps of sub-freezing air. "Somebody is going to have to be around to pick up the pieces...when all of this is over. Escaping that hospital...walking miles through the snow in this cold...with zombies...lurking in the shadows...that's bravery."

"Zombies, Coach?"

"I only mean people who are...infected with the Qilu virus. Zombie is probably a bad word to use."

After a minute of silence, Andre said, "They sure act like zombies, don't they?"

"They sure do, Dre."

They walked on through snow up to their knees, Ross with both the M4 and duffel bag slung across his back and his arms crossed tightly against his chest, and Andre with the blanket wrapped around his upper body like a poncho. They maintained a northwesterly direction, using the east-west alignment of the tree rows for orientation. Moving forward. Forward on feet that felt as if they were encased in heavy blocks of ice. Robotically. One step after another. After a while, it was only the next step that mattered.

They labored on until they came to the slope of a low mountain and stopped only long enough for the steepness of it to fill their hearts with dread. Under different circumstances Ross would have opted to go around, but to do so now would not only greatly increase their time spent in the biting cold, but the route would lead them along the banks of the Wenatchee River, where the chance was too great that they would encounter a police patrol. More than once Ross had thought he heard the beating of rotor blades echoing through the mountains lining the river.

So they went up without a word between them, too exhausted to speak, their bodies bent forward for balance. Halfway up the incline, Andre faltered, fell to his knees and stayed there, his eyes staring at the snow-covered ground but seeing something different entirely—perhaps an extra large supreme pizza and warm flames dancing in a brick fireplace—until Ross urged him up with a waving of his arm.

At last, the slope leveled off, and after about another mile, the lights of the small town of Cashmere could be seen twinkling in the distance.

"You see that, Dre? We're almost there. Just a little further, son." Every breath of the frigid air stung Ross's lungs. "We're almost there."

Andre said nothing. He just kept walking, one step at a time, his body swaying with fatigue.

They descended the mountain into vast acres of fruit orchards on the level ground below. Twenty minutes later, they crossed a dirt road into an open field. Beyond the field was another road, this one paved, which they crossed into another orchard. In the middle of the orchard was an L-shaped house with a covered swimming pool in the backyard and what appeared to be a workers' cabin further back. A dog barked from somewhere, and Ross welcomed the sound of it—the sound of civilization.

Farther was an intersection of two roads: Mission Creek running north, and Binder, which ran east and west. There were houses and metal outbuildings and long pole barns that covered rows of empty apple bins stacked twelve feet high. Ross knelt on one knee and took his map from his jacket pocket and unfolded it across his thigh. He found the road intersection on the map and traced his finger to the airfield.

"Only a half a mile to go. I'll race you there, Dre."

"I don't think I can make it."

"You said that hours ago, and yet, here you are. Come on, man. Just a few more blocks."

Ross stood and folded his map and stuffed it back into his pocket and started down Binder Road. Andre followed. They reached the airfield ten minutes later and came upon a chain link fence behind a row of aircraft hangars at the southeast area of the field.

"You wouldn't happen to have a decent set of bolt cutters on you, would you, Dre?"

"No, sir."

"Well, it looks like we have to climb then."

"I can't feel my hands. My fingers won't move."

"You and me both," Ross said. "We can do this though. Come on. I'll boost you up."

"I don't understand what we're doin' here, Coach."

"I'll explain once we're over this fence, after we find us a nice electric heater in one of these hangars." Ross bent forward next to the fence and laced his fingers and held his hands low in a stirrup for Andre to step into. "Give me your foot. I'll push you up. The faster we do this, the faster we can get warm."

Andre draped his blanket over Ross's shoulders and stepped into his hands. Ross hefted him up to the top of the fence. He threw his legs over one at a time and dropped down on the other side and stumbled sideways as he landed but stayed on his feet.

Ross tossed the blanket over, then the duffel bag, and then went to scale the fence himself. With snow packed into the treads of his shoes, he had no traction with his feet, so he had to rely solely on his upper body strength to pull himself up. He made several attempts but couldn't do it. His arms were too weak after the battle with the starter cord on the snowmobile. Too cold. Too exhausted.

"Get up over this fence, Coach," Andre called. "I'm cold, dang it."

Ross breathed deeply and moved his arms and legs to increase circulation. Then he took his shoes off and flung them over the fence. He checked the safety on the rifle, leaped up as high as he could and grasped the fence chain and dug his sockfeet in, gripping best he could with his toes, and finally managed to get a leg up and over. He dropped down next to Andre and fell backward on his ass. Andre extended a hand and helped him up, and then Ross put his shoes back on and slung the duffel bag across his back.

"Okay then," he said, "let's find someplace to warm up."

The walked between two hangars until they reached the front, then stood in the shadows while Ross studied their surroundings. Directly across the taxiway was another row of hangars, half a dozen of varying sizes. There were additional hangars to the left in a perpendicular row past the curve of the taxiway. A couple hundred feet to the right, beyond the chain link fence and a street that bordered the eastern end of the airport, was what appeared to be a baseball field. There was no sign of anyone anywhere. No security guards making rounds, no aircraft mechanics working late, no evident police presence. Darkness and ghostly silence.

There was a hard layer of snow on the taxiway, but it looked like it had been plowed recently. Ross wondered if the runway was being maintained, so he led Andre along the taxiway until they were looking out over the length of the airstrip. There were snowplows parked nearby, and the runway appeared usable.

"They ain't no planes here, Coach," Andre said. "Somebody done flied 'em all out."

"The planes are parked in the hangars, Dre. That's where we are going now. Keep your eyes peeled for something we might be able to use to pry open a door."

"Can't you just shoot the lock? It don't seem like there's anybody around to hear us."

"Somebody *will* hear us. Even if they didn't, I don't think the caliber of this carbine is enough to break open a door lock. Maybe if we had a shotgun, but we don't. We'll have to get in some other way. I saw a utility truck parked between a couple of those hangers. Let's go see what kind of tools are on it."

They doubled back to the first row of hangars, amongst which was parked a white pickup truck with orange lights atop the roof. There were various toolboxes affixed to the bed, but all were locked. Ross shattered the passenger window with the collapsible stock of the M4 and went to work searching the interior of the truck. He discovered a rusty tire iron behind the seat, and that was all he needed. He found the side door of a random hangar and pried it open without much difficulty, and then he and Andre went inside and closed the door behind them.

The hangar was dark, so Ross used the flashlight on the M4 to look around. Parked inside was a two-engine Beechcraft plane, white with orange and blue stripes along the fuselage, and a red and white single engine Cessna. In one corner of the hanger were a restroom and a set of steel grate steps leading up to a small room just above it. Ross and Andre went up into the room. Inside was a couple of chairs, an L-shaped desk with a computer monitor and some basic office supplies atop it, a five-drawer file cabinet, a coffeemaker on a small table in a corner, and an electric blower heater on the floor. Ross switched on the heater, and then he and Andre huddled side by side on the floor with their backs against the wall and savored the warmth.

Ross removed his shoes and placed them before the heater and peeled off his socks and draped them over his shoe collars. He examined his feet. The skin was shriveled, pale, and waxy, numb to the touch, but as the flesh thawed in the warm airflow, Ross wondered if the agony of it would be much worse if his feet were flayed with dull razors.

Andre was asleep within minutes, but Ross stayed awake awhile thinking about his life, about his future, the future of humanity. He thought about Mickey, and what would become of Mickey's family. Then he thought about Monica, and though his heart ached tremendously, he felt that he had no more tears left to cry. And he was wrong. As he teetered on the precipice of sleep, the tears came, and they continued to flow even after he had passed into the land of dreams. And nightmares.

He didn't know how long he had slept before Andre nudged him awake, but it felt like only minutes.

"They's somebody here, Coach."

Through the wraparound window glass of the small room, Ross could see the overhead lights of the hanger aglow. There came the metallic clank of footsteps on the steel grate steps, and Ross raised his gun. A tall, slender man with a graying beard wearing glasses and a baseball cap and a winter vest over red flannel opened the door and froze when he saw Ross and Andre on the floor. He held a clipboard in one hand and a large, black thermos in the other. A handheld radio was clipped to his belt.

"Be cool," Ross said. "We aren't here to hurt anyone. We only needed some temporary shelter from the cold. Who is here with you?"

The man didn't answer, so Ross asked him again.

"There's no one else here. It's just me. If you all want to stay here and warm up some, that's okay by me. I'm not gonna give you any problems."

"What's your name, and what are you doing here?"

"Name's Robert. Robert Dutton. I work for Mr. Cross. This is his hangar."

"You a pilot, Robert Dutton?"

"Used to be. My eyes don't work all that good any more, so I just maintain the birds now."

"What time you got, Robert?"

Robert turned his wrist and glanced at his watch. "It's just past seven thirty a.m."

"You're here by yourself. You aren't lying to me are you, Robert?"

"Nossir."

Ross stood and told Robert to come inside and have a seat in the desk chair. He had Andre take the radio from Robert's belt, and then he put his socks and shoes on one-handed, keeping his eyes glued to Robert.

"Could you fly one of those planes down there if you had to? Say if your life depended on it?"

Robert looked over his shoulder as if he were studying the planes, although he couldn't see them from the position he was in. "I can fly 'em. I just have some trouble reading the instruments sometimes. My eyes don't work so good, but I'm not blind by any stretch."

Ross nodded and lowered the rifle barrel. "That's good, Robert. Because my friend and I, well, we need a ride."

27.

The Cessna 172 hitched and shuddered and bounced so violently that it seemed as if the plane might drop from the sky like a stone. Ross thought if he had had anything in his stomach, he would have spewed it all over the cockpit by now.

"Are you doing this intentionally?" he asked Robert.

"Look, man, you told me to fly low, so I'm flying low. Down here at this altitude, the wind follows the contour of the mountains. We're gonna get thrown around a little bit. Feel free to take over if you think you can do a better job."

"No, no, you're doing fine. As long as you keep us in the air, that's good enough for me." Ross stared out the side window at the snowy ridges and valleys and rock walls that looked close enough to snag a wing, although in reality were much further away than they seemed. "How far to the airfield in Eatonville?"

"Well, once we get past Mount Rainier, up there on the left, I'd say we have another twenty, twenty-five miles."

"You don't know for sure? What does that GPS there on your steering wheel say?"

"I can't read the numbers on that damn GPS. I told you I have glaucoma."

"You never told me you have glaucoma. You said your eyes don't work so well."

Robert shrugged. "Well that's what happens when you have glaucoma."

"I'm pretty sure you're fucking with me. How the hell would you know where we're going if you can't read the instruments?"

"I can see the purple line leading to the waypoint you typed in before we left. That's all I really need in order to navigate."

Ross shook his head and laughed dryly. "And what if the GPS were to go out?"

"No problem," said Robert. "I'll just keep the autopilot steered on the heading we're on now. It won't deviate between here and there."

"Well, sounds good to me. I've never been one to look a gift horse in the mouth." Ross twisted in his seat and looked back over his shoulder. "How are you doing back there, Dre?"

"Not feeling too good," Andre moaned. "I never rode in no plane before."

"It's not usually this rough," Ross said. "Just try to relax. We'll be there soon."

Before long, they came out of the mountains and dipped into the space between the low cloud cover and endless green forests, the runway of the Swanson Airfield at Eatonville visible ahead. Robert entered a left hand pattern for a short approach to the runway and set the plane down with barely a jostle. The aircraft rolled to a stop about halfway down the airstrip.

"Well, this is it, fellas," Robert said. "It's been real and it's been fun, I just can't say it's been real fun."

"I appreciate you being such a good sport about all this, Robert," said Ross. "We got really lucky with you."

"I don't know how lucky you think you got. I'm just trying to avoid getting a bullet put in me. Don't go thinking I did this out of the kindness of my heart. You fellas are gonna be in a lot of trouble when the law catches up with you."

"They won't catch us," Ross said. "We're taking your radio headsets and hand mic with us. By the time you report us, we'll be in Portland."

"You can't leave me without a microphone. What if I have an emergency and need to get ahold of someone?"

"I hate to be a dick, Robert, I really do, but I'd be a moron to think you wouldn't call this in as soon as you were airborne again. Sorry."

"Man, that's just messed up. I could've given you all a hard time, but I was one hundred percent cooperative, and this is how you're gonna treat me?"

"I'm sorry, Robert. This is how it has to be. Do you need me to enter the Cashmere airport into your GPS before you go?"

Robert thought about it for a moment, then removed the GPS receiver from the control yoke and pressed some buttons and handed it to Ross. "Cashmere is identified as 8S2, that's eight-Sierra-two. Just scroll through until you see it and enter it as a new waypoint just like I showed you back at the hangar. Don't get it wrong. I don't want to run outta gas in the middle of Bumfucked Egypt. I can't believe you're leaving me with no comms."

"You'll be okay. You're a good pilot, you proved that." Ross entered the waypoint and returned the device to Robert. "You take care of yourself, Robert Dutton. I wish you the best."

Robert throttled the Cessna's engine and rolled off down the runway, and Ross and Andre headed across the grass strip that separated the runway from the taxiway. The Eatonville airport was less sophisticated than even the one at Cashmere. There wasn't a hangar in sight, no fencing. A residential street lined with expensive custom homes branched off from the taxiway.

The ground was soggy but snow free, and with temperatures in the high forties, it felt spring-like in comparison to the vicious cold that Ross and Andre had endured the night before. Ross was pleased to see that Andre's demeanor had transformed from one of misery and discouragement to one of awe and wonder.

"I can't believe we just jacked a plane," Andre said. "Isn't that terrorism or somethin'?"

"No," Ross answered, exhilarated by the experience himself, "but it might be considered piracy. I don't know."

"You sayin' we *pirates*? Like Jack Sparrow?" There was obvious delight in Andre's tone.

Ross chuckled softly. "Sort of, I guess. Let's not get confused about what pirates are though. Pirates are the bad guys."

As he walked, he wrapped the M4 carbine in the blanket to conceal it from curious eyes and studied the forested hills in the distance and considered the words he had just spoken:

Bad guys.

"You know, Dre, I don't talk about this much, but my parents died when I was just a kid. My father before I was old enough to remember, and my mother when I was in grammar school. I was taken in by my grandfather, who put me to work on his dairy farm over near Othello. I stayed there until I was sixteen or seventeen, then I went off on my own. Now, most people would consider me a pretty tough guy, and I'm sure growing up on a farm had something to do with that. But, man, you never saw tough until you saw my grandpa. Guys that you and I would think of as badasses, my grandpa would have chewed them up and spit them out and not even brushed his teeth afterward. He used to say, 'Boy, life is one tough son of a bitch, and if you want to make it through, you have to be tougher than life.' I don't know if he was right or not, but there's no denying that toughness helps when times are hard, wouldn't you say?"

"Yes, sir."

"I used to think that if a situation like this ever happened–a catastrophe kind of situation–I would survive because I'm tough enough to bear it. That combined with some common sense and sheer determination would be enough to see me through until the situation improved. But now that the shit has pretty much hit the fan, I've discovered that it's not toughness that has determined my survival so far, but my willingness to hurt others for my own personal gain. I'm not sure how I feel about that. I'm not real comfortable being the bad guy."

"You're not a bad guy, Coach," Andre said. "You're just doing what you have to do to get by."

"Like the guy on the street who can't find honest work and robs an old lady for twenty bucks to buy food," Ross said. "When it comes down to it, we're all just a bunch of animals. Or maybe only some of us are. The fact that I'm more concerned with my own feelings over what I've done than I am the feelings of Robert Dutton, or those security guards at the hospital, or that couple we stole the snowmobile from...I'm not sure what that says about what kind of person I really am."

"This is too deep for me right now, Coach. Let's just get where we're goin'. We'll talk about it then."

And so, again, they walked. They walked south along residential roads. Across open fields. Through thick growths of timber. One mile. Two. They caught a ride in the back of a red pickup truck driven by Mexicans who spoke no English, and were dropped near the private road that led to the cabin on the lake.

"How far now?" Andre asked.

Ross studied the dirt road that wound uphill through the dense forest. "About two and a half miles, from what I remember."

"We gotta walk uphill the whole way?"

"Pretty much."

"Dang it. I'm tired of walkin'. When we get there, I don't want to do anything but sit for about three days."

"You and me both."

They started up and stopped after an hour and sat on a fallen tree beside the road and drank bottled water.

"How come you told that pilot we was goin' to Portland?" Andre asked. "We ain't goin' to Portland are we?"

"No. We're not going to Portland. I only told Robert that so he can relay it to the authorities when they question him. I'd rather the cops think we went to Portland instead of hanging around near Eatonville."

"You're a pretty smart guy, Coach."

Ross laughed. "I'm not nearly as smart as you think I am, Dre. In fact, if you were aware of all the dumbass decisions I've made throughout my life, you probably wouldn't be sitting here with me on this tree trunk."

"You ain't never done me wrong."

"I guess that remains to be seen."

Andre finished his water and tossed the empty bottle into the woods. Ross made him fetch it and put it in the duffel bag.

"I don't think it's a good idea to piss off Mother Nature any more than she already is."

"Yes, sir," Andre said.

An hour later, they reached the cabin. It was constructed of poplar logs, with a tin roof and a banistered front porch. In front was a massive picture window to the left of the door, a smaller window to the right. A rock chimney jutted from the roof on the side of the house. They stood in the yard and stared at the structure and relished the beauty of it, as well as the relief of reaching the end of their journey. Andre bowed his head and said a prayer to God, thanking Him for delivering them safely. Ross joined him out of courtesy, and because he felt the need to express his own gratitude to something or someone. Then they went up the front steps.

The door was locked, as Ross expected it would be. He took the tire iron from the duffel bag and pried the door open best he could without damaging the frame or the latch. They went inside and Ross dropped the duffle bag on the wood floor and laid the tire iron on top of it and leaned the blanket-wrapped M4 against the frame of the picture window. The living room looked smaller than Ross remembered, but still large as far as living rooms go. There was a bear rug on the floor that hadn't been there the last time he had visited many years ago. A square coffee table sat on the rug, and around it was a three-cushion sofa and a pair of reclining chairs. On the rightmost wall was the stone fireplace.

To the left of the living room was the kitchen area. No stove or refrigerator, only a short granite countertop above rustic wooden drawers and cupboards, an overhead cabinet where Ross's uncle had normally kept his whiskey, and a small dining table with four chairs.

Beyond the living room were the cabin's two bedrooms. The door to the one on the left was closed but for a crack, the one on the right wide open. There was a four-tier gun rack on the wall between the doors. A scoped hunting rifle rested in the top cradle. In the cradle below was a pump action shotgun. Ross hoped there was ammunition for the guns somewhere in the cabin.

"It smells like cigarettes in here," Andre said.

Ross took a deep inhalation through his nose. *It does smell like cigarettes. And something else.*

"Where's the bathroom?" Andre asked, heading for the closed bedroom door. "I gotta number two like you wouldn't believe."

Hold on, Dre, Ross started to say, but it was too late. The bedroom door opened and a man stepped out and thrust the barrel of a large revolver in Andre's face.

"Back the fuck up," the man said.

Andre threw his hands up and backed into the living room as the man cocked the hammer of the revolver.

"Whoa whoa, wait a second," said Ross. "We'll go. We didn't know anyone was here. Don't shoot."

"Who the fuck are you all and what the hell are you doin' here?" the man asked.

"My name's Ross. My uncle owns this cabin."

The man cocked his head and squinted his eyes and loosened his muscles just a little. He studied Ross carefully, and after a few moments, he lowered his gun slightly and said, "Colin?"

Ross searched the man's face for familiarity but it wouldn't come. But then it did. He found recognition in the man's eyes. Ross recognized the pain. The hate. "It's been a long time."

"You know this dude?" Andre asked.

"Yes, I do," Ross said. "Andre, meet my brother, Johnny."

The man uncocked his gun and let it hang at his side. He smiled thinly and nodded and said, "Most people call me Rooster."

28.

"You look like you haven't eaten in about a month," Ross said. "How long have you been up here in the woods?"

Rooster stuffed the Magnum into his waistband and reached behind him and pulled the bedroom door closed. He took a crooked cigarette from the breast pocket of his olive drab coat and stuck it between his teeth and lit it with a shiny Zippo. "I don't know exactly. I suppose I been here since day before yesterday. He moved into the living area and took a seat in a black recliner. "Y'all look beat to shit. Pull up a chair."

Ross and Andre sat at each end of the sofa as Rooster's eyes followed their every move.

"So what brings you up here, Colin?"

"Probably the same thing that brought you up here," Ross said. "The apocalypse...and all that."

Rooster nodded and flicked an ash on the floor. "Where's that pretty little wife of yours? Don't tell me y'all got divorced already."

"No. No divorce. Monica...she's uh...well, she's stuck in Europe right now."

"Europe huh? Things any better over there?"

"No. Not at all."

"That's too bad. Well, I'm relieved to hear you and her are still married. When I saw you and the black dude here, I thought maybe you'd gone and turned homo."

Andre sprang up off the couch and puffed out his chest. "You need to watch what you're sayin', I don't care whose brother you are."

"Settle down, boy," Rooster said, unimpressed. "You're gonna wake the old man."

"Old man?" Ross said.

Rooster flicked another ash on the floor and leaned back in his chair. "Oh, I'll introduce you here in a short, after we've done some catching up. Hell, I ain't talked to you in what, five years?"

"Sounds about right." Ross looked up at Andre, whose hands were balled into fists and his face twisted into an ineffective scowl. "Sit down, Dre. You aren't intimidating anyone."

Andre sat but retained his scowl.

"I thought you had to use the bathroom," Ross said.

"Yes, sir. Where is it?"

"There's an outhouse out behind the cabin," Rooster said. "There ain't no toilet paper, so you'll have to use whatever you can find. Plenty of leaves out there now."

"You mean they ain't no *inside* bathroom?"

"Feel free to check yourself into the nearest Ritz-Carlton if you ain't happy." Rooster leaned forward and blew a cloud of smoke in Andre's direction. "Get along now, little doggie. Me and my brother need to talk."

Andre waved the smoke away and gave Rooster the most contemptuous look he could muster and got up and stomped across the floor and slammed the door as he left. From the bedroom came a muffled moaning sound. It was a sound of suffering.

"Well," Rooster said, crushing out his cigarette on the bottom of his boot, "I guess the old man is awake." He stood and walked to the bedroom door and stopped when he got there and turned to Ross. "What the hell you waitin' for, Colin, a formal invite?"

Ross got up and joined Rooster at the door. "Who you got in there, Johnny? It's not Uncle Charlie, is it?"

"Nope, it ain't Uncle Charlie." Rooster pushed the door open and motioned with his head for Ross to go in.

Ross stepped across the threshold, and what he saw made him think he had died back in those cold, snowy mountains in Wenatchee and gone straight to Hell. On the wall hung an elderly-looking man, naked and fastened to the wood by long nails, dozens of them driven through his hands, wrists, feet, the loose skin of his shoulders. There were nails jutting from his chest and his soft, round belly. From the meat of his thighs, his head, and—*oh God*—his testicles. The man's ears were missing, and there was a ragged hole in the center of his face where his nose should have been. His fingers—every one of them—were bent and mangled, broken and then broken again. Blood streamed from his hundred wounds down his body and the wall to which he was crucified, this human pincushion, and pooled on the hardwood floor beneath him.

Ross staggered backwards on legs of rubber and bumped into Rooster. He spun around and gazed upon his brother in horror. Johnny didn't look like a human being any more, but like the incarnation of evil itself. A demon. A walking bag of bones, gaunt-faced with bulging eyes and thinning hair and an aura as black as death. "Johnny...Johnny...Johnny, what have you done?"

"Look at him, Colin," Rooster said, thrusting his finger toward the man on the wall. "Take a good *look*. Don't you see?"

Ross shook his head and kept his eyes on Rooster. He jerked away when Rooster grasped his arm with a hand that felt too strong for such a withered physique. "Don't touch me, you sick motherfucker."

"Okay, okay," Rooster said, "you just need to calm down, bro. Take a breath."

"Don't you dare tell me to calm down. I gotta get away from you, you fucking maniac."

Rooster was blocking the doorway, so Ross grabbed him with both hands and flung him aside. Rooster yanked the Magnum from his waistband, but Ross snatched the barrel in his left hand and smacked Rooster's wrist with the palm of his right hand and dislodged the weapon from Rooster's grip. He then drove his fist into Rooster's nose and knocked him against the wall. Rooster slid down into a sitting position on the floor and Ross stooped forward and shoved the barrel of the Magnum in his face.

"What the hell were you going to do with this?" Ross demanded. "Were you gonna shoot me, little brother?"

Rooster slowly brought the sleeve of his coat across his flattened nose and wiped the gushing blood. "Goddammit, Colin, just take a look at that son of a bitch. Look at his face."

Ross straightened and lowered the gun and looked up at the man on the wall. "What is it, John? What is it I'm supposed to be seeing exactly?"

He moved closer and studied the man's face. A good part of the man's features was covered with an unruly growth of graying red hair, but there was something familiar about the bone structure, the shape of his lips, the long, shiny slope of his forehead. "Do I know you, old man?"

The old man's emerald eyes—the beauty of them seemed out of place in this nightmare—locked onto Ross's. He whispered something Ross couldn't understand. Ross stepped closer, and the man repeated, "Kill me."

Ross stared into the eyes of the man on the wall for what seemed like a long time. And then he began to remember.

I had a little chicken but he wouldn't lay an egg
so I poured hot water up and down his leg.
The little chicken hollered and the little chicken begged.
The little chicken laid a hardboiled egg.
The boy sings the lyrics to the old children's song as he places the green plastic army men in strategic positions on and around the front steps of the mobile home. Johnny sets up his own men in the bushes nearby. War is inevitable, and the boy wants his forces to be ready. He places his tank with the movable turret beneath the cover of the bottom step and is looking for a good spot for his other tank when Lyle opens the door at the top of the steps and pokes his head out and says dammit, I still can't believe that bitch ain't home yet. Then he slams the door, knocking over several of the boy's army men. The boy sets to righting his men, and his stomach begins to grow queasy as he hears Lyle pacing and cursing inside the trailer house. He tries not to think about it and instead focuses his attention on the Jeep-towed howitzer cannons Johnny is lining up over by the bushes. My tanks are better than your howitzers, he tells his brother, who responds with a nuh uh, my housers are better'n your crappy ol' tanks. Then Lyle pokes his head out again and looks around. I'm gonna kill your momma when she gets home, he says. Just you wait and see. After that, the boy can't concentrate much on the army men war.

Not long after, the boy's mom pulls up in the little red Vega. She gets out and takes a sack of groceries from the back seat and starts up the trailer steps. She looks happy, and she is careful not to knock over the boy's army men. She goes in and shuts the door, and there are screaming and thumping and crashing sounds after. The boy can hear his mom crying. No, please stop, she says over and over. But nothing can make Lyle stop when he doesn't want to stop, everybody knows that. So the screams and curses and thumping noises go on for a while longer, and then it is quiet for a couple of minutes and Lyle comes out and tells the boy and his brother they should run on over to the neighbors and call an ambulance, and if anybody asks what happened to their mom, she fell down the trailer steps.

I lost the baby, the boy's mom keeps saying as the paramedics carry her from the trailer house on a stretcher. The boy can see a dark red stain spreading on her pants in the area between her legs. He tries to look away but can't. The baby. The baby. Oh God, I lost the baby.

The boy's mom is in the hospital for a few days, and when she finally comes home, she doesn't speak at all. She looks older and sad and she only sits and stares at nothing. At 3:30 on a Wednesday afternoon, the school bus drops the boy and his brother off at home. They go up the steps into the trailer house and find Lyle sitting in a chair in the living room. His eyes are wet like he had been crying. Hello, boys, he says in a sad voice. You'uns need to go on in me and your momma's bedroom and see what your momma gone and done. That selfish woman. She never gave a damn about any of us. Go on. Get on back there and see. See what she done.

Colin and Johnny Ross cross the threshold into their mom's bedroom. Colin doesn't notice anything unusual at first, but then he sees her. In the clothes closet. Her eyes are half open but only the whites are visible. Her beautiful green irises are rolled back into her head. The skin of her face is as pale as a ghost, like she had been painted in chalk dust. Her mouth is open. A fly skitters along her bottom lip, and then disappears behind her teeth. The fingers of both her hands are tucked into the dog leash—the end that is tied around her throat—as if she had changed her mind and tried to save herself at the last minute. Too late, Momma. Too late.

They stand there and quietly watch their mother hanging from a dog leash in the closet until Lyle comes in and tells them to go next door and call an ambulance. They leave through the front door as Lyle settles back into his chair in the living room and pops open a can of beer. Once they are outside, the tears gush forth in a flood.

"Lyle," Ross said. "How did you find him, Johnny?"

"I was in jail with his son, Justin. Little bastard committed a string of burglaries to support his heroin habit. Once I found out who he was, that he was the biological son of Lyle Gene Anderson, I played friendly to him. He told me everything I wanted to know before I killed him."

"You killed him?"

Rooster got up from the floor and pushed the bedroom door closed, locked it. "I shanked him in the shower. I don't think the guards ever even suspected me."

"Jesus, John, did you ever consider that he might have been just as victimized as we were? Did you really have to kill him?"

"Fuck him. He didn't want to live anyway. He shot himself in the head a couple years back. The bullet followed a trajectory around his skull and came out the other side of his head without penetratin' bone. At least that's what he told me. I told him he was lucky to be alive, and he asked me what was lucky about it."

Ross studied Lyle's face. "He looks the same as he did all those years ago. Older. Fatter. But the same."

"I knew you'd recognize him. How could you forget the face of the Devil himself?"

"Please," Lyle moaned. "Kill me."

Rooster stepped forward and spat in Lyle's face. "You still got a ways to go before you get to taste the sweet salvation of death, so you might as well make yourself comfortable, preacher."

"Preacher?" Ross asked.

"Oh, well, yeah. It's the funniest thing. Old Lyle here went and became a *preacher*, of all things. A full-on Baptist minister. Went by his middle name, Gene. Pastor Gene. Now ain't that some shit?"

"I'll be damned." Ross couldn't take his eyes away from Lyle's. "How the hell did you ever get him up here to this cabin, Johnny? I didn't see a vehicle outside."

Rooster laughed. "Well, bro, it's a long story, but basically, I hijacked a city utility truck and stuffed ol' Lyle here into a tool box in the back and made the driver bring us up here. The truck ain't outside because I drove it into the bottom of the fishin' lake so it wouldn't be seen from the air."

"And the driver?"

"Oh. Well, he's uh...he's still in the truck."

"Jesus Christ, Johnny, what the hell is wrong with you? Seriously, man."

Rooster didn't say anything. Instead, he pulled a large butcher knife from his coat pocket and offered it to Ross.

"What?" Ross said. "What is that for?"

"You know what it's for. You can't tell me you ain't thought about this your whole life, meetin' up with this bastard again."

Ross shook his head "In all honesty, Johnny, I've spent my whole life trying *not* to think about this piece of shit. Whatever he had coming to him, it looks like you delivered in spades. I don't want any part of this."

"Take the knife, Colin. You want to even if you can't admit it to yourself."

"You're wrong. He's just a broken old man now. Look at him. He won't last much longer. This is over, John. Let it go."

"Fuck you," Rooster said. "You stand there all high and mighty, Mr. Career Man with your pretty wife and cute little house in the 'burbs, judging me like your own shit don't stink every bit as bad as mine does. Hell, the only real difference between you and me is that you stuff the past, and all those bad feelins that come along with it, all that garbage that eats you alive from the inside out and wakes you screaming in the middle of the night, you stuff it all deep down inside of you like a bunch of dirty old rags and pretend you ain't fucked up by it, while I *deal* with my demons. Let me tell you somethin' bro, one of these days those rags are gonna catch fire and burn you up. Now take the damn knife. Make him feel what he made our momma feel."

"I won't do it."

Rooster clutched Ross's hand and tried to force him to take the knife. "Remember what he did to us, Colin? He killed our baby brother before he was even born. He killed our momma! Don't you remember, Colin? Don't you remember? He beat you, bro. He beat Mom. He beat me. And there were other things. Things he did to me when you and Mom weren't around. Things I never told anyone about."

Ross saw tears in his brother's eyes for the first time since they were kids. "Johnny...I'm so sorry. I didn't know."

Rooster wiped his eyes with the same sleeve he'd used to wipe his bloody nose. It left red streaks across his face like war paint. He hung his head low and held the butcher knife out to Ross. "Take it."

And Ross did take it. He turned to the man on the wall and moved close enough to smell Lyle's breath. He placed the blade flat against Lyle's blood-streaked cheek and pushed the point up to the curve of his eye.

"Do it, bro," Rooster said in a voice that sounded miles away.

Ross pressed the knife harder into Lyle's eye.

"I'm sorry," Lyle said. The words were weak, raspy, hardly audible, but they nonetheless hit Ross like a fastball.

"What did you say?"

"I said I'm sorry...Colin."

Ross looked deeply into Lyle's eyes, and in those eyes, he saw sorrow and sincerity.

"I'm...sorry," Lyle repeated.

Ross lowered the knife and let it fall from his hand. He nodded to the man on the wall, and then he turned his head to his brother. "It's over, Johnny. Let it go."

And then Lyle thrust his head forward and clasped Ross's right ear in his teeth. Ross cried out and jerked away, leaving Lyle with a mouthful of broken teeth and a bloody chunk of ear.

"He bit me! He bit my ear off!" Ross threw his hand to his head and cupped it over what remained of his ear, then brought his hand away and looked at it. His palm was red with blood.

Lyle spit the flesh from his mouth and let out a shrill cackle and began to rock back and forth on the wall. Ross raised the

Magnum and fired all six rounds from it and blew Lyle's head to pieces.

Ross stood in the bedroom of his Uncle Charlie's cabin on the lake with his ears ringing and the gunsmoke drifting around him and thought that none of it was real. He thought he would wake up any moment with Monica next to him and he would tell her what a crazy dream he had and she would kiss him and tell him she loved him and assure him that everything was okay. Just a crazy dream, sweet boy. Just a dream.

Then fire erupted in his throat and he felt a hot liquid gush over his chest. The air was sucked from his lungs and the world spun around him. There was a flash of light reflected off metal. A spray of crimson. He was drowning. He threw his hands up to this throat. It didn't feel right. A loose flap of skin that shouldn't be there. The hot liquid rushed over his hands. *What's happening?* He turned to run—he had to get air—but his legs gave up their strength and he dropped to the floor and kicked and struggled and tried to breathe, but his lungs filled with his own blood and overflowed. *This is not how I want to die.*

In his darkening vision, he saw Johnny standing over him with the butcher knife in his hand. "Sorry I had to do that, bro," Johnny said. "Old Lyle started gettin' sick night before last. I'm pretty sure it's that Qilu virus. He bit you, so that means you're infected too. I'm doin' you a favor. Trust me, you don't want to end up like *them*. Besides, I can't take the chance that you'll infect me too. So long, Colin."

The last thing Colin Ross saw before the world went black was Monica in her green sundress. She was looking out from the top of the Space Needle and smiling. *There is magic here*, she whispered. *Can you feel it?*

29.

The calendar said May 17. The birds sang and the flowers bloomed in reds and yellows and all shades of blue, and to the east, Mount Rainier rose majestically into a cloudless sky. The two men drank from a creek and filled their plastic water bottles before pushing on through the dense forest, westward to the little town in the shadow of the hills. Their feet hurt and their empty stomachs growled, but they were desperate for a sense of what the civilized world had become since the last of the radio stations within range had stopped broadcasting more than three weeks earlier.

They came to a wooded hill overlooking the town and sat and rested with their backs against a pair of ancient Douglas firs. They remained there for quite some time just enjoying the warmth of the sun and the loads off their feet, and then they sought out a position that would provide them a good view of the town below.

They found a knob that allowed them to examine a good portion of the town, so they lay side by side on their bellies in the tall grass and passed a pair of binoculars back and forth between them and watched the hordes of people make their way along the narrow streets.

There were three or four hundred of them. Some were naked. Others were half so. They staggered along blindly like drunkards and crackheads, or sniffed the air like bloodhounds and rummaged through empty vehicles and alleyways, searching the same places again and again and never finding what it was they were so frantically looking for. There were a few that fought with one another. If one were to fall, it would send those nearby into a frenzy, causing them to attack the one on the ground as a pack of dogs would attack a fox. The attacks were generally short lived, however, and the person on the ground would, more often than not, get back up afterward and go about his or her mysterious business. Occasionally, one would run through the crowd, screaming and flailing his or her arms, and then stop suddenly and look around in confusion before rejoining the others in their aimless shuffle.

Rooster handed the binoculars to his travel companion and took a sip from a water bottle and said, "So what do you think, Mr. Wallace?"

Andre peered through the glass for a minute and then laid the binoculars on the grass before him. "I think we should go back."

Rooster thought about it. "Nah," he responded. He stood up and stretched and swung his arms from side to side to increase blood circulation. "Let's go down there and have us some fun."

THE END

Rocky Alexander is an author of horror and dark fiction who lives with his wife in North Carolina. His work has appeared in various publications since 1990. He currently works as an editor for Bizarro Pulp Press.

Contact him at rr.alexander@yahoo.com
or connect with him on Facebook:
https://www.facebook.com/rocky.alexander.56

CPSIA information can be obtained at www.ICGtesting.com
Printed in the USA
LVOW05s1555271213

367128LV00013B/562/P